CHINA HAND
中国通

SCOTT SPACEK

Post Hill
PRESS

A POST HILL PRESS BOOK
ISBN: 978-1-63758-386-9
ISBN (eBook): 978-1-63758-387-6

China Hand
© 2022 by Scott Spacek
All Rights Reserved

Cover design by David Prendergast
Author photo by Ippei & Janine Photography

Post Hill Press
New York • Nashville
posthillpress.com

Published in the United States of America
1 2 3 4 5 6 7 8 9 10

Map by Peter Hermes Furian

PROLOGUE

SHENYANG, CHINA, MAY 1999

I 've got to get out of here, *now,* but the elevator's as narrow as a coffin and descending so slowly I could be sinking into my own grave.

The elevator shudders to a stop. The floor indicator light goes dark.

There's a grinding noise. I look up, expecting armed security to rappel down the shaft and start carving open the ceiling with Sawzalls.

But the door opens, *finally,* as sluggishly as the descent. I glimpse the lobby through the widening crack. The room appears empty. The escape route in front of me is carpeted bright red. Everything else glitters in fake gold—the plating on the counters and chandeliers, the cheesy reproductions of classic Greek statues.

My reptilian brain screams *Go-go-go!* I grip the straps of my backpack and pray public security agents aren't waiting in ambush.

But Miss Zhang could be watching. She's the super observant "receptionist" at the front desk—undoubtedly a government informant. Hotels in China must register all guest information with the Public Security Bureau and report any suspicious activity. She will definitely be on the lookout for public enemy number one.

Me.

Head down, I glance toward the front desk. Zhang is on the phone, facing sideways, ramrod straight in her red uniform, shaking her head.

She knows.

All my plans are unraveling. How is this happening? I came here to teach "Introduction to American Society" at a Chinese university. But minutes ago, at the railway station, I saw my own face on a wanted poster. Zhang could be staring at it on her computer screen right now.

She's turning toward me. I duck behind a grotesque gold reproduction of *Hermes and the Infant Dionysus* and peek over at Zhang. She's off the phone, studying something on her desk. I need to get over to the cubicle in the corner, where the sign says "Free Internet." I'd kill to log on, to find out how close our hunters are. That's no mere figure of speech. I'm that desperate.

I try to look like a tourist by hunching over my *Lonely Planet* guide. I can see Zhang reflected in a wall mirror, scanning the lobby.

Her phone rings. She picks up the receiver and takes notes. I scurry past several more statues, duck into the cubicle, and open Internet Explorer on the dusty Legend computer. My fingers keep hitting the wrong keys.

Get a grip.

I shift to hunt-and-peck. I'm no good at this—whatever "this" is. I'm still trying to figure out what I've become. Most likely a dupe, a dunce who deserves one of those tall, pointed hats the Red Guards made their enemies wear during the Cultural Revolution.

I peer over the cubicle wall and see Zhang still on the phone. I imagine her reporting, "He's at the computer. We've locked all the doors. Get over here."

I get onto *The Washington Post* website and head straight to "World News," where I skim all the China-related items. The bombing's in there, but so far nothing about us.

I moan under my breath when I see this headline:

CHINA TERROR LINK ALLEGED

WASHINGTON—China has begun funding the Al Qaeda terrorist network, according to Pentagon sources, who are concerned about the increased threat this poses to the US homeland, including of biological weapons…

With China's advanced software and tens of thousands of security officers monitoring internet traffic, running a search is risky, but I need to know what else is out there. My first few queries don't turn up anything concerning. I type General Jiang Guangkai's name in Chinese—江光凯.

Thousands of entries snap into focus. Nothing from the last few days.

I enter my English name, Andrew Callahan, then the characters of my Chinese one—高安祝. The screen fills with my passport photo, the image they used on the wanted posters, and black-and-white stills from Chinese security cameras. *Fuck.* I don't bother to read further. I know what the articles will say.

I gotta get out of here—now.

I look back over at the front desk. Zhang's no longer there. *Where did she go?* I picture the security forces getting ready to storm the building, with her already ducking beneath the desk to avoid the ensuing crossfire.

Now or never.

I snatch up my pack and walk toward the front entrance, barely breaking stride as I push on the door. It doesn't budge, and I slam into the glass.

They've locked the place down.

"*Zenme hui shi?*" Miss Zhang shouts as she emerges from the back office. *What's going on?*

I push again, but it doesn't move.

"*Youbian!*" She yells. *The other side.*

I push open the one to the right and sprint toward the ornate railway station. I'm running out of time.

My companion intercepts me just as I make it past the door to a small tea house. "You're late," he says.

I start to explain as we double back toward the rendezvous point, but he's checking over his shoulder. I see terror flash in his eyes and begin to turn. "Don't," he commands, thinly disguised panic in his voice.

Then I hear the crack of a gunshot.

CHAPTER 1

CAMBRIDGE, MASSACHUSETTS, MAY 1998

I crossed Harvard Yard feeling an insecurity I hadn't known since I'd first arrived on campus four years earlier. The ancient trees corralled me with their gloomy shadows. The centuries-old, red brick buildings made me feel small, insignificant. Something about today's "urgent" summons by Professor Lin, two days before graduation, was setting me off.

Lin was the chair of the Department of Government, a brilliant scholar whom the *New York Times* called "the best-informed analyst of modern Chinese political economy." A freshman seminar with him had opened my eyes to the dynamic China market and inspired me to try to build a career bridging our two countries—starting by taking up Mandarin.

I revered Professor Lin, though there were murmurs among the faculty about his ties to the communist leadership in Beijing, many of whom he had known since he was a graduate student there in the late seventies. He was one of the first Americans allowed in after the normalization of relations between the US and China in 1978. I tried to ignore the suspicions about him, which I saw as professional jealousy or worse—the unspoken racism of envious colleagues toward a professor with a Chinese father and Haitian mother. But even after receiving top marks in three of Lin's courses, my interactions with him were formal.

What does he want today? With him, every meeting had a clear objective. The first time he'd requested to see me that year, I was honored when he offered to be my senior thesis adviser. A few weeks later, he'd asked if I would be interested in applying for an analyst position at White & McInerny, the prestigious consulting firm. It was my dream job. The company had a deep presence in China, and I hoped they would send me there once I'd proved myself at HQ. "You are one of the most disciplined and analytically rigorous students I have ever taught," he'd said. "The head of W and M's New York office is a former classmate. I'd be happy to put in a good word."

I arrived at the Department of Government building, drawing the attention of a middle-aged Asian man in the lobby before he quickly looked away. I continued upstairs.

"Good afternoon, Andrew." The professor's assistant welcomed me warmly and pointed to a familiar seat outside his door.

Within moments, Lin stepped out to greet me. A thin man an inch or two taller than my six feet, his handshake was soft, though he'd once mentioned doing ROTC to pay for college, so had presumably been in the service. What branch he'd never said, and I had never asked. And for all the academic honors he'd received, he dressed modestly, with plain black oxfords, a loose-fitting off-the-rack suit, and simple black-framed glasses.

Now in his late forties, Lin moved easily but with an erect posture as I followed him into his office, which was as staid as his own appearance. His degrees were neatly framed on the wall, bookshelves and desk carefully arranged—though oddly absent of the numerous accolades he'd won, the evidence of influence and erudition that so many professors display prominently. Lin did not wear his worldliness on his modest sleeve. The only decorative touch in his office rested on top of a bookcase, a large conch shell he said his mother had brought with her from Port-au-Prince.

He settled behind his desk, told me to sit, and eyed me closely. I'd say "stared," but I saw more inquiry in his eyes than intensity.

My nervousness compelled me to break the silence. "I can't believe I'm finally graduating."

Lin smiled, indulging me. He anchored his elbows on his desk to ease himself closer. "And now you are going off to become a consultant with one of the world's largest firms, advising the titans of industry."

"I am. Thank you for your help."

That's when he surprised me. "W and M is a great company, but I was thinking about you recently. Have you ever considered continuing your Chinese a bit longer—maybe living and working in Beijing to really understand the culture? You've been studying Mandarin for three years now and have a real knack for the language. I'm sure W and M would be happy to postpone your start for a year if you do something to enrich your skills even further. I know my own experience in China as a young man really helped shape me."

Professor Lin knew me too well. Of course I'd love to go to China. But it hadn't occurred to me that I could head off *now*.

Lin handed me a packet. "It's all in there. The International Affairs University in Beijing. Think about it. I've known the dean for years, and already told him you'd be the perfect candidate. You'd enjoy the IAU. It's a school for future Chinese diplomats, the leaders of the Party. Just imagine the connections you could form and the professional opportunities this might lead to. You'll become even *more* valuable to W and M—you know that business in China is all about *guanxi*." *Relationships*.

13

I didn't need more convincing, trusting that Lin only had my best interests in mind. And, frankly, the idea of doing something completely different before plunging myself into a pressure-cooker job also excited me. Four years of intense study, a competitive focus on always getting top marks, and daily rugby practice had left me burned out. I was looking forward to a spontaneous adventure.

I was still beaming when I left Lin's office, already imagining my stress-free life in Beijing—and nearly ran right into a man standing in the hallway outside the professor's door. He looked away just before we brushed shoulders, but I was certain it was the same guy who'd briefly captured my gaze when I entered the building. If I hadn't looked more closely, I might have mistaken him for Professor Lin himself, or maybe a slightly shorter, stockier brother—those same black frames, plain black oxfords, and a tie as red as the Chinese flag.

CHAPTER 2

BEIJING, CHINA, SEPTEMBER 1998

A gust of grimy air buffeted my face as I passed under the massive concrete beam bearing the Chinese name of the International Affairs University in raised steel letters: 外事大学. My eyes teared up from the grit, and I could taste the bitter, abrasive Gobi Desert silt and see the brownish coal dust in the Beijing sky.

Despite the miserable smog, my mood was sunny. I was dressed in my best blazer and slacks, heading to orientation on the first day of what I expected to be the adventure of a lifetime: living in Beijing and teaching the next generation of China's foreign service. How many future Politburo members would be sitting in my classroom? Maybe even a future general secretary?

I strode past the twenty-foot statue of former premier Zhou Enlai that dominated the quad of concrete buildings, believing I was safe amidst the surveillance cameras stationed at regular intervals along the bare campus walls, which were bereft of the posters or extracurricular flyers so typical at an American university. As I approached the auditorium, its once white exterior now tinged gray with dust and smoke, more lenses tracked me from multiple angles.

"You must be the newbie—Andrew, right?" A dark-haired, square-jawed white guy who looked a few years older greeted me just inside, hand extended. "I'm Will Carter."

"Nice to meet you," I said. "I guess you're a veteran here."

"Here, Bosnia, Liberia—and some other places I'd rather forget," he said, a smooth southern accent coming through. "I prefer it here. No bullets flying around. This is my second tour." He slapped me on the shoulder. "Let's grab a seat."

I followed Will's lead to the front row of the huge room, where roughly a dozen other foreigners were already seated. The rest of the five hundred or so red upholstered chairs were empty.

The speaker system crackled sharply and an unseen woman's voice announced in English, "Please warmly welcome the university leadership and the president of the IAU Foreign Teachers Association!"

The small audience stood and snapped to attention as a portly, mustachioed Caucasian in a gray Mao jacket led two older Chinese men in Western suits and ties to center stage. They were trailed by a striking young woman in a simple black skirt and white blouse.

Mao Man stepped to the podium and motioned for us to sit. The three Chinese settled in chairs in front of the large university seal mounted on the back wall—a blue globe with a white dove flying over an open book.

"Every year," the wannabe Chinese began in a high, scratchy voice reminiscent of the Great Helmsman himself, "it is my honor as foreign faculty president—"

"Trust me, none of us voted," Will whispered.

"—to welcome our new colleagues to the IAU and introduce you to our beloved administration." He clapped toward the three in the middle. We all rose and applauded.

"Name's Tom Blum," Will added as we sat back down. "Fled to Russia to avoid the Vietnam draft and then came here in 1973. Red through and through."

"'Red' like communist?" I sat forward. "Can't wait to meet him."

"You will. He's unavoidable as the Beijing smog."

Blum recited a saying by the *Renmin Lingxiu* in Mandarin, to the beaming approval of the three administrators.

He turned to his less important listeners—us. "For those who do not speak Chinese, the *Renmin Lingxiu* is the 'People's Leader,' Mao, and I said, 'Remember, he taught us that once all struggle is grasped, miracles are possible.' Now, I have the honor of welcoming the Communist Party secretary of the International Affairs University!"

A stout, balding septuagenarian trudged to the podium. We all climbed to our feet again, clapping as he shook hands with Blum. Then the party secretary smiled and nodded to the assembly before motioning for us to take our seats. Blum sat next to the attractive woman in the white blouse.

"Thank you for coming here," he started in slow, heavily accented English, "to help us build the New China." He raised his arms and extended them first toward the three enormous portraits on our right of the men who had ruled the People's Republic since 1949, whom I recognized as Mao Zedong, Deng Xiaoping, and Jiang Zemin. Then he motioned toward eight smaller portraits on the opposite wall.

"The past and current foreign ministers," Will whispered, reading the puzzled expression on my face. "Don't worry—there won't be a quiz."

After another minute of bureaucratic boilerplate, the party secretary plodded out of the auditorium through a side exit as if wearied by the beginning of another school year—or the tedium of trying to communicate with foreigners.

"Thank you, Party Secretary!" the unseen woman gushed over the loudspeaker. "Now, please welcome our beloved Dean Chen!"

More standing and clapping.

"Be sure to always treat this guy with respect," Will said. "He's the former head of State Security in Beijing and accustomed to deference."

"And now he's a university dean?" I murmured, more loudly than intended, as we sat back down.

"You bet. This school's all about enforcing a *patriotic* education," Will replied.

The dean seized the mic as though making an arrest, his eyes roving over the assembled. Mine wandered to the tall woman in the far-right chair.

"I'd much rather deal with her," I said to Will.

"Be careful what you wish for," Will whispered, lips now so still he could have been a ventriloquist. "That's Lily Jiang, the dean's new assistant. She's also the daughter of a top general."

Dean Chen continued to inspect the audience like a drill sergeant. He briefly locked eyes with me. The silence was daunting. Not even my new friend Will ventured another word.

"Welcome to the IAU—the International Affairs University," Chen said finally, so cold he could have been condemning us to the gallows. "We thank you for joining us at our great school."

Blum and the dean's beautiful assistant clapped, a clear signal to the audience, which followed suit.

"We are an open nation," Chen went on. "As a saying goes, China welcomes its friends with fine wine," he added, smiling just for a moment, "but greets its enemies with shotguns."

Jarred, I turned to Will, but he was still looking up.

"Before starting class, you need to understand our red lines," the dean continued. "If you do not respect our rules, you will be expelled and severely dealt with. Have I made myself clear?"

"Yes, sir," we all answered reflexively. I wondered what I had just agreed to as I rubbed my increasingly damp palms.

"The first rule is that while our constitution protects free speech—" Will and I glanced at each other "—we do not permit the spreading of lies or rumors. We will insist that correct facts are taught. You should use your classes this week for basic introductions. But then, starting this Friday, we will put detailed weekly lesson plans into your mailboxes. If you want to introduce other teaching tools, they must be approved by my office first. You certainly must not touch on any subjects that are off limits."

"Be sure to review that list of rules," Will mumbled. "It'll save you from stepping into some of the traps I did."

"I sense a good story," I said, but before Will could elaborate the dean went on.

"Our second rule is that you must understand your place as guests at this institution. We have provided you with beautiful apartments. These are much above the normal living standard of Chinese citizens. We hope you enjoy them. And we expect you to stay together with your kind, as there is to be no—" he hesitated, as if searching for the correct word "—fraternizing between you foreign teachers and our young students, or with our Chinese faculty."

The dean seemed to be staring at a man at the far end of the row.

"The French teacher," Will told me. "Chinese love cultural stereotypes. It's a mostly homogenous society, and they paint others in pretty broad strokes."

The dean turned his eyes to me. "Light-haired, blue-eyed young men like you might be very popular in China," he said, jabbing his finger, "but you need to behave appropriately."

I looked back at him, nodding slightly, beginning to wonder just what I had signed up for. The room was silent.

"Finally," Chen continued, "in China, we take security very seriously. This is most true here at the IAU." He gestured unmistakably at three cameras overhead. "We Chinese do not have the same expectations of privacy that you do. This is a cultural difference that you must respect." He held up what looked like a passport. "In order to ensure everyone can be properly identified, you must carry your passport and Foreign Expert identification at all times. This is the law." He tapped the mic with the passport. "China has been the victim of terrorist attacks by Uyghurs, Muslim separatists from the northwest of

our country—they look a lot like you foreigners with your long noses."
Chen laughed as his gaze swept over the audience.

"Did he really just say that?" I emulated Will's ventriloquism.

"Yup," he replied.

"My assistant Jiang Leilei—Lily—will hand each of you a detailed
rule book on your way out. Study it carefully."

Cued, she rose and walked to the steps by the side of the stage.

"I wish you a rewarding year," the dean added curtly before heading out the same door as the party secretary.

Miss Jiang was now standing in the far aisle, handing out book-
lets to the teachers as they filed out. My eyes had strayed back to her
the moment Chen finished. Up close, she was even taller than I had
thought, almost my height. About my age, too. She wore no necklace
or earrings, and scarcely any makeup, yet was even more stunning for
the lack of adornment.

I saw one of the rule books slip from the stack she was holding and
hurried over to pick it up for her.

I touched her elbow. "I believe you dropped this."

She shook her arm as if to shoo away a fly before looking up and
making eye contact with me, holding it a beat longer than necessary.
"Thank you," she said, with the slightest smile.

"Very chivalrous," Will teased once we were safely up the aisle and
out of hearing range. Then he turned serious. "You already broke a
rule when you touched her. Watch it."

CHAPTER 3

W ill's was a friendly warning. The dean's threats were far less benign. As I passed several more security cameras on the walk to my apartment to pick up my passport, I felt less secure in their presence than I had earlier that morning. I now understood that *I* was among the security threats they were watching.

My students would probably be watching me closely, too. I arrived early for my first class, then stood waiting at the front of the room, carefully reviewing Dean Chen's rule book, "co-authored by Tom Blum." The first page of "updates from the previous edition" noted that the IAU this year had generously exempted foreign teachers from the 10:00 p.m. curfew that Chinese students and faculty must follow. Then I combed over the list of forbidden topics, organized alphabetically, beginning with "anarchism" and concluding with "any other superstitious, pornographic, violent, gambling, or other harmful information."

Very clear.

Eighteen second-year students filed in, ten men and eight women, all wearing navy-and-white tracksuits—the school uniform. A few smiled at me. A handful stared coldly.

"Good morning, class. I'm Andrew Callahan." I mustered as much brio as I could before turning to the blackboard and writing my name in both English and Mandarin, conscious to render the Chinese characters with more confidence than I felt. I was about to continue with my prepared opening remarks when Miss Jiang entered and walked to the front of the class, right beside me, exuding a clear air of authority.

The students rose quickly from their seats. I felt myself straightening as well.

"Teacher Callahan, I will introduce you, as I have been told that people from America's Midwest may be overly modest."

She offered me a quick smile—but not so fast that our eyes failed to meet. I tried to keep my attention on the students as she noted that I was from "America's Wuhan," Chicago. "Like Wuhan, it's a big manufacturing and transportation center in the middle of the country. He studied at Harvard, where he graduated *summa cum laude* in government, with a focus on China. Mr. Callahan has a position waiting for him next year at the very prestigious consulting firm White and McInerny."

The name of the renowned company clearly registered with a number of students, who looked at me with surprise—maybe even respect. Miss Jiang went on. "Mr. Callahan has decided to spend a year here because he knows how important China is becoming in the global economy and he thinks he will be able to make a lot of money here. Isn't that correct?"

The way she put it sounded crass, but I didn't want to challenge her. And I'd heard that materialism in modern China was almost considered a virtue. "That's right, Miss Jiang."

"*Wo tingshuo Meiguo ren kanbuqi Zhongguo ren,*" said a thick-necked man in the corner by the door. *Americans look down on Chinese.*

I wondered if he thought I couldn't understand his Mandarin—or didn't care that I could. Miss Jiang didn't intervene as he went on in English. "You think we are inferior."

I suspected that he was testing me in front of the dean's assistant. I was familiar with how Western powers had taken advantage of China and didn't want any of my students or Miss Jiang to think that I shared those prejudices. "Most intelligent Americans do not look down on the Chinese. They respect the amazing developments taking place here."

He smirked in obvious disbelief.

Only then did Miss Jiang join in, not to redress but to introduce him. "Mr. Callahan, this is Zheng Jianguo. He is your class monitor."

"My name is probably too difficult for you," Jianguo spoke up in the same derisive voice as before. "You can call me Rick."

Miss Jiang went on, "The class monitor's job is to make sure that only the correct facts are taught. He provides regular updates to the administration." I presumed this included her. "We don't want anybody to get into trouble by saying or doing something inappropriate." She held my gaze, though I couldn't tell whether it was to challenge or warn me. I noticed her strikingly high cheekbones and big brown eyes.

"Class, you should feel fortunate to have Mr. Callahan as your instructor this year. While we know that in general American students perform very poorly on international academic tests, I can say that he is the rare exception."

She turned to me. "I will leave you, Mr. Callahan. If you need any assistance from the dean's office, you can come see me."

"Thank you, Miss Jiang."

I forced myself not to watch her walk away.

A stern, round-faced young man with pouty lips wasted no time in speaking up. "Why did you choose to come to this school?" His suspicion could not have been more evident.

I told them about my wonderful Professor Lin, and how he had encouraged me to teach there because it was a first-rate university and the experience would allow me to master the language and understand the ancient culture—leaving aside the self-serving motivation of expanding my network and furthering my career ambitions. "So, what about you students? How are you enjoying university life so far?"

They looked back and forth, as if daring one another to respond. A short, slight woman in the first row finally answered.

"We spent our first year at another campus in the countryside. We're excited to be in Beijing." She didn't look excited. She looked exhausted.

A boy blurted out, "Last year, we had to do military training and study Chinese socialism."

"Interesting. And very different from my university experience."

"Really? How?" asked the sleepy-looking girl.

I looked at Rick and sensed that I'd started across a minefield. The missions of Harvard and the IAU were starkly different. Their respective mottos said it all. Harvard's was "Veritas," Latin for "Truth." IAU's was "Unswerving Loyalty."

"Obviously, both schools only accept brilliant students," I began, earning a few laughs. "But we didn't have military training, uniforms, political lectures, or curfews, so I guess we had—"

More freedom? Had I almost let that volatile word slip out? I worried my sudden silence was now saying it for me. "I guess we had less structure," I added finally.

Rick squinted at me. I moved on as fast as I could. "Any other questions?"

"I heard Americans believe in God and other superstitions," said a long-haired girl from the back.

I shrugged and smiled but refused to go down that prickly path. Good move, too. Rick's squint had turned into a glare. Those cameras might have been finding their focus as well. Their dark eyes appeared no less cold than his.

I pivoted straight back to compliments. "I must say, I am impressed by how fluent everyone's English is."

"We have four hours of English class every day, beginning first year," said a young man who'd been silent till then. "We need fluent English to attend foreign graduate school programs or work for Western companies—so we can bring technologies back to China," he added, then looked around, as if he shouldn't have told me that.

Sure enough, the class cop was now glaring at him.

"I guess that explains why you speak English better than many of my fellow Americans."

That sparked a few chuckles and a flurry of self-congratulatory smiles.

We continued our back and forth until the hour ended with a shrill ring from the loudspeaker, which swiftly roused even the weary-looking girl in the first row. As the students gathered their materials and headed for the door, I hastily mentioned that my office hours were Friday afternoons from one to four at my apartment. Teachers didn't have offices, so this was standard practice, as odd as it would sound to students and faculty back home.

The last to leave was Rick, who stood by his desk staring at me. I nodded at him and gathered up my materials. Moments later, I saw that he'd left and shut the door with unnerving silence.

I peered out of the classroom's small window at my new campus. I should have had a clear view of the peaceful, tree-studded campus featured in the IAU brochure, but it was hard to see much through the brownish-gray air.

I walked out and headed across the quad toward my apartment. Only a few students were outside, and they were moving with purpose. A solidly built man in a gray suit standing beside one of the nearly leafless trees was eyeing me openly and jotting in a little black notebook.

Distracted, I bumped into a young woman before quickly apologizing in Mandarin for my clumsiness.

"*Mei shi*," she said, waving me off. *No thing.*

When I checked again, the suited man was gone.

CHAPTER 4

Will and I could hear the thumping bass of "Ghetto Supastar" reverberating ahead of us, down a dirt alley near Peking University. Our feet picked up the rhythm, hurrying us along. So did our excitement. We had just finished the first day of class. Will wanted to show me the Beijing that didn't appear in most guidebooks, starting with a bar called Solutions.

He greeted the doorman by name as we walked into a wall of sound and waving arms. Cocktail waitresses in body-hugging gold and black minidresses with prominent Yanjing Beer logos weaved through the crowd with heavily laden trays.

We slid into a small corner table. Will ordered two drafts, which swiftly arrived. We clinked glasses as he toasted my boldness in coming to China, then we took in the scene.

DJ Aki was the big draw that night. Decked out in a Rastafarian hat, Vans Old Skools, baggy gray pants, and a sheeny black shirt, he worked the pulsing, multinational crowd from a raised platform. The sea of Chinese, European, American, African, and other Asian students and local hipsters dancing to the droning beat could have been in Berkeley or Cambridge.

"Another beer?" Will asked as the DJ announced a break. We'd all but inhaled the first Yanjings. I nodded and scanned the crowd for a waitress.

I waved one over. "*Eh, xiaojie, zai lai liang ge zhapi.*" *Excuse me, could we get two more beers?* I was pleased to finally practice my Mandarin in the wild after so much time in the classroom. She responded with an approving smile.

We watched her work her way through the crowd, ducking past a shoving match among four Asian patrons.

Will turned back to me. "Hey, I should take you over to the Beijing Fight Club."

"Like *Fight Club*, the book?" I had just read the Chuck Palahniuk novel.

"A real boxing club. I stopped by once—met some of the guys on their way out. Seems cool," he said. "I've done some boxing over the years."

I wasn't surprised, given his lean, sinewy physique.

I didn't consider myself a fighter, but wasn't averse to contact sports. I had gone through a karate phase as a kid, then quarterbacked my high school football team and captained the Harvard rugby squad. And hadn't I come to China to do something a little crazy? "Yeah, I'd love to check it out. But will we have time?"

"Plenty, once you get the lesson planning and grading down."

"Is it expensive?" We only made two thousand RMB a month, about two hundred and fifty US dollars. I was thankful I'd saved a few thousand dollars from an internship a year earlier.

"You can handle it. I've managed to get by," Will said as the waitress delivered the next round. "*Ershi kuai qian,*" she announced.

I handed over twenty renminbi. China was one of the few places left where the equivalent of six American dollars could still get you two pints and a cab ride across town and back.

"She's kinda cute," I said as our waitress walked away.

"Then go talk to her. She clearly approves of your Mandarin. Maybe she'll feel the same about your manhood."

"I don't have a lot of experience with waitresses." Or with women generally, although I saw no need to confess that to my new friend. But glancing around Solutions at all the pretty faces did make me wonder if I'd taken school and rugby a little too seriously.

"Here's a hint with waitresses: try tipping them," Will laughed. He patted me on the shoulder. "If it's the last thing I do, I'm gonna loosen you up this year. We're young, single, and far from home."

As DJ Aki reentered his booth and the music started pumping again, Will pointed across the room. About fifteen feet away, two young Asian women sat at a table by themselves, appearing and disappearing in our field of vision depending on the gyrations on the dance floor. I doubted they would go without company for long. A number of men in the crowd were eying them openly, including a tall, thick-necked Westerner bellied up to the bar. The woman facing me was wearing a short black skirt and a shiny silver top. Her dark, shoulder-length hair sparkled with blond highlights. Except for a brief, enticing glimpse, her face remained in the shadows. I couldn't make out her friend's face at all. She'd settled sideways, shrink-wrapped in a white tank top and snug jeans. Two tumblers sat on their table.

Will waggled his eyebrows. "Take some initiative," he shouted. "Or I'm going over there to say my Harvard friend is too shy to introduce himself, and his name is—"

"Seriously?"

"I'm counting down: five…four—"

"All right."

I ran my hand through my hair as I started over to them. The first woman came into view quickly and was as cute as she'd first appeared. But as soon as I caught sight of her friend's features, I shielded my face with my hand and pivoted back to my seat.

"What the hell?" Will said above the din.

"It's Dean Chen's assistant—Miss Jiang!"

"Maybe she'd like to give you detention." Will laughed. "Tell her you've been a baaad boy."

"That's a terrible idea." But I did wonder what she was doing here. I assumed that, like other Chinese staff, she lived in the teacher's residence on campus, with a strict ten o'clock curfew.

Will sipped his drink. "So, other than your instant infatuation with the dean's assistant—"

"Don't go there, please." I held out my hands in protest.

"Forget it. How'd it go in the classroom?"

"My students definitely don't fit the deferential Chinese stereotype." I glanced back to see if Miss Jiang had noticed me. I didn't think so. "And don't you find the school kind of strange? It's like part university, part military base. The dean is literally an ex-cop. There's a class monitor? And I'm pretty sure I saw a plainclothes policeman watching me after class."

"You probably did. They've got a lot of them. Last year we heard they were getting threats—from Uyghurs maybe. The ones Dean Chen mentioned."

Will looked like he was about to say more, but loud jeering in what sounded like Russian suddenly broke through the music. We turned to see the big Westerner who had been at the bar—and two equally bulky buddies—elbowing dancers aside as they closed in on three Chinese women standing with their dates. They shoved aside the smaller men, grabbed the young women, and hauled them onto the floor.

"Assholes," Will hissed. "And people wonder why the Chinese don't like foreigners. Guys like that give *laowai* a bad name." He glared at them. "It'd be fun to give them a little smackdown, wouldn't it?"

"Uh…no. I don't think so." I could take a hit on the football field and deliver one on the rugby pitch, but had no misperceptions about being some street fighter—and didn't want to throw away my career in a brawl with some Russian thugs.

Besides, the girls had managed to extract themselves and were fleeing the club with their boyfriends, passing the bouncers who'd done nothing to stop the bullying.

Like me, I winced inwardly.

"The least we can do is go sit with Miss Jiang and her friend," Will said. "Those guys are already raping them with their eyes."

The Russians did appear to be on the verge of drooling. I hesitated to go over, though, wondering how it would look if we were spotted in a club drinking with the dean's assistant. But Will was right—they might welcome a less rapacious male presence.

Miss Jiang saw me before I made it halfway to their table. She smiled and pulled over a chair for me to sit. A warm flush prickled my face. I hoped it was less conspicuous to her than her tight jeans and low-cut tank top were to me. She caught me looking but it didn't seem to bother her.

"Funny to see you here," she said with a smile.

"I didn't plan on seeing you, either, Miss Jiang."

"Call me Lily. We're not at the IAU."

"And I'm Andrew."

"Well, Andrew, let's keep this," she gave the club a once-over, "our little secret, okay?"

She nodded at Will and patted her friend's hand. "This is *Wu Wei*, or Sophie."

"Do you both live in the *Waiguo Zhuanjia Lou*?" Sophie asked. The *Foreign Experts Building*.

"Yeah, we're real 'foreign experts,' *Zhongguo Tong!*" I replied, joking. *China Hands*. "Like Edgar Snow, the renowned journalist—"

"We're not in school now." Will nudged me. "Who wants a drink?"

"I'll have a rum and Coke," Sophie said.

"And you, Lily?" I asked.

"Rum and Coke sounds good," she replied.

"My pleasure," Will said, mouthing "good luck" to me as he headed to the bar.

I wondered what to say to Lily. Dean Chen had made it clear that there would be serious consequences to any impropriety, including "fraternizing" with a fellow staff member.

As I leaned closer to Lily to be heard over the music, a heavy hand slapped down on my shoulder. I turned, startled, to see a grotesque tattoo of a naked woman tied spread-eagle on a rock on the thick arm of one of the big, drunk Russians. He was leaning over me, ogling Lily up and down.

"You cute," he said in his thick Slavic accent, coating me with beery, garlic breath and spittle. "We dance." He pointed at Lily. "Later, other things."

He laughed uproariously, hardly seeming to notice that I'd pushed his hand away.

"I'm not dancing with you," Lily told him.

"Come on." He grabbed her hand roughly. The muscles in his forearm tightened, making the naked woman in the tattoo writhe obscenely.

He tried to pull Lily away but she resisted.

I started to rise, looking the man in the eye. "Get your hands off her."

He pushed me back down. "Nobody ask you." He was smiling, and appeared confident that he could snap me in two like a stick.

I tried to steady my voice. "Seriously, leave her alone. Go hit on someone else."

"Okay. I hit on you."

He shoved me to the side, almost spilling me off the chair. Then he yanked Lily to her feet like a rag doll and pulled her away from the table. I glimpsed panic on her face and glanced at the asshole's buddies. Where was Will? At the bar, I remembered, hidden by a curtain of dancers.

The barrel-shaped guy was leering drunkenly at Sophie, who was backing up in her chair. The third Russian was sucking suggestively on the mouth of a beer bottle, laughing. Then he shouted at the guy who'd grabbed Lily. It sounded as though he was egging him on, but all I really caught was his name—Igor.

I jumped up and grabbed Igor's wrist with two hands. "Let go of her."

"Fuck off."

"She doesn't want to dance with you. Don't you get that?" I heard the pleading in my voice and hated it.

"Don't be tough guy," he said, jabbing the meaty index finger of his free hand into my chest.

Tough guy? That was the furthest thing from my mind, even as I tried to shove him away from Lily.

He backhanded me so hard I heard the crack of his knuckles on my skull. I had never taken a hit that hard, even in my unpadded college rugby days. My legs buckled, and I felt myself falling.

Lily screamed, then others did too, as I hit the floor.

It took a moment to regain my senses.

"What the fuck is wrong with you guys?" Will shouted in his distinct southern voice.

Still woozy, vision shaky, I looked up and saw the Russian release Lily and turn toward Will. She helped me to my feet as the Russian spat on the floor in front of him.

"You guys should get the fuck outta here," Will said. "Nobody wants to fight."

Igor's response was a hard right at my friend's face.

Will ducked the punch easily. As the Russian staggered off balance, Will smashed his elbow into Igor's nose. He went down faster than I had—so fast I could scarcely believe it.

Igor's friend charged Will, who seized the man's collar and snapped him to the side so suddenly that the guy's own momentum sent him sprawling onto the floor. Will followed up with a kick to his ribs. It was like watching a Steven Seagal movie. I was in awe of Will. So, apparently, was bottle-sucking number three, who ducked into the crowd to get away.

"You okay?" Will asked me. He appeared to be the only one completely unfazed.

"Yeah, I'm fine." Although my head was throbbing, I mostly wished I hadn't been taken down so easily.

Lily squeezed my hand. "Thank you for stopping him."

"I didn't really do—"

"Yes, you did. No one else helped." She glanced at the gapers in the crowd. "Sophie and I have to go. You should, too. The police will come."

They hurried to the door, where the bouncer ushered them out of the club as if they were celebrities.

Will took my arm. "She's right. We gotta move."

But as we headed for the entrance, four uniformed officers rushed in. They stopped us and demanded to see our passports.

Will pulled his out right away. I reached for mine, but it wasn't in the right front pocket of my khakis, where I'd put it. I patted my pockets again. Nothing. Dean Chen had been clear about carrying our passports at all times. And these cops looked like they wanted to come down hard on someone for the fight.

Oh, shit.

I tried to tell Will *sotto voce* that my ID was missing and maybe he could help me talk my way out. I wasn't *sotto voce* enough.

"You do not have passport?" the officer closest to me said. "You know this is the law of the People's Republic of China! This is another law you have broken."

"I have one. It was in my pocket," I tried to explain as I patted my pants yet again. The officer shook his head dismissively.

Two of the other officers were looking at the Russians' papers and waving them out the door, as I wondered if the guy who'd grabbed me had also taken my wallet. But he was the opposite of light-fingered. More like heavy-handed in every way.

Then I remembered crossing the quad after class hours earlier and accidentally bumping into that young woman while I was distracted by the suited man taking notes.

That was no accident. *She* must have bumped into *me*. And then picked my goddamn pocket.

I felt like I'd been set up—maybe from the start.

CHAPTER 5

D J Aki stopped the music and the lights blazed on as the officers rammed us up against the wall. All I could hear in the next few seconds was the furious *click-click-click* of the cuffs clamping around our wrists, tight as tourniquets. Then I watched Will dragged past the stunned crowd toward the front door.

My turn came next. The cop seized my arm, his fingers hard as steel bands. But what I felt even more in the seconds that followed was the sweat streaming down my face and back.

As we stepped outside, a cold breeze turned the perspiration into a full-body chill, which seemed like the icy grip of fear itself. I'd never been arrested, much less handcuffed.

A cop grabbed the top of my head and shoulder and shoved me next to Will in the rear of a small police car. The space was so tight that even shifting sideways left my cuffed hands jammed between my lower spine and the stiff back seat. The cuff's steel edges were biting into my wrists.

When I looked at Will, he must have sensed I was going to say something, because he shook his head to discourage conversation.

By the time we pulled up to a two-story police station with barred windows, the cuffs felt like they'd sawed down to the bone.

The bigger cop dragged me out of the back seat and shoved me forward so hard I started tumbling down—before he seized my cuffs to catch me and nearly dislocated my shoulders.

The other officer was pushing Will toward the entrance.

Inside, they took down our basic information, including our positions at the IAU, then hauled us off to separate cells. I heard the door to Will's slam an instant before my guard kicked me into the one across the hall. This time I did hit the floor as the metal door banged shut behind me.

"It will be easier if you confess your crimes," he said in stilted English as he walked away.

Alone, I managed to clamber to my feet and take a seat on a concrete bench that extended from the wall. I made another effort to ease the constant pain of those cuffs. The more I struggled, the more my wrists throbbed.

The physical pain was only part of it. I was confused—in shock at what was happening. *Confess my crimes? Not carrying a passport?* Then I imagined the worst—the inside of a Chinese prison.

I told myself to stop. *Be patient, everything will be—*

An officer screamed at Will, jolting me. His cell wall started getting pounded. I hoped that was what it was. I was terrified they were beating him and that I would be next.

I didn't have to wait long to find out. A burly officer whom I didn't recognize stormed into my cell, grabbed me up off the bench, and threw me against the wall, face first. I managed to take the brunt of the blow with my chest and shoulder, but the harsh impact still thundered in my head.

The cop harangued me, his mouth an inch from my ear. I could feel his hot breath and spit as he forced my arms up my back until they felt like they would pop out of my shoulder sockets. I begged him to stop in Mandarin and English, but when he paused it was only to grab the hair on the back of my head. I tensed up, sure he was going to smash my face into the cinderblock.

He shook my head and shouted in English, "Fistfights and hooliganism may be acceptable in your country, but they are serious crimes in China. So is trying to hide your identity. You should confess your crimes or face more serious punishment!"

Then he used my face as a door knocker against the wall. Hard enough to hurt like hell, but not to break bones.

I tried to apologize, but the officer's mouth was still close enough to bite off my ear. He yelled that I should stop my "insincere groveling." He was right. I *was* insincere. And groveling. But I didn't know what else I could do. I thought any second he'd lose all restraint and pound my face into hamburger meat.

I was so shaken I would have confessed to any crime, but I didn't know what he wanted me to say or do.

A female officer burst into the cell and said she needed to speak to him, "*Xianzai.*" Now.

I strained to listen to their agitated talk as they hurried away. All I caught was the woman saying, in Mandarin, "The supervisor suggested a better way."

For all I knew, they were debating the merits of a rubber hose versus a wooden baton.

I stared numbly at the door, too fearful to sit down for several minutes. When it was thrown open, the burly cop looked livid. Spittle still coating the corners of his mouth, he smacked the back of my head and marched me into the hall, forcing me to face a wall again. I anticipated the worst—and was dumbstruck when he unlocked the handcuffs.

"*Zou kai!*" he shouted, pointing to the entrance. *Get lost.*

What?

I stumbled down the hall on wobbly legs, not daring to turn around. With each step, I expected to be chased down or shot in the back for "trying to escape."

My hands were shaking so badly I needed to use both to push open the exit door. I was in disbelief as it closed behind me. Then I spotted Will on the sidewalk, just outside the iron fence surrounding the station, no visible wounds on him. I doubted that I looked unscathed. Or had those cops perfected torture that left no trace?

When I started to talk, Will put his finger to his lips to hush me.

He nodded toward a waiting cab—another surprise. Who called it? Or had someone been dropped off? The woman officer?

We piled in. Will told the driver to take us to the university.

"What the hell just happened?" I asked, rubbing my abraded wrists. I couldn't see Will's.

"Honestly, I don't know. I expected a good cop, bad cop routine, and got it, but then they just told me to get outta there. I guess it's just the typical mysteries of the Chinese"—air quotes—"justice system."

I forced a smile—a sick-looking one, I'm sure. I was hugely relieved to be out of jail, but also rattled physically and emotionally. I'd only been in China for a few days and already I'd been singled out for a warning by the dean at orientation, had my passport stolen, been humiliated in a bar fight, and been arrested and hauled off to jail. Nothing like this had ever happened to me before. What the hell was going on? I imagined my job offer with W&M being taken away—everything I'd worked for down the tubes.

I was reeling with regrets, and filled with curiosity about Lily, who'd had the luck—if that's what it was—to duck away from the nightclub just in time.

CHAPTER 6

T he shrill ring of the phone jarred me awake. I bolted upright and glanced around. I was battered but thankful to be in my own bed and out of jail.

I forced my bare feet onto the chilly tile floor, gritty with Beijing's inescapable coal dust, and stumbled out to the living room. "*Wei.*" *Hello.*

"*Gao Laoshi*," a woman replied, calling me *Teacher Gao* in grim-sounding Mandarin. "Dean Chen wants to see you *on your horse.*" In a hurry. "Be here by eight."

In twenty minutes? My heart was already racing. *This can't be good.* She hung up before I could respond.

I switched on my coffee maker and dashed to the shower, pausing only to examine my face. The Russian's fist had left a purplish lump on the side of my forehead, but otherwise there were no conspicuous signs of what I'd endured. Running my finger across my scalp, I couldn't even feel where that cop had used my head as a door knocker. He had managed to assault me without leaving a trace. Will might have been abused in the same way.

Ten minutes later—showered, shaved, and dressed in my best shirt and tie—I downed some coffee and tried to clear my muddied head, still pounding with the aftershocks of what was probably a mild concussion. As I gazed out my top-floor window, Beijing appeared as hazy as my brain. I could just make out a white pagoda temple hovering in the skyline like a ghost.

The best approach to this meeting with Dean Chen was also unclear. Given the omnipresent surveillance and his previous role in State Security, I was sure he'd already heard about last night's debacle.

I considered just throwing myself at his mercy—if he had any.

Or was I becoming paranoid? I didn't think so. Too much had already happened since arriving at the IAU.

I scowled at the motion detector overhead and headed out, hurrying down the stairs from my sixth-floor apartment, past the office of the *fuwuyuan*, the building attendant who doubled as a security guard on the ground floor. She was hunched over, eyes fixated on the array of video screens and blinking lights linked to all the cameras and sensors in our units.

With the dark-suited "note taker" on my mind, I avoided the quad and even more surveillance, instead following a tree-lined path. It might have been a lovely walk if I wasn't so anxious.

When I arrived at the dean's office, his secretary waved me to a brown pleather sofa under photos of Chen shaking hands with various party chieftains, all with perfectly combed, coal-black hair. I stared blankly at yesterday's *China Daily* on the coffee table, too preoccupied to even pick it up.

By twenty after eight, I wondered if Chen was deliberately delaying our appointment to further mess with my mind. But then, suddenly, he appeared, as if summoned by a tic that had just started taunting my left eye.

I sprang to my feet like a jack-in-the-box, recovering barely enough of my senses to greet him. My efforts brought no response or warmth to his wrinkled face. The dean simply stared at me before saying, "My office."

I wiped my sweaty hands on my pants and followed him into the simple room. A wooden desk stood with chairs on either side, backed by a crowded bookshelf. A mullioned window offered a view of the quad.

He ashed a cigarette I hadn't noticed. "Take a seat, Mr. Callahan," he said in his hoarse smoker's voice, glaring at me through thick, black-framed glasses. Then he sat, studying my bruise with a frown. "Mr. Callahan, we had high hopes for you, coming from Harvard."

Had? "Yes, sir," I managed.

"But you clearly have failed to conduct yourself with the dignity we expect of teachers who come to our university. Let's start at the orientation." His voice rose as he slapped the top of his desk so hard that I jerked back in my seat. "Do you really think I did not notice you and Mr. Carter gossiping while I was talking?"

Still startled, I couldn't respond.

"Then, in your first class, right after we gave you a list of forbidden topics, did you really say that at Harvard you had more freedom than IAU students have?"

"I never said that." I'd thought it, to be sure, but was certain I'd swallowed those words.

"We have reviewed the videotapes, Mr. Callahan. You implied it so clearly that only a fool wouldn't have understood, and the class monitor is no fool. Rick is my nephew. We are not idiots. I'm not sure the same can be said of you." His last words were as cold and pointed as icicles.

"I'm sorry. I never intended to imply that."

"Mr. Callahan, don't insult me with your lies. We haven't even gotten to your behavior *outside* the classroom. Tell me, what were you doing in a drunken barroom brawl last night?"

"It's a…I was…these Russians were…" I couldn't think of any way to demonstrate my innocence—and certainly didn't want to say anything that would call attention to Lily's presence.

"Enough. I can't bear to hear you struggle for an honest answer. We cannot have IAU instructors behaving in such a disgraceful manner."

At least he hasn't mentioned Lily.

Chen pulled himself close to his desk and leaned forward, like a cat about to pounce. "Then the police stopped you, and you didn't have your passport. Not even a copy. What did we tell you at orientation? *Always have your passport.* You can't follow even the simplest instructions, yet you presume to teach Chinese students? To do what? Get drunk and carouse?"

"Dean Chen, I know this doesn't look good, and I'm sorry—"

"'Doesn't look good?' It looks atrocious. Why didn't you have your passport? Did you get so drunk you lost it?"

It had been years since anyone had sneered at me so openly. I felt belittled, humiliated. I tried to explain. "I'm pretty sure it was pickpocketed by a woman who bumped into me yesterday."

"Chinese?"

"Yes, I think so."

Chen suddenly rose to his feet and stubbed out his cigarette in an ashtray crammed with butts. He was towering over me, smoke pouring from his nostrils. "You—*you*—of all people are accusing a Chinese woman of stealing your passport. Is that what you're saying, Mr. Callahan?"

"No, not really," I hedged, fidgeting in the seat. "I just don't know how—"

"Who is she?"

"I don't know. She bumped into me and then—"

"Where did you keep your passport? Perhaps you can remember that."

"In my front pants pocket."

"So tell me…how did it end up in the bushes near the Foreign Experts Building? Because that's where a Chinese security officer found it this morning."

I breathed a sigh of relief that my passport had been found. I shouldn't have. Chen slapped my passport down on the desk with the same vehemence that he put out his cigarette. "What were you doing in the bushes to make your passport fall out of your pants? Tell me, I want to know."

I was so blindsided by his sordid suggestion that I didn't know what to say. I stammered, "S-s-s-someone stole it and must have dropped it there. It's not what you think."

"Did they put this there, too?" He reached into a desk drawer and pulled out a plastic bag containing a used condom, holding it by his finger and thumb, a look of total disdain on his face. "Is this part of the plot against you?"

I touched my injured forehead, inadvertently setting off a stabbing pain. My skull was pounding, my eyelid spasming. "What are you talking about?"

"It was right by the passport. *Your* passport. In the bushes."

"No way that's mine. Who found it?"

"Our excellent security service. A respectable woman had to pick this up." He had a look of pure revulsion as he threw the bag on his desk.

I felt more trapped than in that concrete-walled police cell, and had no idea how or why it was happening. "I...I...I was set up, Dean Chen!" What other explanation was there?

"By Chinese officials? Are you saying that you are so important that we would send someone to steal your passport and then plant a used condom in the bushes? *You* disgust me even more than this evidence of public fornication. Do you know that falsely accusing someone is defamation? Defamation is a serious crime in China, Mr. Callahan. You could go to prison for a very long time. And if the young lady was one of our students, she will be expelled." He glared at me.

"I wasn't with any student. There was no public sex—or any sex. And I'm telling you, someone set me up and planted...that." I gestured vaguely towards the used condom. "Can you do a DNA test?"

"And waste even more money on you? We have all the evidence we need. You would be wise to admit your crime." He pointed to my passport and the condom, then held up the police report from last night. "We have never had a teacher get off to such a disgusting start, Mr. Callahan."

I had no reply. It seemed like he already had me tried and convicted.

"Are you sure teaching here is what you want to do?" he demanded.

"Yes, of course."

"Is this what *you* wanted to do, or did someone send you here?"

What? "No one sent me here," I said forcefully. "I came here on my own. I thought it would be interesting to live in China and teach." Was he insinuating that I was somebody's stooge?

Dean Chen put the baggie into a drawer as if he could no longer bear the sight of it. Then he sat back in his chair and lit a cigarette. "You thought it would be interesting to live in China and teach." He shook his head, exhaling a gray cloud. "We have reviewed your activities since arriving at the IAU. Your behavior has been so stupid, so completely irresponsible, that it's highly unlikely anyone would have entrusted you to spy on us." He leaned forward. "But it does seem that *someone* has an interest in you." He paused, dramatically, to let that sink in. "Who might that be, Mr. Callahan? We want to know why you're so important to them." He smiled—either at his own speech, or just because he delighted in watching me squirm.

"I really don't think I'm important to anyone."

"I agree that your importance to anyone is almost impossible to fathom. But if you *are* important to them, then you are also of great interest to us, no matter how disgraceful your behavior has been."

His eyes bored into mine even more intensely. I looked up and to the right before remembering that unpracticed liars often shifted their gaze in that direction. I couldn't do anything right, even tell the truth.

"Mr. Callahan, a person you were drinking and carousing with last night is of most importance. Do you know who I mean?"

"Will Carter?" I was about to tell him that Will was innocent, too, but Dean Chen cut me off.

"No, not your fellow carouser. *Think.* Who else's company did you keep?"

Not Lily, please. I was certain that if he learned I'd been drinking with Lily, he would expel me immediately. My expression must have given me away.

"That's right, Mr. Callahan, Miss Jiang. She is very, very important." He nodded slowly, expressionless.

Feeling too hopeless to argue further, I just sat on the edge of my seat, hands out, palms up, the body language of a beggar.

He drew deeply on his cigarette, eyeing me above the fiercely burning tip. "You were buying drinks for Miss Jiang and her friend."

"No, I swear. We ran into them there, and then this big Russian guy was trying to manhandle Miss Jiang and…"

"You can't even remember her friend's name? You must have been very drunk."

"Sophie!" Her name came to me in a flash.

"Bravo, Mr. Callahan."

"I also remember that those Russians had been bullying some others in the bar, and we wanted to make sure Lily and Sophie were safe."

Chen took a deep breath. "Miss Leilei is more than my assistant. Her father is General Jiang Guangkai, chief of the People's Liberation Army staff and a member of the Central Military Commission. He is a powerful man. Some people might want to harm him and his family. We've had to tighten security here because of threats like these."

What? Will had said Lily's father was a general, but the chief of the People's Liberation Army staff? And someone might want to harm them?

"He spoke with his daughter last night. I was on the phone with him when you arrived. Do you want to know what he said?" Chen's gaze dipped to my passport.

I nodded.

"He said Miss Leilei believes you saved her from being attacked by that big Russian man, and that your intervention came at a personal cost to you, Mr. Callahan." He glanced at my bruise. "That much appears true."

"Yes, sir."

"That's the only reason you're not in jail right now. You protected an important man's daughter."

He stubbed out his cigarette. "We will continue our investigation into the disappearance of your passport." He slid it across his desk. "And that condom. And we will keep IAU Foreign Teachers Association President Blum informed of your actions, as this reflects badly on all of you. Behave, Mr. Callahan. You are on thin ice, as you say."

"Thank you, Dean Chen."

"Don't thank me. Everything about your behavior offends me. But I am willing to abide by the general's wishes."

"The general's wishes?"

"That you be spared immediate expulsion because of your aid to his daughter." Chen gestured for me to stand, then rose and thrust his face so close to mine that I could smell his tobacco breath. "But I would advise you to reflect on your actions. And if you ever lie to me again, you will be finished."

Jesus…what does that mean?

My hands shook as I put my passport into my pocket and walked out of the dean's office, wondering what the hell was going on. I tried to dismiss the idea that I was caught up in a big conspiracy or had been set up. For what? But then I realized that if Chinese officials had indeed engineered this, Dean Chen would have said exactly what he did, just to scare the shit out of me. Because wouldn't that be the whole point?

You're under their thumb now. You'll do exactly what you're told.

But who am I to warrant such attention?

My head was spinning. But thank God at least Lily had stood up for me. If her father hadn't intervened, Will and I might still be in jail. Then a surge of questions stopped me in my tracks: *Why would a Chinese general help us? What's in it for him? What will he want from me now?*

Besieged by doubt, I walked on to the classroom building. My students wouldn't arrive for an hour, but I sure as hell couldn't go back to sleep. I figured I might as well go in early and try to prepare for my lesson.

When I arrived at the door to my classroom, another thought struck me numb: Dean Chen had asked who had sent me to the IAU. It was Professor Lin who had suggested it.

When I considered all that had happened, going back months, I found it hard to believe that the events of the past twenty-four hours had been mere coincidence. But who was the puppeteer? Professor Lin? Was Chen trying to make me suspect him? I thought they were close.

All I knew for certain was there were no strings in my hand. Only keys. But the classroom door was unlocked, and the lights were already on. And there was Lily, sitting at my desk. She smiled at me. Despite all my misgivings, I was drawn to her, finding desire in the slipstream of doubt.

CHAPTER 7

"Hello, Mr. Callahan."

Lily spoke formally but offered a most informal smile. She sat a couple feet from the desk, legs crossed in her navy skirt. Her arm was draped over the back of the chair, her posture confident.

"You can call me by my first name," I said softly, standing before her like an errant pupil.

She rolled forward, the wheels of the old wooden chair creaking. "We address each other formally, Mr. Callahan." Her eyes rolled up to her left. I followed them to the security camera and felt like an idiot.

"Of course, Miss Jiang. My apologies."

She got up. "Take your seat. I'm not here to usurp you."

She stepped to the side as I put my gray canvas messenger bag on the corner of the desk and sat down. I felt her warmth on the wood. She stood a few feet away, but her lingering perfume made her feel closer. I found it as inviting as her hands when they rose within inches of my face. I thought she was about to cup my cheeks and searched her eyes for the same attraction I felt, but she was clinically studying my bruise. Without touching me, she directed my head to the side so she could view the injury more closely.

"That must have hurt." She nodded. "When that beast grabbed me, I felt completely alone…but when you grabbed him, I knew I wasn't. Thank you."

"You told your father."

"Of course." She was still standing right in front of me. "Those Russians must be dealt with according to the law."

According to the law. "I guess I would have been, too, if—"

"No." She shook her head.

The firmness of her response stopped me from asking for clarification. Her point was made: she held power. She was her father's daughter. She was the dean's assistant at one of the most important universities in China. "No" said all that and more.

"But we must not meet like that again," she added warmly.

"I understand." Then in a whisper, I dared to ask, "So how will we meet?"

She might have offered a fleeting smile. I couldn't be sure. She said nothing. The silence held for several fraught seconds. I began to perspire, as if her floral perfume had humidified the air.

Then the door opened and Will stepped in.

"Sorry," he said, squinting as though even the gray light from the windows was too strong, his hangover too painful. "I didn't know you had company. Good morning, Miss Jiang."

She gave him a nod and eased away from the desk.

"Come in," I said, wishing he'd turn around and leave. "We were just talking about last night."

"I was examining Mr. Callahan's battle wound," she said.

Will grinned, no more immune to her charms than I was. "I'm just glad you made it home safely, Miss Jiang."

"Thank you," she said. "How are you feeling?"

"Honestly, my head hurts. I've been taking aspirin but it's like throwing pebbles at the Great Wall and expecting it to come tumbling down."

Lily laughed. I did, too. That was the Will I was getting to know. Quick-witted, gregarious, charming.

"What about *you*?" he asked me as he came nearer, training his eyes on my bruise, which was starting to make me feel self-conscious. "You really took one for the team."

"The team?" Lily said. "He was trying to protect *me*." She was proprietary with her tone but playful with her manner.

"He sure was," Will agreed.

"But really, where would we be without *you*, Mr. Jean-Claude Van Damme?" I said. "You turned Solutions into a scene from *Bloodsport*. Did Dean Chen call you in, too?"

Will started to nod, then stopped, as if the pounding inside his head would allow no more movement than necessary. He propped his hip against a front-row desk. "I'm supposed to go in there at eleven. You?"

"He said I'm on thin ice." That was all I offered, mindful of the camera and hidden mic that I presumed was recording every breath we took.

"So I guess we shouldn't go to the skating rink across town," Will said with a wink.

"If you do, don't expect me to fish you two out if you fall through again," Lily answered, not missing a beat.

I didn't join in their bonhomie—but then again, I was the only one nursing an obvious injury.

"I should leave you to your lesson planning," Will said. "And you, Miss Jiang, to your duties."

I watched him close the door before speaking again. "I wonder if they polish those camera lenses to keep them sharp," I said brightly to Lily, bringing her attention to the eyes that were upon us.

"Every day," she answered without hesitation. "A clear eye leads to clear thinking."

"Sounds like Confucius."

Her eyes widened, as if she might laugh, but she didn't. "I'm glad you're feeling better, Mr. Callahan."

"Thank you," I said as she turned and walked away. I tried not to study her shape. I failed, even though I knew that the security camera was watching me as closely.

Seconds after she left the classroom, the students marched in. So much for lesson planning. I was going to have to wing it. Most greeted me in English. A few asked about my bruise. I realized too late that I'd given them the stock answer of a battered spouse: "I ran into a door." No one questioned my response.

The dean had said to use the first week for introductions, so after focusing on me the first day, I wanted to hear about them. *Like if your father's in the Politburo and some terrorists might come here to kill us all.* "Anything you'd like to say. I'll be all ears. That's an American idiom, by the way."

No one smiled, but a tall boy in the back corner took the initiative. "In Chinese, my name is Yang Yiyong. I don't have an English name. I am from Beijing. I like to play basketball. In China, I am so tall I am like Shaquille O'Neal," he added with a nervous laugh.

"How about if we come up with an English name for you? How does Shaquille sound?"

"Like a girl's name."

"I don't think I'd tell Shaq that," I said to scattered chuckles. "What about Michael—like Michael Jordan?"

"Good one," he agreed.

I turned as casually as I could to another student who announced that her English name was Dolly.

"For Dolly Parton?" I asked.

"No," she laughed, "for the cloned sheep," referring to the first mammal produced from an adult cell, and announced the year before to great fanfare.

She wasn't kidding, and I laughed along with the others. Dolly wore blood-red lipstick and gesticulated freely when she spoke of her love for skiing, interjecting "like" and "I mean" into her speech, as though she were a Valley girl. She reported that she had, in fact, gone to Deerfield Academy, the Massachusetts boarding school, for two years. After her leg was broken in a car accident, though, she returned to China.

"I couldn't afford the medical treatment in the United States," she explained.

"Neither can many Americans," I replied, trusting that the remark would meet with Dean Chen's approval. His nephew, the class cop Rick, nodded.

I eyed the young man next to Dolly. "What about you? Do you have an English name?"

"No, but I have a French name—Napoleon Bonaparte."

I tried for another dash of humor. "Okay, but you seem too tall for a Napoleon."

The observation didn't sit well with the would-be emperor. "Napoleon Bonaparte," he insisted.

"Do you have any hobbies, Napoleon Bonaparte? Anything we should know about you?"

"In our military training, I liked shooting guns."

"What did you shoot at? I ask because when I go to my grandparents' farm, I sometimes go rabbit hunting with a shotgun or shoot cans with a pistol."

"I like to shoot the AK-47. It is good for hunting. Hunting Americans. Ha ha," he added, without a trace of real laughter.

Stunned by his open hostility, I scanned the room for a friendly face. Seeing mostly neutral stares, I settled on a young woman named Qianyi, who told me her parents were diplomats.

"And do you have an English name?"

"Why do I need an English name? We live in China." She gestured out the window, as if I needed a clue to where I'd landed several days ago.

"Uh, I was told that in English classes the students often take English names. And maybe because foreigners can't pronounce or remember Chinese ones very easily."

"Does that not seem lazy? Chinese people will not always be so accommodating. More and more people are tired of that."

Feeling the pressure, I tried to explain. "All right, but when I took Mandarin, we all took Chinese names. Mine, *Gao Anzhu*, is a rough transliteration of my real name."

"As I said, my parents are diplomats, but I am not. Chinese are always giving, always accommodating. The time is coming when that will have to stop."

Qianyi's sense of national pride may not have been appreciably different from that of some Americans, but I did not expect this sort of attitude from a student at a top university. I was thankful when the rest of the class responded with less antagonism.

As the end of the hour neared, I thanked them for their introductions, adding that I'd enjoyed hearing from each of them. I wasn't beyond stretching the truth. "I was also thinking about fun ways to introduce you to American culture and thought of showing some classic movies. For those of you who are interested, I'd be happy to hold an occasional 'movie night' at my apartment." I knew it would need to be approved by the dean's office, but Will said that he and others had done it last year and that you could find any popular title on the street for less than a US dollar in video disc format. All of them pirated, of course.

Class monitor Rick appeared to weigh my suggestion. "It would depend on the movie."

"Do you like comedies?" I thought those would be safer than action-adventure films, given the genre's penchant for American heroes.

Before anyone could respond, the bell rang, and we agreed to finalize plans next time.

I watched everyone leave. So did Rick. For several moments, I thought his glare would see me out the door, too. After offering him a smile—and wishing I hadn't bothered—I gathered my materials, determined not to be intimidated by him. When I looked up, he'd once again slipped away quietly.

His absence seemed to clear the air, along with my thoughts, and I accepted that the second class had gone reasonably well. The students were responsive, a few quite friendly, with more diverse backgrounds than I'd expected.

And only one seemed to want to shoot me with an AK-47.

CHAPTER 8

By Friday, I figured I'd settled into an irreproachable routine, with the subtle exception of making eye contact with Lily several times on the grounds or in the hallways, little lures that I hoped kept us fishing in whatever pond we'd found ourselves.

After a quick lunch alone in the canteen, I was tempted to skip office hours back in my dusty, poorly lit apartment. Not one student had bothered to make an appointment, and there were more pleasant places to spend my time. Still, I told myself, a week that had begun on such a rough note should not end on an indolent one. I had to make sure that if anybody—especially Dean Chen—decided to stop by, I would be there.

I settled at the desk in my living room and began reviewing my students' homework assignments. To gauge their English levels—and with the administration's permission—I'd asked them to write short essays about what they did over the summer. I started with

Rick's. He had taken GRE prep classes at New Oriental—China's version of the Princeton Review—in hopes of attending grad school in America. I was surprised Rick would have much interest in visiting the US, but he explained it in his essay using a maxim from Sun Tzu, the ancient Chinese warrior-philosopher: "If you know the enemy and know yourself, you need not fear the result of a hundred battles." It sounded like he was a coconspirator with Napoleon Bonaparte, Mr. AK-47.

I turned to Qianyi's report. She had apparently spent July through August in Rick's same GRE class and wanted to attend Stanford because "by working with professors there, I can bring back technologies for China," a goal that I soon discovered was a recurring theme among several students.

Reading these essays and several similar ones made me feel protective of my country in ways I never had before. Our neoliberal economic professors at Harvard had emphasized the benefits of the free flow of labor and goods but, frankly, I was having second thoughts after noting how many of my students considered the theft of intellectual property a national prerogative.

I heard footsteps on the stairs and looked up, taken aback to see Lily poking her head in the door. My smile appeared immediately, as if of its own volition. Lily was also beaming. This was our first moment alone together since—

You're *not* alone. Don't kid yourself. I glanced up at the motion detector flickering in the corner of the living room. It would have been foolish to assume there weren't hidden cameras or microphones tucked away, too.

"I hope I'm not bothering you," she said, with no hint of regret.

"Not at all. None of my students seems interested in coming, so—"

"So I'm your first visitor? I'm honored."

"Can I get you something to drink?"

"Water?" she asked, touching her tongue to her teeth. "The air is so dry and dusty."

"Of course."

I walked over to take a bottle from the refrigerator in the entry-way—the kitchen was too small—when she asked if I had *hot* water.

"Oh, right." Most Chinese preferred it that way.

I retrieved the *reshuiping*, an insulated hot water bottle the maids dutifully filled each morning and left just inside the front door. Lily smiled as I brought her a full plastic cup. She was standing in front of my bookshelf, flipping through a CD organizer she had taken down.

"I like some of these groups." She placed her finger on one by George Michael. "'Fastlove.' I like that song. Everyone in China says that loving fast is typical in the West."

"So you know about George Michael."

"My father always buys CDs for me when he travels abroad. I ask him to get the most popular ones."

"Sounds like he travels a lot."

She strolled over to my desk chair and took a seat. "You're not really guessing, are you? That's the first thing people usually hear about me. My father the general."

"Yes, I did hear that." There was no forgetting that he was also the chief of the People's Liberation Army General Staff and a member of the Central Military Commission. "What does he say about the places he visits?"

"He doesn't talk about them much. But ever since I was little, he's brought me back music, books, movies, and magazines from places like America and England."

"You like Western pop culture, it seems."

"I do. The music and stories are much more *real* than anything here. Even though I am Chinese, I feel like I can really relate to what Western artists are trying to say—and, of course, it helps me practice my English."

"It's working. You speak perfectly. Have you ever traveled abroad?"

"No, never. But I really want to—my father definitely 'whetted my appetite,' I think you say. Have you seen *Before Sunrise?* The Ethan Hawke movie?"

"Of course."

"It's so romantic. After I saw that, all I wanted to do was travel around Europe by train."

I smiled. "Hoping to meet Ethan himself?"

"Maybe. But even if I did he'd probably ignore a Chinese girl like me. Didn't they say every man's fantasy was to meet a *French* girl on the train, make love to her, and never see her again?"

I saw all sorts of ways to take this conversation but, titillating as they were, every one of them led directly back to Dean Chen's office. For all I knew, he was listening in at that very moment. I skirted her question. "Not every guy."

"Hmm. Anyway, I had hoped that after graduating from the IAU—"

"Oh, you went here, too?"

She nodded. "I wanted to go to graduate school in the US and then get a posting abroad in the Ministry of Foreign Affairs, but with my father always traveling, there was no way."

I got it. The Chinese government feared the defection of top officials—especially generals with their military secrets—if they and their families were out of the country at the same time.

"That's gotta be frustrating," I said.

"It is. You know, I love China, and I am very proud of my father, but being his daughter here is really very constraining. I can't have my own life. Sometimes, I wish I could just move to the US or Europe and reinvent myself." She closed her eyes, as if imagining it all. "But of course I can't." She shrugged. "So, after graduating the Foreign Ministry assigned me to help Dean Chen here on campus—to train people to take the positions I wanted and live in the countries I hoped to see." She glanced out the window at the usual bustle of students on the walkways below.

I felt for her, and wanted to know her so much better, but again was conscious of who might be eavesdropping. "Well, at least it's a prestigious school, with smart students and a peaceful campus."

"Sure, but there are too many rules and restrictions. I guess you've noticed that every morning the students wake up to the national anthem and then have to attend political lectures on how the US is trying to keep China down."

"I think they're sparing us all that over in the Foreign Experts Building."

"At Peking University, they have a lot more freedom."

I was shocked at how openly Lily criticized the IAU, whether out of exasperation or perhaps confidence that as the daughter of a general she was untouchable. I kept my response as neutral as possible. "So why do so many students choose to come here?"

"Their parents make them. Many of the top officials in government graduated from here, and they send their children. You know Rick, the class monitor? His grandfather was the foreign minister."

"And his uncle's Dean Chen."

"That's right," she said. "Powerful families in China stay powerful for a reason."

I hesitated, not knowing what to make of that. An implied criticism? Of her own father, no less? I was trying to thread these verbal and ideological needles with care, so I merely agreed that it was a strict school.

"Too strict," she added in a lowered voice. "Like that ridiculous ten p.m. curfew. For me, too, even after I've graduated."

"But that doesn't seem to have stopped you from having fun…like the other night." I whispered. "How did you get out?"

"Promise you won't tell anyone?" she asked quietly.

I nodded.

"Through the bathroom window."

"What about the school's security cameras?"

"You just need to figure out where they are. There are no cameras outside that bathroom window, and it's a short jump to the ground. Then I climbed the fence on the north side of campus, away from the guards. I got back in the same way. I'm strong." She held up her arm and flexed her bicep. "Feel."

I couldn't resist, and squeezed it. "Impressive."

"I do lots of yoga and pull-ups." She suddenly reached out and grabbed my own arm. "Still not as muscular as yours, though."

I wanted to pick her up and kiss her right there, but just thanked her and safely changed the topic. "What would they do if you got caught sneaking out?"

"Not much. My father, the general," she repeated, gazing directly into my eyes.

"What's your mother like?"

"Her friends say we have similar personalities, but I am not so sure. She is much more strong-willed than I am. But I might be more of an adventure seeker."

"Maybe when she was your age, she was more like you. Maybe that's the person your mother's friends are comparing you with."

"I'm not sure. She and her friends, growing up during the Cultural Revolution, didn't have time for fun and adventure. Radicals took socialism to an extreme. They persecuted millions—including my mother and her family. Many starved or even died. I think it hardened her in a way. She doesn't like to talk about it." Lily paused. "I think that's why she and her friends recently started taking dance lessons. That's their idea of doing something wild—reliving a youth they never had."

"I know it's not exactly the same," I said, aware of the trauma the Cultural Revolution brought to millions of Chinese, "but I think I can relate to the generational gap you feel. My parents both grew up poor—my mom on a farm and my father the son of a laborer on construction sites. Like your father, my dad joined the Army for a few years to pay for college. And while I didn't grow up rich, my parents' childhoods definitely shaped them in a way I can't fully relate to. They thought I was crazy to 'waste' a year teaching in China."

"So, are your parents taking dance classes now, too?"

"Believe it or not, they did a few years ago!" I laughed, delighted to find this connection between us.

"Yes, there are lots of schools here, too." She looped hair behind her ear, charming me with the simplest gesture. "Speaking of schools, have you enjoyed teaching about American society? Must be easy for you," she added with a laugh.

"I'm just getting started—and it seems I'll basically be reading off the," I chose my words carefully, "very *detailed* teaching notes. I mostly came to prepare for a business career in China. Though after burying my head in books for so long I suppose I was also eager to travel—no pressure, no commitments."

"*Before Sunrise.*"

"Maybe," I smiled. Though some of my friends thought it was more *Heart of Darkness.*

"Someday I'd like to teach Chinese to pay for my own travels. Do many Americans want to learn Mandarin?"

"Not as many as Chinese who want to learn English, but more and more, as China's economy and influence grow. You can always help me with my Mandarin."

"That could be nice." She rose and walked over to the window, staring at the skyline. "You must be excited to join a company like White and McInerney next year."

"I felt very lucky to get an offer from them."

"When I was an undergraduate, I attended one of their recruiting events in Beijing. I met the head of their office here. He said they worked 'behind the scenes' with governments and corporations. I thought it sounded a lot like your CIA, so I talked to my father about them."

I took the bait. "What did he think?"

"He laughed. 'Them?' he said. 'They're just here to make money off China. That company's the least of our worries.'"

My expression must have changed because she asked, "Did I say something wrong?"

"Isn't that how you described me in class—someone who was just here to make money?"

"Well, from what I saw in the bar, you certainly didn't come here to fight." She smiled. That stung. But then she gave my hand a reassuring touch.

"You know I was just joking. You were really brave. It took a lot of courage to stand up to that jerk like you did. He was huge."

Lily picked up her backpack. I looked at my watch. She'd been there for half an hour. I was shocked by how quickly the time had passed. Although I had been warned of the risks, I wanted to see her again. Soon.

"Maybe we could have coffee some time. Or lunch?" I suggested.

You idiot. I pictured her father in his military uniform, covered in ribbons, ordering my immediate imprisonment. My facial tic felt like it might start firing any moment.

But she agreed right away. "Yes, that would be nice. And it reminds me why I came here—I almost forgot."

My eyebrows raised. "Oh, yeah?"

"My father is hosting a dinner on the eighteenth, two weeks from now, for some American diplomats, including your ambassador. He told me he wanted to invite some other foreign guests and asked if I had any suggestions. I thought of you."

Dinner with a general and the ambassador? "Really?"

"Yes, *really*, you should come. You might find it interesting, and the food will be some of the best Chinese cuisine you'll ever have. It will be held at the Diaoyutai State Guesthouse."

I was flabbergasted. "Thank you. I'd love that."

"Wonderful. My father knows how you tried to protect me." She seemed to choose her next words with care. "He's a typical father and military officer, so he said he'll decide for himself about you. But I'll make sure we sit together."

"Sure…but what would Dean Chen say?"

"My father the general," she replied once more.

I walked her to the door with a smile so broad I could feel it. When we said goodbye, I noticed that Lily had turned my office hours sign from "Open" to "Closed" before she came in.

I laughed to myself, picturing a romantic scene from a coming-of-age comedy. Maybe she'd gotten that idea from an American movie, too. Then I shuddered as my thoughts turned to darker genres.

My mind rewound through everything we'd said, praying there really weren't any listening devices, and wondering how I could explain myself to the dean if "my father the general" wasn't enough to stop him.

I started inspecting my apartment all over again, tormented by the idea that the real purpose of the conspicuous motion detector in my living room might be to distract a foreign teacher from the stricter surveillance of concealed cameras and mics.

After cranking up the volume of the BBC World Service on my short-wave radio—it was on a long list of "necessities for China" in Professor Lin's packet, and a godsend whenever I began to go crazy watching China Central Television—I started removing books and CDs from shelves and checked behind the cabinets. I got down on my hands and knees to follow the floorboards. And that's where I found a tiny silver mic, the shape and size of a pencil eraser, tucked into a little groove against the wall below my desk.

I followed its wire, white as the floorboard, along the seam toward the corner of the room, behind the television cabinet. I felt the exposed copper before I actually saw it, and I smiled with relief. The mic wire must have been clipped at some point. But by whom? And I realized that security services might blame *me* for cutting the wire.

Report it.

Then it occurred to me that the cutting of the wire might not have been an accident at all. Maybe it was designed to distract me from a better concealed mic. And if I reported this one, they would surely grill me about why I was digging around my apartment. I could just hear Dean Chen's voice, "And why do you think you are important enough to spy on?"

As the questions piled up, it became clear that the wire might have been cut for reasons that someone like me couldn't possibly imagine.

And that might be the greatest danger of all.

CHAPTER 9

Will and I choked on leaded-gas fumes as we negotiated the chockablock madness of Beijing traffic on our heavy, single-geared Forever brand bikes. I had never seen such horrendous gridlock, even in Chicago's worst rush hours. We pedaled past a barrel-chested policeman struggling to impose order on the incessantly honking bumper-to-bumper cars, buses, and the cyclists swerving in between everything and everyone.

Battling through the mess felt like a warmup for our destination: the Beijing Fight Club. I'd told Will I wanted to try out the place. The knockdown at the bar was humbling, and—even if she was joking—Lily's comment yesterday about not being a fighter only rubbed it in.

Only inches separated my handlebars from Will's as we rode past barbers who'd set up chairs under white canvas tents, and a sidewalk market where hawkers—their skin dark and leathery—sold fresh fruit and vegetables from the back of tricycle wagons. A swarm of kids was unloading pears.

"Shouldn't they be in school?" I shouted over the din.

"Can't. They're not legal," he yelled back. "Everyone in China has a *hukou*, a household registration that determines where they can live or get social services like education or healthcare. These people from poorer provinces aren't legally allowed to be here. They gotta live in the shadows, like illegal immigrants in the US."

We spotted more as we passed a huge construction site with hundreds of workers scurrying about. Unlike building projects in the US, where heavy machinery handled the biggest jobs, men here were digging entire foundations, dozens of feet deep, with shovels. Others were fastening bamboo scaffolding with rope around growing high-rises.

"They live over there." Will pointed to a tent city.

"Tough life." I remembered that one of the first words I had learned in Chinese class was *chi ku*, which meant "eat bitterness." It could describe how migrants endured hardship, but it was also applied to the resilience of Chinese people as a whole.

We finally locked our bikes near the entrance to Fuchengmen Station and pressed ourselves into a mass of bodies on the newly built train to Dongzhimen in northeast Beijing. That's where we got off and grabbed two seats at the front of a small, beat-up old bus. Our position gave us an unobstructed view as the balding driver crept through the chaotic traffic, beeping his horn and shouting obscenities the entire time while miraculously avoiding the vehicles and pedestrians swarming all around us. If I really were the subject of surveillance, I didn't think anybody could possibly tail me through this maze. Nevertheless, I kept looking back, only to be met by the curious gazes of people squeezed into seats and standing shoulder-to-shoulder in the aisle.

Our driver hit his horn hard and swerved suddenly, then slammed on the brakes. Will and I were thrown against the metal barrier in front of us. The impact bruised my forehead but spared my temple, still sore from my clumsy heroics in the bar. Someone on the teeming pavement screamed in agony. The driver quickly reversed.

We stood and looked out the window.

We'd crashed into a cyclist, who lay halfway under his twisted bike, moaning horribly. His leg stuck out at an unnatural angle. His companion jumped off her bike and rushed to his side, crying and wringing her hands. But not for long. She turned on the bus driver, pointing her finger furiously at him. He swore back at her in a guttural tone I couldn't decipher.

The injured man pleaded for help as she carefully tried to free him from his mangled bike. A noisy crowd gathered but, to my amazement, no one else made any effort to aid them.

"We need to call..." I shouted, straining to find the word for "ambulance" in Mandarin before settling for "...a doctor."

"Stay seated!" the driver yelled at me as he climbed out.

We watched through the front window as the young woman and driver pointed angrily to each other and shouted. I could understand her fury and was baffled by the driver's lack of remorse.

"Pay the woman so we can get moving again," someone behind us yelled out the window.

Pay?

That's when I realized the woman and driver were bickering over what the accident would cost him. The driver finally handed over 1200 *yuan*, about one hundred fifty dollars. Several pedestrians helped the young woman lift her friend and carry him and his bike off the road.

The bus driver hoisted himself back behind the wheel and merged into traffic, swearing and honking all over again. I looked at Will in disbelief.

"One or two thousand RMB to the right person can get you out of some serious shit," he said.

The bus dropped us off at a stop near a tiny Thai restaurant with a big red pepper on the front. From there, we hoofed it down noisy, busy streets where the rich aroma of spicy cooking was soon overcome by the stench of raw sewage. I kept checking over my shoulder, but anyone following us would be impossible to spot in the packed streets.

"Lai wanr ma?" a halter-topped young woman shouted at me from the front of a massage parlor. *Want to play?*

"You like her?" an older woman asked in English. "Come inside— we also have others."

We smiled politely and kept moving.

Across the street, vendors called out to us, their carts full of Want-Want Rice Crackers, spicy wheat sticks, packaged buns stuffed with bean paste, instant noodles, and White Rabbit and other Western candies. Nearby, a group of old men squatted in front of Chinese chessboards, oblivious to it all as they moved their cannons and elephants into position.

We finally arrived at a large karaoke bar. Will signaled for me to follow him inside.

"Where's the Beijing Fight Club?" I asked.

"This is it."

The fusion of karaoke bar and fight club was not subtle. Evander Holyfield and Mike Tyson cocked their fists at us from the walls of the main lobby. Sugar Ray Leonard and Rocky Marciano glared from posters in the corridor that led to the bar. Incendiary English words were spray-painted in neon yellow and orange on the black walls all around the room in oddly alphabetical order:

> *Animal! Asshole! Attack! Beast! Brutalize! Crush!*
> *Death! FIGHT BIG! Monster! Sucker! Willpower!*

The exhortations seemed more ridiculous than intimidating, but what did I know?

A boxing ring stood incongruously in the middle of the main room of the karaoke bar. The ropes on one side drooped to the floor. Above the ring, customers could watch fights from a second-floor balcony.

A balding man in his fifties in a black Beijing Fight Club T-shirt ambled toward us with a cigarette hanging from his lips. Without a word, he ushered us through a door to a gym in the back, where a younger, six-foot guy with a military buzz cut greeted us with a grunt, then sized us up. Apparently satisfied—or at least not disgusted—he introduced himself as Liu Jun, the head coach.

"*Wo jiao Will*," the more formidable of us replied.

I also offered my name.

"*Nimen yao lai da quanji ma?*" Liu asked. *Do you want to box?*

I said we wanted to learn how and had come to check out the club. Liu led us farther into the back room, where a well-worn practice ring stood, along with an assortment of dumbbells, pull-up bars, free weights, and some of the biggest Chinese guys I'd ever seen, all grunting and shouting. The whole place stank of sweat. The coach noticed my surprise.

"Bodybuilding," he blurted out in English. "What country are you from?" he asked in Mandarin.

"*Meiguo*," I replied. We are Americans.

"America has the best boxing," he said.

Finally, something positive about my country.

A few of those bodybuilders scowled at us fiercely, as if they wondered what we were doing in their gym. Sizing *them* up, I had to agree.

Liu asked us something, but I couldn't catch it with all the clanging of weights and the thumping of DMX's "Ruff Riders' Anthem" in the background. I cocked my head.

"Have you boxed before?" he asked again.

Will said he'd had some experience with boxing and martial arts. After his efficient dispatch of those Russians, this was like Picasso conceding that he'd picked up a brush or two.

Liu nodded his approval and offered us a free class.

We'd brought workout clothes. After a quick change in a narrow, pungent locker room, we returned to the floor. Liu was waiting, another cigarette drooping from his lips. He introduced us to the rest of the boxers. Will exchanged nods and a perfunctory smile with one squat guy named Wu who had scars on his face and arm. It looked like maybe they had met before—or were challenging each other to a throw down right then and there.

"Shadowbox!" Liu commanded, transforming instantly from genial guide to tough coach.

Will impressed me once again with his skill, while I had only a vague notion of what to do from the *Rocky* movies.

Liu stepped over and said he'd show me the basics. A dozen pairs of eyes studied us as we threw jabs and crosses, body shots and uppercuts, ducking and parrying the counterpunches of invisible adversaries.

"*Shoutao, shoutao!*" Liu barked for us to stop. Time to put on the gloves. "Akihiro!" He gestured at a short but muscular Japanese with a spiked haircut to put on his gloves, too. A bodybuilder said in stuttering English, "Akihiro very good boxer."

"Will!" Liu shouted, pointing toward the ring, where Akihiro now waited.

Will confidently ducked between the ropes.

"*Kai shi!*" Liu yelled. *Begin.*

Akihiro stepped forward, eyes intent on Will, who moved out of his corner as if he craved body contact. He threw an aggressive combination at the Japanese fighter, as if to finish him off quickly, only to get pop-pop-popped by counterpunches so quick they blurred.

"*Shang xia, shang xia!*" Liu yelled at Will. *Up down, up down!* "*Baohu ziji!*" Protect yourself! "*Baohu lian!*" Guard your face!

More weightlifters tromped over to check out the spectacle. "*Zhongguo! Zhongguo!*"—China! China!—one shouted, thinking he was seeing a fight between an American and a Chinese.

Another—maybe assuming I couldn't understand—answered that he wanted to kick some American ass next. "I hate America," he growled.

"That's that Japanese boxer," a guy with arms as large as holiday hams pointed out. If there was one subject Chinese could all agree on, it was that they detested Japan more than any other country, even America. Their mood shifted instantly.

"U-S-A! U-S-A!"

Before leaving the States, I wouldn't have considered myself particularly patriotic, much less nationalistic. But at that moment, watching

Will box—with everyone around us viewing the fight as a bitter contest between Japan and America—I actually did feel as though my country and I had something on the line. I really wanted Will to win.

The coach, though, would have none of it. "Knock it off!" he shouted at the gathering crowd. No nationalism in his boxing club.

About three minutes into the fight—the length of a pro-boxing round—Will was picking his spots, looking for openings. Akihiro jabbed steadily with his left, occasionally mixing in a hook or cross.

After one of Will's left hooks, Akihiro tried to catch him with a fast right. Will saw it coming. He ducked and rolled his shoulders to the right, then threw a thunderous left hook to the side of Akihiro's head, a right feint to his face, a left to the body, another left to the chin, and finally a quick right hook to the side of the head. Akihiro stumbled back, then crumpled to his knees. It was primitive, but I was captivated.

"*Hao, hao. Keyi le.*" Liu had seen enough.

Will climbed down from the ring and pulled out his mouth guard. I slapped him on the shoulder. "Way to go!"

"Thanks," he said, not nearly as animated as I was.

Liu pulled his cigarette out of his mouth, exhaled a huge gray cloud, and put on a pair of gloves. He didn't bother to tape his hands. Why would he? He pointed at me. I was next.

"*Shanglai, ba.*" *Come up here.*

He looked about thirty-five, past his prime, and was clearly a heavy smoker. But still, he was a boxer and I wasn't. I stepped into the ring expecting butterflies. What came alive was a whole belly full of bees, as if the hive had just been kicked.

Liu started off flicking telegraphed jabs and looping hooks that I could block. I knew he was taking it easy on me, but I was high from the sudden physical contact and began to go after him harder, punching wildly and trying to look badass.

Uppercut, I told myself.

I launched the blow. Liu evaded it without difficulty, like all my others. As my fist sailed upward, I found myself suddenly breathless, drained of adrenaline. As I gasped for air, I never saw his punch coming. It hit me square in the temple, not far from where those bare Russian knuckles had done their damage at Solutions. I'd been spared on the bus but not in the ring.

I tried to cover up, ducking my head into my body and gloves. Too late. Liu carpet-bombed me with blows to my face. My brain felt like it was bouncing around inside my skull. I'm sure it was. I launched a haphazard combination in a futile attempt to defend myself. Liu backed off and lowered his gloves. The fight was over.

As I wiped my face with my glove, I saw a streak of blood from my nose. I didn't even remember being hit there.

"Not bad for a beginner," Will said, patting me on the back.

Not bad? I'd hate to see what "bad" looks like.

"That's it for today," Liu announced to the group, handing me a filthy rag to stop my nose from bleeding on his gym floor.

I heard one of the bodybuilders say in Mandarin that he couldn't wait to kick my ass.

Liu took a drag on a fresh cigarette, then gave Will and me a rundown of the schedule and fees. I hadn't left a single mark on Liu, and he didn't seem even the slightest bit winded. "Hope we see you here again," he added, shaking our hands.

Will told him he would as we headed for the showers.

"We should go drink to your first time in the ring," he said to me. "I know a lady from the US embassy having a party nearby."

"Sounds fun—but we may be celebrating my one and only trip here." My bell was still ringing and my ribs ached.

Will just gave me a look, like he knew that I was hooked. And I realized it, too. I'd had a taste of blood, and even though it was my own, I wanted more.

CHAPTER 10

A steely-eyed guard blocked the entrance to the Diaoyutai State Guesthouse and shooed me away.

"General Jiang Guangkai himself invited me," I said in Mandarin as I held up my passport and pointed to the list of names on his clipboard.

The man's glare didn't soften. I couldn't blame him. I must have looked completely out of place, showing up at a formal dinner in the same khakis and gray blazer I'd worn to orientation, plus a button-down white shirt and blue tie, the best outfit I'd brought to China. I was caked in sweat, and my brown bluchers were covered in dust from the forty-minute trek there. In the diplomatic land of Brioni, I was L. L. Bean.

He snatched my passport, stepped into the guardhouse, and picked up the phone.

I looked at my watch. The event was to begin in three minutes. I glanced around to see if I could find Lily or someone else to help. Right then the guard returned, head slightly bowed. "Excuse me for the delay. Please follow the signs." He pointed the way.

"*Xie xie.*" I thanked him as I hurried through the gate and along the tree-covered path.

I didn't want to offend the general by showing up late. He was a legend in China, with hundreds of internet citations. He'd fought in China's 1979 conflict with Vietnam, and in the eighties had directed military intelligence efforts that successfully stole US submarine, stealth, and radar technologies—thefts so compromising to American security that they hadn't been revealed to the US public until recently. By the early nineties, he was in charge of the Nanjing military region across from Taiwan, a highly prestigious command, before being tapped to lead the Army General Staff.

I crossed a stone bridge over a slow-moving stream as weeping willows swayed on both banks. Then I saw Villa 18, the exterior beautifully lit for the banquet. The building was a classic Chinese design: broad and symmetrical, with red and green trim and a yellow-tiled roof that swept up at the corners to encase golden gables.

I approached the end of a line, behind the well-heeled dignitaries. A young man in a black suit came out, pulled me aside, and led me through a side entrance to an ornate bathroom. Handing me a small white towel, he pointed to my sweaty face and dusty shoes.

After sorting myself out, I followed the attendant across a fine blue carpet to the main ballroom, which was framed by a floor-to-ceiling window overlooking an illuminated lake.

I checked around for Lily among the fifty-plus Americans and Chinese in attendance, about a quarter of them military officers. I didn't see her but did spot General Jiang at the center of the room. He looked like photos I'd seen of him online, right down to his dress uniform. Unlike the American officers, whose chests were adorned with a fruit salad of ribbons and medals, the general's uniform was plain, save for the yellow epaulets and red and yellow pins on the lapels of his dark green jacket. He was leaning close to the US ambassador, a man whom I recognized as the former Democratic senator from Tennessee.

I also spotted a woman from the US Embassy who'd hosted a party after our first night boxing. I hadn't caught her name, but she worked for the Commercial Service, helping American companies sell into the local market. She'd been charming two Chinese gentleman, gently touching their arms. When she had excused herself to greet several late arrivals, one of the guests beside me had whispered that he'd heard a rumor she was actually CIA and organized these events to cultivate contacts from the nearby Chinese Ministry of Foreign Affairs.

Now, as I watched her and the ambassador and so many others attired in the crisp creases of the deeply influential, I could almost feel the undercurrents of spy craft swirling throughout the room in real time. It felt surreal, as though I'd stepped into a grand scene from a Cold War movie.

At that moment, Lily walked into the Great Hall in a long red dress and heels. She wore pearl earrings, which for the first time appeared quintessentially Chinese to me. Her elegant presence only contributed to my own sense of not belonging. But then she waved at me with such a welcoming smile that it washed away my misgivings. She motioned to meet her beside her father.

The general's gruff expression softened as she approached him, and I could see adoration in his eyes. I wondered if I would one day feel the same about a daughter of my own.

Lily might have been whispering my name in her father's ear because as I drew near, he put out his hand and in a booming baritone said, "*Gao Laoshi!*" *Teacher Gao.*

"Andrew, this is my father." I heard pride in her voice and found it endearing as the general held me firmly in his grasp.

"It's an honor to meet you, sir," I said in Chinese, concerned about how I should converse with a general. He exuded power and was physically intimidating. A few inches shorter than I was, he had broad shoulders, a bristly military haircut, and a long scar below his right eye. I doubted it stemmed from a gardening mishap.

The ambassador filled the conversational void by introducing himself to me in his gentlemanly Tennessee drawl. His grip provided only the slightest pressure, as if a diplomat's understated strength extended to the most quotidian gesture. Then he turned to his blond daughter Elizabeth and introduced her, adding that I was teaching IAU students about American society.

"I'm really enjoying it," I said, surprised that he knew who I was. Was there an American Embassy dossier with my name on it? Perhaps it wasn't just the Chinese keeping tabs on me.

General Jiang added, "My daughter told me that Professor Gao is an excellent teacher." Professor? Hardly. But I wasn't about to correct him.

A slender woman with a delicate face and sharp cheekbones stepped to the general's side. He introduced his wife, Lily's mother, Jiang Xin, to me. She belied her apparent frailty by looking me in the eye and shaking my hand firmly.

"Lily tells me you went to Harvard," the general said, looking me up and down. "You must be very...intelligent."

"I don't know about intelligent," I said. "I had to work very hard at Harvard."

"Modest, that's good—not very typical for Americans." The general squeezed my arm tightly. I instinctively flexed it, sore after lifting weights only hours earlier at the Fight Club. I'd been careful not to spar, however, for fear of showing up with a swollen eye or crooked nose.

General Jiang spoke quickly in Mandarin to Lily. I didn't catch what he said, so I looked at her for help. She smirked. "My father said that in China, bookworms aren't usually as big and strong as you."

Coming from a military man, I took that as a compliment. I didn't mention that my boxing record consisted of one loss by knockout at a bar and several more defeats at the hands of Coach Liu, an over-the-hill chain-smoker.

Lily guided the conversation with ease, pausing only when guests were asked to take their assigned places for dinner. A half-dozen notable Americans, including the ambassador, defense secretary, a high-ranking admiral, and a few Fortune 500 executives sat at the head table, along with their Chinese counterparts, with General Jiang and his wife at the center. Lily and I settled at one of several smaller tables beside a handful of others. I was awestruck to find myself at a momentous bilateral summit, and couldn't help but selfishly think, *These are exactly the sort of business contacts I hoped to make in China.* Professor Lin was right about teaching at the IAU. And that was before I ever met Lily.

"Thanks again for inviting me," I told her.

She surprised me by discreetly pressing her leg against mine under the table. She didn't say anything, just locked onto my gaze, but there was no mistaking her overture.

I held my leg against hers for another moment before pulling back, worried that her parents could see us. I breathed a sigh of relief to see that the tablecloth blocked the view.

A staff member served each of us a plate of what the menu called, in Mandarin, a "garden full of spring blossoms," a colorful dish of ham, salted duck eggs, carrots, snow fungus, oranges, sweet beans, and other garnishes served on blue and yellow china. I asked Lily about the origins of the dish's name, which seemed to have little to do with the ingredients or taste. "We often place more emphasis on the overall appearance or sensation," she said as her fingers gently touched the back of my hand.

I smiled, while desperately trying to control the chemicals coursing through my body, a mix of desire and fear. My rational side was telling me this general's daughter was off-limits, which seemed to make me want her even more.

I attempted to focus on the food as another appetizer was served— "three flowers competing with each other," delicately arranged pieces of shrimp, pig ear, and a mystery item I couldn't even recognize. As I sampled the succulent dishes, their delicious aroma almost overwhelmed the entrancing perfume Lily wore.

I asked her about the Chinese dignitaries, particularly an Asian man at the head table, who looked familiar.

"That's Ed Lee, the Managing Director of White and McInerny in China," Lily said.

"Really?" I recalled her saying she had met the head of W&M at the recruiting event.

"Yes, you should introduce yourself to him tonight."

After several more delightful cold appetizers, the hot dishes began to arrive in small portions, starting with a variety of soups, including one made from chrysanthemums and tofu. Then crispy fried mango and quail rolls appeared before king crab, baked snails, black pepper beef, and what they called "shrimp and dragon ball dumplings."

As I enjoyed the Chinese *haute cuisine* and unique company, I learned that the dinner had two purposes. Officially, it was part of a series of meetings to improve US-Chinese relations, which had been on rocky terms since 1996, when America sailed the USS *Nimitz* aircraft carrier right through the Taiwan Strait. China's humiliation might have been on the mind of two US military delegates at my table who were discussing the need to avoid a "Thucydides Trap," a historical tendency for established and rising powers to go to war.

Unofficially, the evening celebrated General Jiang's recent return from the United States, where he'd been part of a delegation negotiating China's entry into the World Trade Organization.

Even without such a high-stakes backdrop, the dinner would have been a memorable event. The glasses of *baijiu*, a Chinese rice wine, came one after the other in quick succession, and so did the general's stories. His parents, he lamented, must have wanted to prevent him from having a successful military career because the "*kai*" character in his name (凱) was the same as that of an infamously ambitious general from Chinese history, Yuan Shikai, who was tasked with suppressing a revolution but then took the opportunity to install himself as president. "Were my parents trying to signal that I could not be trusted?" he joked to wild laughter—as I took his daughter's hand under the table.

The general looked over at Lily, who then added the most encouraging pressure to her touch. I could feel my heart pumping faster as I tried to reassure myself that our flirtations remained hidden.

The general continued his storytelling, saying that he'd always wished he'd played an instrument. "I tried to encourage my daughter Lily—" Her hand froze on mine. "—to play the piano, but she was too stubborn." He looked at her with open affection. "I have commanded great armies but cannot make my own daughter obey a simple order."

Everyone roared once more. Lily's hand relaxed and she smiled, I suspected for more than one reason.

As the banquet wound down, we enjoyed a "coffee oil mousse cake," a plate of kiwi, dragon fruit, and ice cream, and a custard pastry. After the general signaled an end to the event, guests started milling around as they prepared to depart. We had just left our table when I felt a tap on my shoulder.

"Andrew Callahan?"

I turned and nodded.

"Ed Lee, from White and McInerny." He reached out to shake my hand.

That's when I recognized him as the man in the Department of Government building at Harvard, the one I'd seen while visiting Professor Lin. What had Lee been doing there? W&M recruited at all the Ivies, but I wasn't aware of any formal events at the time. Maybe he'd been following up on prospects, though clearly those efforts hadn't included me.

"Great to meet someone from W and M." Feeling a reminder was in order, I added, "I'm supposed to start working there next year, actually."

"Yes. I heard it through the grapevine and I wanted to say hi."

The grapevine includes a new hire like me? I recovered enough to thank him and add, "It's good to meet you, too."

"It's great that you're spending some time in China first, learning fluent Mandarin," Ed said. "I can think of some situations where we could really use someone with your profile." I smiled, unsure of how to respond. Ed appeared Chinese, but he sounded as if he had been raised in Texas or Oklahoma. "That's very reassuring," I answered finally. "I wasn't sure if I was making a mistake, taking a year off to teach in China, of all things."

"No, not at all," he replied. "Back when Japan was booming, we hired a number of people like you. Guys who'd spent a year or two teaching English there, learning the language." He glanced at Lily, who was talking to Elizabeth. "Maybe meet a girl."

Ed was a senior partner at my future employer. I thought it best not to pick up on his comment.

"We should speak more, but not here," he said. I was curious about his need for discretion. Then he smiled and nodded in Lily's and Elizabeth's direction. "You probably have other things on your mind. But next month, we're having a cocktail party to celebrate the opening of our new Beijing office. You should come."

"I'd love to. Thank you."

He handed me the address. "Thursday, October 8th, seven p.m. See you then."

I went over to say goodbye to the general and to thank him for the evening. He pumped my hand, even friendlier after all the food and wine.

"I am pleased Lily has an opportunity to work with such a smart, strong colleague as you." His eyes shifted to Ed Lee, who'd stopped to talk to the ambassador. I thought I saw the general stiffen. He turned back and appeared suddenly sobered. "Please look after her for me."

"Yes, of course," I assured him, perplexed by his abrupt change in demeanor. I was tempted to ask if he was okay but felt that might be presumptuous.

Besides, he was already walking away. Not toward the ambassador or his own daughter, or to his wife, who was making her way slowly from the head table, but toward the door. Suddenly, he seemed strangely alone amidst the celebration.

CHAPTER 11

Lily asked me to walk her home, a welcome sign that she didn't want the evening to end. An even stronger signal came when her hand slipped into mine as we passed over the stone bridge bookended by those lovely willows.

"How about stopping for a drink?" I asked. It was only eight thirty, and I wanted to make the most of our unexpected time alone before her ten o'clock curfew.

Lily snugged her silver merino shawl tightly across her chest, which was all the answer I needed—and a great excuse to put my arm around her. She pressed closer and offered a theatrical shiver and a smile.

"Did you enjoy the dinner?" she asked as we approached the main gate.

"The food was every bit as delicious as you said it would be. I just hope I acted appropriately."

"You were perfect," she said. "My father quite liked you. He said you were just as described."

"Thanks for putting in a good word for me."

"I did, but I think it was mostly Ed Lee, from your company. My father said Mr. Lee had told him a lot about you yesterday…said you were quite the 'outstanding young man.'"

Really? It seemed a lot of flattery to pass along from the "grapevine."

Lily and I maneuvered carefully past dozens of uniformed security officers stationed side by side on the road fronting the compound, then meandered—still arm-in-arm—toward a little restaurant bustling with locals eating and sipping beers in small groups.

"Let's stop in here," Lily said, nudging my lower back.

Two young women in bright red *qipaos*, the tight-fitting traditional Chinese silk dresses with seductive slits running to mid thigh, greeted us by announcing that their "foreign friend" had arrived. This was a common expression; it didn't necessarily denote familiarity.

"This place is like a zoo." I was commenting not on the patrons toasting one another, but on the posted menu. Most of the items were still alive in cages and tanks. I saw nearly every creature you'd possibly want to eat—chickens, fish, shrimp and other shellfish—and a fair number you might not: turtles, eels, and snakes, not to mention other critters I couldn't readily identify. A gray cat and a white Pekingese dog scurried about the feet of the diners.

We were shown a table in the back corner, just below a television playing a hit music video by A-Mei, a Taiwanese singer. Wearing black latex pants and a red sequin shirt, she repeatedly returned to the hook and pointed directly into the camera to declare that he really was a bad boy.

It was easy to find meaning in coincidence when I saw Lily smiling at me.

A waitress in a green skirt handed us menus. "Beer?" I asked Lily. She nodded.

"Two draft beers," I said in Mandarin to the waitress.

"We have a six-day holiday coming up for National Day and Mid-Autumn Festival," Lily said. "Do you have any plans?"

"I completely forgot about it." The Chinese National Day was October 1 each year. Mid-Autumn Festival was a Thanksgiving-like celebration always held on the fifteenth day of the eighth month of the lunar calendar, which this year happened to fall on Monday, October 5. "I don't know. You?"

"I was thinking of taking a trip to Shanghai." She took a breath, then spoke quickly. "Want to come with me?"

"Lily...you know I can't," I said, though my emotions were telling me the exact opposite. "It would look bad—terrible. Dean Chen definitely would fire me and kick me out of China."

"I guess I thought American guys were a little more...adventurous." She looked me in the eye. *Does she realize how provocative she's being?*

"You really should go with some of your other friends." I ached saying that.

"Would you go if you weren't my colleague?"

"Lily..."

"Just tell me."

"Yes."

She was quiet for several pressing moments. When she did speak, her voice was low. "What would you say if I told you I've thought about leaving the IAU?"

"Really?" I thought she had a fixed commitment to the Foreign Ministry, which had posted her there. "And do what?"

"You said more and more Americans want to learn Chinese." She looked at me intently. "What if I just went to the US?"

"But how, with your father in his position?" Lily had made it clear that the Chinese government would not allow her to go to graduate school overseas with her father out of the country so much. The perceived defection risk of a top military leader was too great.

"That's what I'm asking *you*. I thought you might know."

Maybe I was being paranoid, but something didn't feel right. Was she trying to lure me into saying that she should violate Chinese law? Did Dean Chen or the Chinese security services give her a recording device and put her up to it? As much as I was falling for Lily—and I thought the attraction was mutual—I also suddenly worried that I was being used or set up. *How well do I really know her?*

I looked over and saw a turtle staring blankly at me and imagined myself in a cage of my own soon.

"Lily, I have no idea about those things. And what would your father say?" *And do?*

"Oh, he's not the problem. I've asked him. He says he wishes there was a way."

"If the government doesn't allow you to leave, and if your father can't help, I can't imagine there's anything I can do. I'm just a teacher." Saying those last few words had never made me feel more powerless.

She shrugged. "Well, think about it. Maybe I'm just dreaming crazy things."

Our beers arrived. I held up my mug. "Cheers. Thanks again for tonight." I smiled in an attempt to improve the mood—and set aside my sudden suspicion of her.

Lily started to join the toast but then paused, staring at someone over my shoulder. I turned to see two sturdy, middle-aged men sitting at a table, both looking directly at us, faces red. One was wearing a black leather jacket. He whispered to the other man, in a gray sweater, then looked toward the entrance, where another hefty guy was just coming in. He joined them.

I didn't like the vibe, and neither did Lily, whose eyes darted back and forth. "We should get out of here," she said. "My father has some enemies, you know."

So I'd been told by Dean Chen, when he snarled that Will and I were released from jail only because we had protected Lily. He'd noted in less scathing tones that potential threats to Lily were among the reasons for the IAU's armed guards.

"Yeah, let's take off." I wouldn't be any match for the group of men staring at us. I squeezed Lily's hand, about to stand when her eyes widened again. The man in the leather jacket was approaching us.

He inhaled deeply on a cigarette. Smoke quickly clouded his pockmarked face.

"Hey, young lady," he said in Chinese, "this foreign friend of yours—who is he?" He reeked of alcohol.

Lily replied calmly—even as she white-knuckled my hand—that I was a teacher.

"Oh, he is your teacher?" He laughed.

"No, not my teacher."

He ignored her comment. "What are you learning? To be a Chinese slut?"

Beijing bars were starting to feel more prone to violence than the fight club.

"Look, I understand what you just said to the lady," I told him as politely as I could in Mandarin, hoping he would be less likely to bother us if he realized I spoke his language. "That's uncalled-for."

Laughing again, he turned to his friends at the table. "He sounds like a child when he speaks Chinese!" He leered at Lily and puffed up his chest. "You should be with a Chinese man."

I took a deep breath and offered what I hoped was a confident-but-not-looking-for-trouble smile.

This time Lily asked the man to leave us alone. He glared at me and clenched his fists. I thought he was about to coldcock me, so I rose to my feet. He spun and strode back to his table, where the two others had remained.

"What a jerk," Lily said to me in English as I took my seat, relieved that they seemed to be local thugs rather than enemies of the general. Still, if they got physical, what was I going to do against three guys? And if we left, what if they followed us outside?

After he rejoined his friends, their conversation became boisterous with drunken laughter, using vocabulary that I'd never been taught in any Mandarin class. "What are they saying?" I asked Lily.

"You don't want to know." Then Lily swore. Leather Jacket was coming back to us, this time with a wine-sized bottle of Yanjing beer and a glass.

"Excuse me," he began in gruff Mandarin. "I would like to toast my foreign friend." He slopped beer into my glass and then into the one he'd brought for himself.

"*He si ta!*" his friend in the gray sweater shouted as he came over. *Drink him under.*

"*Eh, pengyou,*" I began—*Hey, friend.* I stood and motioned for the pair to go back to their table.

"*Bizui.*" *Shut the fuck up.* Leather Jacket wielded the now-empty beer bottle by the neck like a club. How had I gone from never getting into a fight in the US to feeling as though I were wearing a sign in China that said "Bring It On"?

The answer was the beautiful Chinese woman sitting across from me.

I once more urged them to leave us alone, but Leather Jacket grabbed my collar with his left hand and cocked his right, preparing to swing that bottle at my head.

With no time to think, I jerked my hands up to shield my face, then ducked as the red and yellow label arced overhead. My muscles fired before my brain as I unleashed one of the combinations I'd practiced endlessly on the heavy bag at coach Liu's direction, delivering a hard left to his body, swiveling back to fire a left hook to his jaw, before finishing with a compact right jab to his nose. The restaurant fell silent.

I was no Mike Tyson, God knows, and I'd only been doing this for a couple weeks. But I'd taken the boxing seriously and had mastered enough basic moves to stop a drunk throwing a big looping right—and a beer bottle. The thug's knees were buckling, his nose oozing blood, but he managed to woozily brace himself against our table.

One down—almost—*two* to go. I snatched Leather Jacket's hair—what there was of it—and shoved him into the arms of Gray Sweater.

That's when I heard someone bellow, "Hey!" Two burly Chinese men in gray suits were shouting from the entrance. "You!" They both pointed to the three thugs. "Get the hell out of here. Now!"

Leather Jacket wiped his bloody nose and limped away with his friend. Together with the third man, they hurried past the two strangers who now rushed toward us.

"Miss Zhang," the broader of the two said in Mandarin, "are you all right?"

"Yes, I'm fine." Lily turned to me. "My father's security detail." The pair drew closer as she stood and glared at them. "Where were you? Why didn't you stop them sooner?"

The smaller one laughed. "Your father said Teacher Gao was strong. We wanted to see for ourselves."

I looked at the Yanjing bottle lying on the floor and considered the damage it could have done to my face while these two were evaluating my fighting skills. "I'm glad you stepped in," I said finally.

"You two should get going," the bigger one replied. "It's almost curfew," he reminded Lily. "We'll make sure those hoodlums are gone."

Lily and I headed out of the restaurant. As we stepped into the street, we could see Leather Jacket and his buddies weaving down the road. The two bodyguards followed us out. The big one assured us that they'd keep their distance, but we'd be safe.

My body quivered as we walked toward the IAU. My right knuckles were blood streaked from his nose and my left wrist felt sprained. But I had to admit that I was proud of myself.

Lily, too, was giddy, now rehashing the blow-by-blow like a soldier telling a war story. Without even thinking about it, I started to put my arm around her, careful to keep my blood off her shawl— but then I turned around, saw the bodyguards again, and thought better of it.

When we reached Lily's building, I noticed moonlight falling on her face. Her skin looked luminescent, her eyes playful. I wanted to kiss her, and I would have, but I spotted the ever-present camera above the front doorway—and was conscious that the security detail was lurking somewhere just out of sight.

She took my hand. "Follow me."

Lily hurried me to where she'd climbed out of the bathroom window, embracing me in the next breath. Her shawl fell to her sides as we kissed for the first time. Through her thin red dress I could feel her breasts against my chest, while my hands found her lower back and the firm rise of her bottom.

Her hands also shifted, and I delighted in the greedy touch of her desire. To be free of surveillance felt far more intoxicating than any drink.

The next moment I froze, feeling a visceral panic. I didn't know what came over me; I wanted so badly to continue, to bury myself in her enthralling scent. But then Lily spied the source of my unease— her father's bodyguards standing twenty feet away.

No longer witnessing my strength, but my weakness.

CHAPTER 12

The unflinching stares of those two bodyguards paralyzed me. The general's security detail appeared equally incredulous that a foreign teacher would be so bold as to pursue the daughter of such a powerful man. Or were their mouths agape over Lily's temerity? They watched as we walked past, no longer hand-in-hand. We didn't dare say a word or make direct eye contact with them. The guards fell in behind us, clearly determined, this time, to keep us in sight.

It took only minutes to reach the entrance to Lily's building. She parted with the formality of a princess. "Good night, Andrew."

I felt summarily dismissed.

The two heavies trailed me toward the Foreign Experts Building. I quickened my pace, each step more angst-ridden than the last. I worried they wanted to punish me—finish the job that was started by the drunks. Fists clenched, I sprinted to the entrance of my building.

When I turned, Lily's guards were nowhere in sight. Still, I raced up the stairs to my apartment, bolted the door behind me, and collapsed onto the couch, racked by desire and fear.

Tonight, it had all come to a head. Was I so weak and spineless, so *stupid*, that I couldn't resist the temptations of a woman who I *knew* could lead to my personal ruin? Or was I strong enough to risk every-thing—my freedom, even—for her affections, and maybe even love?

Or, I again wondered, is she simply using me? A misgiving that now felt as sharp as a paper cut.

I was about to turn on my short-wave to try to escape my quaver-ing self, when I spotted a slip of paper nudged under the door. I must have missed it in my panic. I doubted the delivery was good news—I wasn't having that kind of night.

> *Breakfast at my place? Inquiring minds want to know.*
> *—Will*

A talk with Will was just what I needed. Maybe he could help explain what the hell was going on around here. From orientation on, my experience in Beijing had involved surveillance, fights, and now being openly followed.

I fell asleep quickly but awoke no more than six hours later. I threw myself together and headed two floors down to Will's unit, hungry for his usual bacon and eggs and strong coffee. What greeted me first, though, were his raised eyebrows and immediate question. "Good date last night?"

"Depends what part of the night you're talking about."

As Will served up his fare, he listened to my account of that diz-zying evening—the sparkling gala and Ed Lee's appearance, and my recalling that he'd been at Harvard. Realizing I needed to protect her, I didn't mention Lily asking if I could help her leave the coun-try. But I did tell him about the wicked combination I'd landed on Leather Jacket.

"Prince Valiant to the rescue."

"Hardly. It was all downhill from there. Turns out her father's security guys were watching the whole time—said they waited to see if I could take care of myself. Then they followed us back to campus. We thought we'd lost them when we went around the back of Lily's building for a goodnight kiss, but they'd sneaked up on us and they were watching. Christ, they even followed me part of the way back here."

"Holy shit," he muttered.

"There's more. Lily thinks the two of us should go to Shanghai for National Day."

"You, my friend, are playing with fire. You definitely should not go with her—though I was thinking Shanghai might be a cool city for us to visit one of these days."

I trudged back upstairs even more worried.

I waited nervously through the weekend for the arrival of Chinese security agents or a summons from Dean Chen, but nobody had shown up by the time I headed to class Monday morning.

The students filed in, ready as ever with their smiles or shyness or insolence. I tried to focus on reading off the IAU teaching notes about the leading role the Communist Party played in the civil rights movement in the US, but couldn't help repeatedly glancing at the door. I was too distracted to question or strategically moderate any of the propaganda I was spreading. I expected at any moment to be perp-walked out in shackles—with a solid punch to the gut for good measure.

But nothing happened.

For the rest of the week, I endured the same grinding anxiety, acutely aware of every camera and uniformed security officer I passed—as well as the gazes of plainly dressed men and women who might also be part of China's secret security apparatus.

Friday, Lily walked into my classroom as the students were filing out, making eye contact with me for the first time since we'd said goodbye at her dorm. Rick had already stood to leave but slouched right back into his seat and thrust his leg out into the aisle, as if settling in to watch a show.

Lily stepped to my desk and, with her back to the class cop, offered me a warm, reassuring smile. "Mr. Callahan, I have a question about grammar. As you know, in Chinese, we don't have verb tenses. Sometimes, when I speak English, I use the present tense when I am trying to refer to something in the past or the future."

She tilted her head to the side, as though to say, *Catch my drift?* This didn't seem to be about grammar at all. My face was getting warm. Rationally, I knew we needed to slow down, but I wasn't thinking entirely with my brain.

I looked at Rick's smug expression as I formulated my reply. "Communicating precisely in a foreign language can be difficult. Maybe you could come by for office hours this afternoon and we can sort out any confusion?"

She opened her pack, pulled out a little black daily planner, and briefly examined it. "Yes, that should work. Thank you for accommodating me."

Lily sounded so formal that I almost believed her only concern was linguistic—until she gave me that same look she had seven nights earlier.

When she left, so did Rick—subtle as a fire alarm.

I hurried to the school canteen, bought two bland meat-filled buns and a serving of cashew chicken swimming in oil, and rushed back to my apartment, checking the clock every other mouthful. Then I brushed my teeth, brewed coffee, and turned my office hours sign to "Open."

She arrived within minutes in tight jeans and a patriotic red silk blouse, which contrasted strikingly with her shiny black hair. The pointed collar framed her exquisite face so perfectly that I didn't even notice what she had in her hand.

"I bought an English grammar book," she said, holding it up. "I thought it might be a good reference guide." She fanned it open until she came to a page with a handwritten note. Placing the book open on my desk, she went on. "It explains everything so clearly."

She turned the book so the note faced me and offered another smile, which scattered the last of my reservations like a gunshot sending birds into the sky.

The note listed a time and place and ended with, *Nod if you can make it.*

I nodded, mouth so dry I might have been rolling in sand. I got up and poured each of us a cup of coffee. She raised hers as I did mine, and, without a word, we toasted to each other.

CHAPTER 13

Before leaving for my rendezvous with Lily that evening, I reread her note, finding reassurance in the first line: "11:00 tonight, behind my apartment, where we said goodbye...." Where we'd had our first kiss. Every instinct said I should see her.

Go with your goddamn gut.

I hurried down to the lobby of the Foreign Experts Building, my mood buoyant, until I glanced at the CCTV camera perched on the exterior wall, its raptor-beaked lens dutifully recording my 10:35 departure. But I had a plan.

I walked to the main gate—the only one still open after the ten o'clock curfew—and exited past the guard station. The officers nodded at me as I headed out and strolled north on Zhanlan Road. A couple cars passed by, but otherwise the night was unnervingly quiet. I followed the imposing iron fence toward the North Gate, where the guards appeared to have locked up right on schedule.

Farther on, I snuck back onto campus at the same point where Lily told me she'd climbed the fence to go to the bar with Sophie. She mentioned that spot lacked camera coverage, but navigating through the overgrown grass and past a series of spotlights was still daunting, with only sparse patches hidden from the powerful beams. And I knew I would have no excuse if I were discovered. I might even be labeled a stalker or potential rapist if caught prowling the grounds of the Chinese faculty apartment.

And did you climb the fence by mistake, too, Mr. Callahan? Dean Chen's accusing voice haunted my every step. If I were caught, at best, he'd expel me from the IAU and China. I would probably find my position at W&M taken away as well. Foreign companies went to great lengths to appease their Chinese hosts. But I found myself drawn to Lily, willing away any reservations about her motives.

My eyes adjusted to the dim light as I moved closer to the building and gleaned the outlines of the stairs that led down to the door where Lily had told me she'd be waiting.

"Knock once," her note in the grammar book had instructed, "then count to ten and knock again. If I don't open it after the second knock, it's not safe. Go. Don't wait."

The steps felt damp, almost greasy, as I descended, bent forward with my hands pressed against the loosely pebbled concrete walls on both sides. There were small holes where stones had come loose and crunched underfoot with every step I took. The pressure of my hand loosened a larger rock. It tumbled down the stairs and clunked against the door. I froze, terrified of who might have heard, realizing seconds later that Lily might have believed it was my first knock.

When I stepped cautiously forward again, my heel slipped, landing me flat on my butt and crashing my feet into the door. It opened so quickly I thought I'd broken it. I looked up with pure dread but saw no one, not even Lily—only a faint light from a hallway sconce. Then she stepped around the door in gray sweatpants and a loose white T-shirt, looking alarmed.

Silently, she reached out to help me. I took her hand and climbed to my feet. She drew me into the hallway, closed the door, and turned the lock.

She led me forward. The hallway smelled of must and mold. Light leaked from the base of a door to our right. She opened it and pulled me into a laundry room, where the odors of the hallway surrendered to the scent of fresh sheets and towels stacked neatly on broad tables to my right. Industrial-size dryers, still emitting residual heat, rose on my left.

Lily flicked the switches on a wall panel and all the lights but one shut off. I heard her take a steadying breath as she guided me to the end of the room, where it doglegged enough to accommodate a table the size of a single bed. Several sheets and a large towel were laid out. Smaller ones formed two pillows.

"I wanted us to be comfortable." She sounded unsure of herself, as if I'd find her efforts improper—or that she herself might be having second thoughts.

"I want you to be comfortable, too," I whispered back.

Lily cupped my face with her hands. "I'm so happy you're here."

My reply came in the kiss she'd invited. My hands fell to her hips, and I drew her close. She pressed against me, making me feel more alive than ever, and whispered in my ear, "The staff come in at three a.m. Till then, we're safe."

I kissed her again, my hands now moving up her shirt, until I filled my hands with her firm breasts. When I started to remove her shirt, she raised her arms to help me. I surged at the sight of her nakedness, then leaned forward to kiss her chest. Her nipples grew keen, and she inhaled with a start when my lips opened for one and then the other. I pressed my face between her breasts as her hands threaded through my hair. I savored the sweet pressure of her fingertips and her warm breath on my ears.

She trembled and her legs shook. I picked her up and eased her onto the table.

potential consequences of my relationship with Lily were
g into focus. If Dean Chen or the general—or someone I
en met—wanted to get rid of me, it would be easy. They could
a "bike accident" or another bar fight or invent a reason to
arrested—I wasn't carrying my passport, or they "discovered"
used condom. At best, they'd put me on a plane and bar me
e country. My career with White & McInerny would be over
even started. I'd never see Lily again.

n I had walked out of my building, I'd intended to drop by
tment…. But that would be foolish now, with Dark Suit—and
ew who else—eyeing me. Surveillance hovered over me in
ke…like the growing realization that I was enthralled by Lily,
ted to keep seeing her, despite the potential consequences.

ded to talk to Will.

oon as I was out of sight, I looped around and reentered the
Experts Building through the garden in back. I rushed up the
the fourth floor. Thankfully, Will answered on my first knock,
and gym bag in hand.

leaving?" I asked.

anymore. You look like you've seen a ghost."

t of."

ook a couple steps forward to glance down the stairs, then
me by the arm to pull me inside before locking up behind us.

going on?"

member I told you about the creepy guy in the dark suit?" Will
"When I left just now, he was outside on the bench, taking
soon as he saw me."

what? You slept in on a Saturday. That's no crime, even in China."

ispered, "I was out until three in the morning…." I looked
he apartment as if I might actually spot the invisible devices
ew were there. "With Lily," I mouthed.

?" he asked in a hushed voice.

it's just what you're thinking."

In seconds, we lay only in our underwear, facing each other, hands still chaste. She held my face again as we kissed. When I pulled her close, all restraint dissolved.

I held her bottom firmly, grasping it, following those lovely curves. Our hips were moving with nature's own rhythm. She reached down and, for the first time, took me in hand. Her fingers felt perfect, her thumb at home.

I touched her gently, found her moist, and began to suckle her breasts again. My hand guided her legs. And then my lips found her belly, and moments later, her deepest pleasure. I thrilled with her scent and taste, relishing her instinctual desire to press into my mouth.

My hands rose from her thighs to her breasts, caressing her nipples. I was possessed with the desire to give her every pleasure possible.

She shuddered. A moan escaped from deep inside her, holding me still as she bucked in silence.

I looked at her. Lily's eyes fell to my nakedness.

"We have to be careful." She handed me a condom.

"Yes," I whispered, tearing open the wrapper and easing it on.

Then she reached down and slipped me inside. Her arms and legs swept around me, tightening with shocking speed and strength. I held her hands in mine, our lips and tongues a tangle as our most fundamental instincts took over.

I muffled the sound of my pleasure, as Lily had. My heartbeat surged as I looked at her. Her hands cradled my face as we kissed and I caressed her, relishing the length of her supple body and the smile that never left her face.

"You're wonderful," I said. The connection I felt was so strong it shocked me. I realized I'd never really been in love before, and wondered whether she had.

"*We're* wonderful," she replied.

Although I'd set aside my earlier concerns about Lily—and was glad I had—I still worried that there were cameras watching us. My eyes darted around the shadowy space.

She sensed my panic. "It's okay, Andrew. We're safe. I love being with you."

I pulled her closer, surrendering to the moment.

We dozed off in each other's arms. When I awoke, I was stunned to see it was ten of three.

I shook her. She gasped and leapt off the table. "Go, *leave*," she said.

We dressed in haste. In less than two minutes I was at the door of the laundry room with Lily standing beside me.

"Go," she repeated.

I rushed into the early morning darkness, hoping that Lily had time to remove the sheets and towels she'd arranged so carefully.

I retraced my original route, arriving back at my apartment thrumming with a mixture of wild joy and lingering panic.

CHAPTER

When I walked into the crisp autu[mn] I spotted the suited man I'd se[en] my first day of class—minutes [...] stolen and the condom was planted. He sat [...] bench that faced the entrance to my buildi[ng] my pocket for my passport. He jotted in his li[...] then, but this time he also smiled at me. I se[...] the chilly menace of a man making the cruel[...]

As I passed him, I wondered, who the [...] reminded me of one of the bodybuilders at [...] jawed and easily filling out his bulky overc[oat] teacher, training IAU students in soft power [...] tip of the spear.

I wanted to confront him, but where wou[ld]

He grabbed me by the arm again and led me into his small kitchen with a window overlooking campus. He handed me a glass of water. I hadn't realized how thirsty I was. I must have sounded it, too. I glugged a few mouthfuls and looked outside. The guy was gone. "I don't think his being here was a coincidence."

"Did anyone see you last night?" he asked.

"I don't think so, but it was damn close. We were down in the laundry room of her building. Lily said the work crew would arrive at three, and we woke up just in time for me to run out. I hope Lily was able to get out of there before they arrived."

"So you don't know for sure?"

"I was heading over there to check when I saw the guy in the suit."

"Could be nothing special. The school has security everywhere, and the Public Security Bureau assigns people to monitor Americans. This guy might just have been assigned to you."

"Or maybe he's working for Lily's father."

Will nodded. "Possible. But it's also possible he was sent by some rival of the general."

"What are you talking about?"

"This country's in a major transition. There's a lot of factions competing against one another. Not openly, but it's serious. *The Washington Post* has had a few articles about it recently, and I've heard rumors. There might be people with their own reasons to keep tabs on her and her father—and now you—if that's what's happening."

I must have looked gobsmacked because Will hurried to reassure me.

"It's probably just regular IAU security. Why don't you call Lily?" He handed me the campus directory, and I found her home number. My finger shook as I worked the rotary dial.

"No answer. Maybe she's still sleeping."

"That's a reasonable assumption, considering the hours you two have been keeping. Let's make another one—that you won't be arrested if you go outside right now. Grab your gear. Let's get a quick bite and head over to the Fight Club."

Not a bad idea. I needed to do *something* to keep my fears from eating me up inside.

"If you're really being watched, you'll want to keep to a normal routine. And let's face it, there's nothing that focuses the mind like getting punched in the face."

We headed out the front entrance and grabbed our bikes, which were parked just outside the North Gate, then walked them to a roadside stand across the street to buy fried pork and cabbage dumplings. They were so good I had to remind myself not to overdo it or I'd be tasting them on their way back up in the ring.

As I relished the last bite, I almost choked when I looked back towards campus. "Over there!" I sputtered, nodding my nose at Dark Suit.

He was walking on the other side of Baiwanzhuang Road with someone else, but I couldn't get a clear view of his companion. They were on the sidewalk, studying the ground, covering the same path that I'd taken along the iron fence last night.

As thousands of people do every day, I tried to tell myself.

"That's the guy tailing you?" Will asked.

"Yeah, the big guy."

"He looks like a hit man from a movie."

"That's not helpful," I said, ducking behind some stacked baskets of steamed dumplings.

"And is that the dean's nephew?" Will asked.

I stole another look. "Yeah. My class monitor."

What are they doing together?

As they moved farther along the fence, I stepped out from behind the baskets to watch them. They stopped at the exact spot past the guard station where I'd snuck back onto campus for my tryst with Lily. Dark Suit pulled out his notebook and flipped through several pages. He said something to Rick, who pivoted and headed onto campus through the North Gate, while Dark Suit scowled and marched toward the main entrance. I ducked behind the baskets again.

Will joined me, wondering aloud what they were up to.

"It looks to me like Rick's retracing my steps," I said.

"I doubt that, really." Will was smiling. "Look, Lily is sleeping, no doubt blissfully, and there's no APB out on your ass, so let's go box."

We hopped on our bikes and raced toward Fuchengmen Station. My right buttock throbbed from the fall on those concrete steps on my way to Lily's arms. Last night, the intense pleasure had anesthetized me to the pain. But now, I ached on the bike seat, even as I stirred with the memory of Lily.

At the station, we took a train to the other side of town, then shoe-horned ourselves into a bus as it plunged back into traffic. I hoped this one wouldn't run over a bicyclist.

The bus disgorged us near the Fight Club.

As soon as I walked in the door, Coach Liu said I'd be facing off against Wu Dazhuang again, a squat, pug-faced guy who loomed larger than his frame, thanks to his battered looks and his scars, including a long, jagged keloid on his shoulder. I'd noticed it when I was intro-duced to him before our first sparring session. He was on a bench in his boxing trunks when my eyes landed on that knotted skin. He must have caught my glance because he muttered, "*Dajia da de*." *A fight.*

He also had a chipped tooth, which he claimed he'd gotten, along with the scar, coming to the aid of a waitress in the high-end restau-rant where he worked near the Swissôtel in northeast Beijing. Three drunks were yelling at her. When she tried to calm them down, one slapped her. Wu made short work of the guy who had attacked the young woman, as well as a second one who came after him. What he hadn't anticipated was the broken beer bottle the third one used to slash Wu. "*Xingkui mei diudiao xiaoming*," Wu told me. *It's all right. Not like I lost my life or anything.*

As I stepped back into the ring with Wu, I tried to calm my mind. I'd been gaining skills and confidence, learning to parry, slip, block, and sometimes duck his shots before counterpunching. This session, I found that I was boxing better than ever. Maybe Wu had worked late, or I was flying high on lust and love. Whatever the cause, I landed a hard left that sent him reeling into the ropes and down onto his knees.

My first knockdown. I rushed up to ask if he was okay.

Wu waved me off. "You've become a better fighter. No more for me today."

Suddenly, I was floating on air. Wu was no pushover. Several other Chinese fighters nodded at me, which I took as grudging respect.

"Nice work," Will said, patting me on the back.

I watched him box three rounds, better able to appreciate his skills now that I'd picked up a few myself.

Afterward, we lifted weights for about forty minutes. I was already exhausted, but Will always insisted, repeating a Muhammad Ali quote about suffering now and being a champion later.

After we showered and were getting dressed, Will asked if I would be interested in some "more realistic" training.

"What do you mean?" I pulled on my pants.

"I could teach you some other stuff. You know—jiu-jitsu, sambo, hapkido. Might come in handy if that big guy really comes after you and doesn't abide by the Queensberry Rules."

"Here?" I hadn't seen anyone doing martial arts at the boxing club.

"No, maybe in back of our building. We can still come here, too."

I nodded, not wanting to look a gift horse in the mouth, then reminded myself to teach Lily that well-worn expression. Thinking of her on the bus back to the IAU softened all the muscles that I'd pumped up in the ring and weight room.

Will nudged me as we neared the university. "I'm thinking of throwing a little party. Help you get to know some of the other teachers. There are some oddballs, but they're mostly interesting people— wouldn't be a bad thing to hang out with someone other than Lily."

"And you."

"Two bad influences." He patted me on the shoulder. "But seriously, people are watching you. You should mix up your routine."

I nodded. He was right. But I also knew I wasn't going to stop seeing Lily. I couldn't.

"I'm not gonna lie to you," he went on. "I've been there, too. We all have hormones, and it's tempting to go a little crazy with your Chinese girlfriend who's also a colleague you've been explicitly told not to date. It's all good fun until someone loses an eye. I'm just warning you."

Lily was much more than a girlfriend I wanted to go "crazy with." But Will's warning felt so ominous that I had to restrain myself from reaching up to shield my right eye, as if I already knew the target.

CHAPTER 15

After our night of passion, it was impossible to concentrate on anything but Lily. I took the class through "America's Usual Imperial Ambitions Led It into the Vietnam War, but the Working Class Led It Out," a lesson sure to appeal to them, but my mind was elsewhere. I kept wondering when I could be alone with her again.

I was dreading our imminent separation for National Day, when Lily was going on her six-day trip to Shanghai with friends. Traveling with her was out of the question, though a little more than a week ago Will had also made the suggestion that I go there with him. I was thinking about this when Lily appeared at the classroom door.

"The dean wishes to see Rick now."

As he gathered his study materials, Rick looked worried, which buoyed my spirits. Despite being the dean's nephew, maybe he'd acted horribly enough to warrant a suspension or even permanent removal from the school. I would have loved to be rid of him.

When the bell rang twenty minutes later, the students departed with their typical alacrity. Within moments, Lily surprised me by reappearing and walking up to my desk.

"Good morning, Mr. Callahan," she said quite loudly, for the benefit, I presumed, of the camera and probable hidden microphone nearby. "We need your assistance with a small matter." Then she barely whispered, "I've missed you so much," as she tilted her head toward the door and led me into the crowded hallway. Subtly, she slowed enough to let most of the other students and teachers pass. I realized she had a plan.

At the end of the hall, she nudged me toward stairs leading to the basement.

We hurried down. I was thinking of my panicky flight from the laundry room when she pulled me into the shadows under the staircase.

We stood close but motionless, listening to the receding footsteps and conversation above. Then she dropped her bag and cupped my face, kissing me deeply. I thought I should keep my eyes open and alert, but they closed instinctively as I focused on her lips, her warmth, her body pressing firmly against mine.

I pulled away. "Did you get out of the laundry room okay?"

"Yes and no, but we don't have time now. Have you given more thought to meeting in Shanghai? You think you can go?"

"Maybe. Will actually said he and I should go there for a few days. If I travel with him, I'd have an alibi."

"Alibi?" She looked at me quizzically.

I smiled. Her English was so good that I was always surprised at the rare instance she didn't understand something. "A cover story."

"Yes!" She gripped my arms, nodding emphatically. "Yes, yes, yes. I will have an…alibi, also. I will tell my friends I have an aunt in Shanghai and will stay with her for one day."

"So I'll be Auntie Andie?"

We had to stifle our laughs.

"Which night can we meet?" she asked.

"I'll only be there three days. I can't abandon Will the whole time. Let's plan on the second night." My heart was already pounding with anticipation.

"I know a good hostel with private rooms near an indoor climbing wall I want to try."

"You climb?"

"Yes, I love it. I do it whenever I can." Lily certainly had a climber's body—that lovely fusion of strength and tone. "What about you?" she asked.

"I tried it once but I'm no good."

"I can teach you." She winked. "And if you're a really good student, maybe I'll reward you with a kiss."

She laughed again. I flashed back to our night together and wanted her right then and there, but even standing under the staircase with her felt dangerous.

I gave her a quick kiss and headed back up, worrying I'd run into Dark Suit or Rick, freshly released from the dean's office, but I recognized no one in the nearly vacant hallway. As I swept out of the building, relishing a renewed sense of joy, Rick and Dean Chen himself intercepted me.

"Mr. Callahan," the dean said, pointing at me.

I must have startled visibly because he asked, "Are you all right?"

"I'm fine, thank you, Dean Chen." I struggled to maintain my composure.

He smiled for the first time in my presence. Rick looked less pleased, as if I'd intentionally interrupted them.

"I'm glad to hear that," the dean said. "You must be adjusting to life here."

"I've enjoyed exploring the city. And this is a wonderful school." I eased toward the Foreign Experts Building, hoping to cut the conversation short, but they stayed beside me, Chen with a collegial air at odds with our earlier encounters. I wondered why. Surely, Rick, glowering by his side, had reported his suspicions about Lily and me.

Seizing on the opportunity to work on my cover story, I mentioned the possibility of going to Shanghai with Will.

"I am pleased you and Mr. Carter are going to explore more of China. Shanghai has a fascinating history. It is a former treaty port, taken over by foreign powers after the Opium—" He stopped abruptly, maybe realizing the colonial reference could ruin the mood. "You should make a point of seeing the Yu Gardens. They really are beautiful."

He patted my arm. "It is good to see that you have recovered after your rocky start, Mr. Callahan. I hear good things about you from your students. I hope you have a safe and pleasant journey."

"Thank you—and thanks for the tip." I was so astounded by the dean's friendliness that I failed to ask about his own plans—or immediately consider why he was so interested in mine.

But I thought about him plenty as I hurried back to my apartment. What explained the dean's abrupt charm offensive? Something was off.

And, as I reflected on it, the same might be said for Will's sudden eagerness to go to Shanghai. He had never brought it up until I mentioned Lily's suggestion. He warned me about "playing with fire" but then seemed to be nudging me toward the flames. Why?

As I opened the door to my building, I reminded myself that Shanghai was one of the most visited tourist destinations in China, just as Dean Chen had said. Having Will and Lily propose going there was no more suspicious than if they had mentioned the Great Wall. I needed to calm down.

I started up the six flights of stairs, relieved to lose myself in the effort. Before I realized it, I was bounding up them.

I arrived breathless at my door—and a surge of anxiety riddled my body, as I realized I was trying to run away from my growing suspicions about the two people I felt closest to in China.

CHAPTER 16

By the time Will and I stepped out of the taxi at Beijing Railway Station, I was prey to nothing more than exhilaration as I gazed at the building's gilded eaves and clock towers, a curious combination of classic Chinese architecture and mid-twentieth-century Soviet designs. We were on our way to Shanghai for the long break, and I felt liberated from the constraints of the IAU and the personal concerns that had plagued me of late.

Lily had departed two days earlier, but I still found myself unconsciously searching for her as we pushed our way through the throngs of travelers to the cabin Will had reserved.

"Just remember...I'm on record that your meeting Lily is a bad idea, buddy," he said as we settled into our "soft sleeper" bunks. I had told him about my plans when we booked our trip.

"Maybe, but it's a done deal."

A few kids parted the fabric door and peered into our room, giggling. I was eager to change the topic and must have looked as excited as they were as they began peppering us with questions. "Do you like Chinese food?" a plump boy asked.

"Yes, Chinese food is the best," Will and I agreed.

A girl asked if we knew how to use chopsticks.

"You bet," I replied. "I can do it with both hands."

She looked impressed—until I mimed scooping up noodles with one chopstick in each hand.

"Not like that!" She laughed.

The others did, too. Another boy asked if we knew kung fu.

I pointed to Will. "He's a master. Like Li Xiaolong." Bruce Lee.

Will, who'd given me my first few lessons in the days before—basic hand and leg strikes, plus some simple joint locks and counters—smiled and shook his head. But the children stiffened, hands up, pretending to be scared before running off laughing.

Minutes later, the train lurched and we were off. As the hours went by, we sped past small villages of red-brick and concrete buildings, tall cityscapes in the distance, and innumerable small plots of agricultural land. We snacked on the instant noodles we'd brought along, then dozed off, eager to rest up before our long weekend.

We pulled into Shanghai some twelve hours later, and immediately headed for our run-down hostel that Will had booked at the north end of the "Bund," an art deco strip built by the British in the early twentieth century. It was hard to believe that, only sixty years earlier, the city was still carved up into "concessions" run by foreigners. Dean Chen's comments about the colonial influence came back to me, and suddenly I could sympathize with the humiliation so many Chinese still felt about their subjugation by Westerners.

As Will got ready in the bathroom, I thought about my rendezvous with Lily the next day—then wondered if seeing her was a huge mistake.

So much for leaving my growing paranoia in Beijing.

SCOTT SPACEK

I looked in the mirror and saw the drawn expression on my face. I needed to shake off my anxiety or this would prove a dismal getaway, not only for me but for Lily and Will. And I couldn't do that to my closest friend in China, the guy who'd saved my skin already more than once and who had made this trip happen.

He emerged from the bathroom, pulling my mind out of the psychological abyss. "Can't let you go soft after that long train ride," he said with his inimical smile. "Last one to one hundred pushups buys the first drink."

I chuckled, but he was already on the floor pumping them out. I dropped down, too, secretly relieved to let physical exertion, once again, put my qualms at bay. In seconds, I caught up and then beat him for the first time in a physical competition.

"First beer's on me," he announced.

And the second and third, as we hit several bars and clubs. At the last one, Will showed off his pyrotechnical dance skills, executing a flawless routine from Michael Jackson's "Billie Jean" music video. The rapt audience gave him a huge ovation.

"You've got quite the fan club here," I said as an attractive woman in a tight skirt and T-shirt waved toward him. "Maybe you should take advantage of it."

"Nah, man. I learned our first week that I need to keep you out of trouble at nightclubs."

The next morning, I woke up woozy but didn't want to be late for Lily. I downed a couple aspirin with some instant coffee and steamed buns from the hostel café, and was rushing to pack my bag when Will grabbed my arm.

"You be careful. I mean it."

"Thanks, man." He was a good guy. I felt guilty for doubting him earlier.

My Lonely Planet guide said Lily's hostel and the climbing center were about half a mile away. As I negotiated the mob of locals and tourists, the crisp autumn air and boats bobbing on the Huangpu River energized me, though not as much as the sight of Lily. She was on the

110

sidewalk in front of the climbing center half a block away. She turned and saw me, and we ran toward each other and embraced tightly. I knew we should be discreet, but neither of us could help it.

She took my hand and hurried me inside. "I've already paid the climbing fee. It's my treat." Lily was bubbling with excitement. "Get dressed. You can pick up your shoes and harness over there." She motioned to a man in front of the equipment room.

When I emerged from the lockers in my gym clothes, she helped me get fitted with a harness.

I'd had such limited exposure to climbing, with its colorful ropes and assorted gear, that I might have been intimidated by what I saw as I looked up at the three-story wall with its angled juttings and numerous hand and footholds, all so brightly painted. But Lily proved a skillful teacher. By midafternoon, with her strong hands on the safety rope, I grew more comfortable on the wall, and I was happy to reciprocate for her.

I admired her strong legs through her Lycra climbing shorts. Her snug tank top revealed her tight abs and toned arms. By watching her closely, I saw how she reduced the effort on her upper limbs by using her legs to drive herself upward.

On my last climb, I made it to the top of the wall, happy to ring a bell to announce my modest triumph. Lily clapped, along with other climbers who'd witnessed my earlier, ungainly efforts.

After showering, I met Lily in the lobby store, where she held up a harness. "They have good prices on really excellent equipment."

I wouldn't have known good from bad, but I'd been seduced by the sport and purchased a harness, shoes, and a neatly coiled royal blue rope. The prospect of more outings with Lily motivated me as much as the climbing did.

She suggested we drop off our things at her hostel on the next block, and we headed out. We avoided holding hands, and no one appeared to take interest in us as we entered the lobby together. We took the stairs to her room and locked the door, then tumbled onto her bed. Our pent-up desire sustained us for the next two hours.

As we lay together afterward, I finally asked what had happened after I left the laundry room that night.

Lily smacked her forehead and left her hand there. "It was *so* close. I quickly folded up all the sheets and towels and crammed them on the shelves, then just as I was opening the door to get out of there, the head of housekeeping walked in."

"Oh, no."

Lily slid her hand down over her face. "It was humiliating. I think she knew right away that I'd been down there with someone. I was sure she was going to report me when she said, '*Fang xin.*'" *Don't worry about it.* "'We are all human.' She was so kind." Lily choked up. "This is silly, I know, but kindness makes me cry."

I held her close until my stomach rumbled.

"I know what *that* means," Lily laughed, shooting upright in the bed. "And I know a great place to eat near here."

Out in public again, I kept my head down, worrying that people could tell the nature of our relationship in a glance. Both of us refrained from any displays of overt affection on the way to a small neighborhood restaurant. Half of its tables were occupied with families and friends chattering away, while a few single men smoked and read the paper.

"This is an authentic local restaurant," Lily said, eyes on the chalkboard menu. "Foreigners never come to a place like this."

The offerings were not extensive. They didn't need to be. Hungry from climbing, we ate a full meal, cooked to perfection: *xiaolongbao*, traditional Shanghainese dumplings; *xiehuang doufu*, tofu and crab meat casserole; a braised pork belly dish called *hongshao rou*; some *siji dou*, sautéed string beans; and white rice.

The sun was setting when we stepped back outside and made our way to Nanjing Road, following it from the famous Peace Hotel on the waterfront all the way past People's Square on the grounds of a colonial-era horseracing track. We eventually stopped for ice cream at a Baskin-Robbins. I didn't know where they sourced the ingredients, but it was the best tasting rocky road I'd ever had. Maybe it was having Lily by my side.

When we returned to her room, our lovemaking, for the first, time, assumed slower rhythms, as though we understood that we wouldn't be doing this again for a while. Will had made plans with me for the next day, and Lily needed to keep up appearances—in every sense—with her friends.

We fell asleep as I held her close.

Over tea the next morning in the hostel, Lily noted the obvious. "We can't meet in the basement of my building again."

I agreed and told her about anxiously watching Rick and Dark Suit in front of the North Gate. "It seems like there's no way to have privacy on campus."

"I was thinking of the hostels in Beijing," she went on. "There are so many, and we could be anonymous there, too."

I was increasingly sure that this was no mere fling, and that we were both steering toward a real future together. I was so certain of this that I didn't question our ability to find a safe harbor for our love.

CHAPTER 17

I took the bottom bunk on the train back to Beijing, replaying my most passionate moments with Lily as the lullaby of the tracks rocked me to sleep.

I woke up with a start, realizing that we hadn't gone to the Yu Gardens, which the dean had specifically said we should visit. Would he be offended? The memory of his scowling face answered that question.

"Bad dream?" Will looked down from above.

"You could put it that way." I explained that the Dean was probably expecting a report on the visit to Yu Gardens.

"Just tell him you loved the gardens. Say the rockeries were—"

"The what-eries?"

"*Rocke*ries. Stone walls with lots of plants and flowers. The main attraction—those and some koi ponds and ginkgo trees. Just riff on that and you'll have it covered."

Taking his word for it, I fell back asleep, and we both returned to Beijing reenergized for Will's potluck dinner party on the last night of our long break. He'd invited the nine other teachers—American, French, Korean, and Japanese—asking us to bring a "taste of home."

I arrived early to help him prepare, setting my bowl of neon yellow Kraft macaroni and cheese on the table. Not gourmet, but definitely American. I'd found the familiar blue boxes at the Western supermarket across town. Will, of course, outdid me with a fragrant pot roast—culinary skills honed at his family's small restaurant in Asheville.

The other Americans added barbecued ribs, buffalo wings, and fruit salad—with dragon fruit as an exotic addition. The Frenchman Philippe brought beef *bourguignon*, the Korean couple *bibimbap*—a mixed rice, meat, and vegetable dish—and the Japanese couple Yukimi and Makoto contributed a perfect platter of *tonkatsu*, a fried pork chop breaded with panko. For dessert, Will made Toll House chocolate chip cookies, and we all regifted piles of bland, red-bean-filled mooncakes—the fruitcakes of China—that we had received for Mid-Autumn Festival.

Everybody filled their plates—*sans* mooncakes—as Will handed out cold beers and wine.

"Let's toast to tonight's spectacular example of international collaboration—at least on cuisine!" he announced to shouts and claps.

"Salut!" yelled Philippe as he uncorked a bottle of champagne.

"I do believe we've assembled a menu almost as diverse as the Cheesecake Factory," Will added.

"*Chi-zu-kei-ki?*" Yukimi asked her husband, her eyes darting around.

"An American restaurant chain," I explained to slow nods.

I'd been eager to get to know the other teachers but was immediately buttonholed by the one man I'd been avoiding since orientation, when he introduced Dean Chen: Tom Blum, with his fly-away mustache, intense dark eyes, and Mao suit. Blum was a committed Marxist, and Will had warned me that Tom was always on the prowl for new converts to his cause.

As the long minutes turned into an hour, I tried to numb myself by downing a second and then a third Yanjing while Blum droned on about how he came to understand the superiority of communist systems—first in the Soviet Union and then in China.

"It was 1973, toward the end of the Cultural Revolution, and I went to Beijing to see for myself how Mao's great mobilization of the proletariat was working."

What he saw instead was the inside of a Chinese prison—officials arrested him as a suspected spy for the Soviets or the US. They didn't seem to know or care which.

But Tom's faith in the Communist cause never wavered, and it paid off handsomely. He joined the IAU faculty in the eighties, then became a foreign policy advisor to the Chinese government and the author of the standard high school and university propaganda textbooks on American history. Growing fame helped him promote his lucrative private English school on the side. That profitable enterprise didn't strike me as good Communist behavior, but I was learning there were many contradictions inherent in "Socialism with Chinese characteristics."

"You never married?" I asked, noticing how Blum hadn't uttered a word about his personal life. He'd arrived alone—and who could suffer a guy like him for more than a few hours, much less a lifetime? He confirmed my assumption.

But the Chinese state-run media loved Tom. Despite the long-time presence at the IAU of *bona fide* scholars like the tweedy Professor Paul MacDonald, with his doctorate in history from Yale, reporters flocked to Tom. He was always ready with a quote that could be summarized as "Why America Sucks and China is Awesome."

Will and Professor MacDonald evidently took pity on me and joined us. I thought Tom had finally exhausted even his keenest listener—himself—when he piped up again like a propaganda-spewing Energizer Bunny.

"It has been my great pleasure to watch China's development, achieved entirely through its own efforts. The secret is Confucianism and the government's unrelenting focus on the common good."

"This is such nonsense." Swept up by the passions of the moment, I forgot about the possibility of listening devices. "'Entirely through its own efforts'? China sends more foreign students to the US than any other country, and it's gotten huge benefits from our open economy. What if the US had embargoed China the way it did the Soviet Union?"

Will piled on. "'Unrelenting focus on the common good'? The Great Leap Forward and the Cultural Revolution were disasters, and if everything is so great, why the need for all this surveillance and iron-fisted control?"

Tom was undaunted, condescendingly patient, as if used to dealing with people brainwashed in the West. "Mao knew that to build Chinese society, he first had to tear it down. And human rights—like Einstein's physics—are about relativity, balancing the needs of the individual against the group. I'll bet you'd rather walk through downtown Beijing right now than any major American city—at least you won't get shot. And even if troublemakers are dealt with harshly, the average person in China is getting a lot richer while the so-called American Dream disappears. Someday, it'll be the Chinese Dream we talk about."

By the time I returned to my apartment, head throbbing—and already anxious about the need to make a good impression at White & McInerny's party the next night—I found that a message from Lily had been slipped under the door. It noted the location of a hostel where we could meet after the W&M event. Her suggestion sparked my biggest smile of the evening, and pushed aside any concerns about what could happen with my powerful future colleagues.

CHAPTER 18

The elevator doors opened directly into White & McInerny's wood-paneled reception area, alive with the sounds of the party. A tall woman with a bobbed hairstyle in a red *qipao* greeted me with a smile and ushered me into a room where a hundred and fifty or so well-dressed guests mingled, a mix of Asians and Westerners. The wall to my left was a floor-to-ceiling window, providing a brilliantly illuminated panorama of Beijing. A Filipino band was playing the Rolling Stones' "Start Me Up" on a small stage to the right.

Ed Lee approached quickly. "Andrew, great to see you again." He shook my hand heartily. "Drink?"

I looked down at his Heineken. "Beer, thanks."

He signaled a waiter carrying canapés and drinks, who handed me one from his tray. "How have you been?"

I told Ed I was settling in and exploring the city. "Taken up boxing, too."

"In a gym, I hope."

"Of course." I laughed, though his joke was more on point than he could have realized.

"I imagine China's changed a lot since you first came," I said. "I'd love to hear about your experience."

"China's so different from when I first got here. It still gets a lot of bad press, but it's improved. Hopefully, the liberalization will continue."

"Is your work as a consultant here any different from what you'd be doing in the US?"

His brow furrowed for what might have been a revealing second. "Our clients here want help on much more strategic questions, like how to enter the market or how to expand overseas. The Chinese government also engages us on research and public relations—some top officials are even here tonight." He sipped his beer. "We joke that with all the high-ranking Party members coming through we're almost a second Zhongnanhai," the Chinese leadership complex. "I should give you a tour—we can chat more comfortably where it's quieter."

He led me through a sliding glass door into the main office area, handsomely appointed with minimalist furniture and contemporary Chinese paintings.

"W and M seems to be doing well."

"An RMB here, an RMB there, and the renminbis add up to real dollars." He laughed as he led me down a hallway and into his own impressive office.

"Make yourself at home," he said, closing the door behind us.

I took a seat across from a tufted leather couch where Ed crossed his legs. My eyes drifted behind him to another majestic scene—this time down Chang'an Avenue, all the way to Tiananmen Square and the Imperial Palace. I wondered if he'd designed the seating according to *feng shui* principles, or simply to dazzle visitors with the view and, by implication, W&M's own lofty position in the Chinese and global economies. I had already signed on the dotted line, but if I hadn't I would need no more convincing. I tried to imagine myself one day having an office like this—not to mention whatever ungodly salary they paid Ed.

He rested his beer on a marble coffee table. "Andrew, I was hoping we might get to know each other better. And I wanted to make myself available in case there is *anything* I can do to help you while you are here in China."

Ed opened up about his own background. Turned out he was from Arkansas. His parents were born in mainland China but fled to Hong Kong during the revolution before immigrating to the United States in the early fifties. "You know, it wasn't always easy being the only Chinese growing up in a small Baptist town in the middle of the Cold War, speaking Mandarin at home. But I can tell you, my parents, with their experience, were the most rabid anti-Communists within a hundred miles."

I appreciated his candor, but still didn't quite know what to say. And with all the surveillance I'd seen at the IAU, I wondered if there weren't also listening devices here. "So how did you end up with W and M?"

"I studied Electrical Engineering at MIT—like all the other Asians," he added with a wide smile. "Then one of my professors asked me if I'd considered joining W and M. Said they were looking for people with my profile. And I guess the rest is history. And what about you?" Ed asked politely. "I'm familiar with your outstanding resume. But how has your experience been in China so far?"

"Well, I admit there's been a settling in period at the IAU." I sensed that I couldn't bullshit him. He already seemed to know everything about me.

"Settling in period?"

"Well, there've been a few weird...I don't know what you'd call them...misunderstandings about—"

"That sounds diplomatic," he interrupted.

"I'm trying," I laughed.

"Don't try so hard. Just say what happened."

I saw no reason to mention the awkward questioning about the condom by Dean Chen. And I certainly wasn't going to tell him about

Lily. I did describe getting hauled out of the club with Will and a little of what we went through at the police station.

Ed sat forward, showing a level of interest that worried me.

"And did your colleague—'Will'—did he get the same treatment?"

"Yeah, he did." I remembered how cool he had been about it. "The thing is, the cops didn't leave any bruises on us."

"But they scared the shit out of you, right?"

"Yeah they sure did."

"You know, that whole 'confess your crimes now or we'll make it *really* hard on you' act is par for the course here. And the cops take special pleasure in foreigners with Chinese girls. Have you gotten any grief about that?"

Is he guessing about Lily? I hedged. "At orientation, the dean pointed right at me when he told us all not to 'fraternize' with students—which I would never do—or colleagues."

"So you would 'fraternize' with a colleague?" Ed's expression was blank for the first time.

Neither of us spoke, and I now feared I'd really fucked up. And I knew lying wouldn't help. "Yes, I am."

"And how's that going?"

"She's a really, really nice woman."

"So we've heard. But you're taking a big risk. You understand that, right?"

"Yes, sir." I had thought about this before, of course, but now it was really hitting home.

"You seem like someone who's not afraid to take a risk, Andrew."

I couldn't read him. I felt like I'd dropped down a rabbit hole. "I'm certainly not reckless, if that's what you're saying."

"Definitely not. But you're not afraid to take chances if something important is on the line. Like being with this woman."

While I paused over a reply, he went on.

"Have you noticed all the surveillance around you?"

"Of course." I hoped he was changing the subject.

"Are you comfortable operating in this sort of environment?"

"It's like living in a straightjacket, to be honest. I feel like I can never really relax and just be myself."

Ed uncrossed his legs and leaned back. He'd put aside his beer. I hadn't touched mine since we walked into his office.

"That's well put," he said. "We've been reviewing your files." I swallowed deeply. "*Phi Beta Kappa*, fluent in Chinese, invitation to try out for USA Rugby."

What the hell does rugby have to do with W&M?

"Your major was 'government' but you've taken so many extra classes you're only a few credits shy of a degree in computer science."

"I wanted to get my money's worth while I—"

Ed cut me off. "You like challenges. You achieve your goals. You can handle pressure. From what we've seen—"

"Seen?"

"We have lots of eyes at W and M. We knew about your arrest and, as you've probably surmised, we know about your colleague Lily Jiang. It seems you're learning fast how to operate even in a straightjacket." He stood. "Let's finish our tour."

He locked up behind us and led me down the hall to a steel door. "Welcome to our SCIF. Our sensitive compartmented information facility." Ed used a plastic keycard to trigger the automatic door. "I think you know someone else who's visiting us tonight."

"Oh my God."

Professor Lin was sitting at a conference table only a few feet away.

CHAPTER 19

Lin smiled as calmly as he had during office hours back in Cambridge. "*Hao jiu bu jian.*" *Long time no see.* He stood and extended his manicured hand. "So wonderful to see you, Andrew. How are you?"

"I'm...shocked." Here was my senior thesis adviser and the man who'd urged me to apply to W&M before suggesting I first spend a year teaching in Beijing.

"Take a breath, Andrew. We'll explain." Lin sounded more informal than he'd ever been at Harvard as he ushered me to a chair.

Ed sat across the table from me. "What I'm about to say can never leave this room," he said. "If you want to walk away, you can." I glanced at the sealed door. "But if you stay, you cannot tell a soul or there will be *grave* consequences. Understand?"

My breath caught in my throat. "I do." I understood his words but not where he was headed, which made me uneasy—but also deeply curious.

"Good. In addition to working for W and M, I'm also an intelligence officer with the Central Intelligence Agency," Ed said.

What the—?

"I'm also with the Agency," Lin added, "and sometimes that involves identifying talent at Harvard. Obviously."

As I looked from one to the other, my molars clamped together, superglued by shock.

"The professor and I—and others—are involved in a critical US intelligence operation, right now, here in China," Ed continued. "You are here because you may be in a position to help Lily, her parents, and the United States of America."

Help Lily? The US? I studied Lin and Ed. I'd read about false flag operations, where spies from one country pretend to represent another. What did I *really* know about my former professor—the one noted for his close relations with the Chinese Communist Party—and this man from W&M?

"Are you serious?"

"As life and death." Ed let that sink in. "For two years, we've been meeting with General Jiang. At first, just casual get-togethers to exchange views without the diplomatic posturing. But then he said he wanted to defect."

"Defect?" I'd heard about Soviets defecting to West Berlin in hidden car compartments. But how the hell would someone escape from China's surveillance state?

"That's right. We asked the general why, and at first he fed us the usual 'democracy' line. But as we pushed him, he revealed that there's a Maoist 'New Left' faction within the Chinese government that's trying to seize power, through a coup if necessary. He thinks they could succeed, and if they do, it'll be disastrous for him and his family, and for China—and the US, too."

"He wants to defect to flee a potential coup?" This wasn't the badass General Jiang I thought I had met.

"The general is a patriot and wants to stop this, but he says he can't from within China—it's too dangerous. The leader of the New Left, Bo Zhongqi, is the son of an 'untouchable,' a close former comrade of Mao's. Bo and Jiang despise each other. Bo would love any excuse to lock up the general and his whole family for good. We want to help Lily's father get out of the country, and we need to move fast."

"Why should we…" I thought again about false flags. "Why should the US meddle in all this?" We didn't have a great track record when it came to interfering in other countries.

Lin stepped in, assuming his familiar, professorial role. "Since the 1980s, under Deng Xiaoping, China has been moving toward a more open economy and better relations with the US. The New Left Maoists don't want any part of that. They think market reforms have been a disaster for the average worker, and they see America's post-Tiananmen Square sanctions and military protection for Taiwan as attempts to bully China or even overthrow the government."

"So they want to fight the US? They couldn't possibly win."

"Not right away," Ed clarified. "But they view conflict as inevitable, and they want to choose the time and conditions."

I wanted so much to be with Lily. If she and her family could get out, maybe we could be together in the US. But a cloak-and-dagger exfiltration of one of China's most important generals was a magnitude beyond what I'd ever thought I'd have to do to be with the woman I loved. And I was still dubious. "You're actually saying these Maoists are so powerful that General Jiang, the leader of the People's Liberation Army, can't stop them without leaving China?"

"These Maoists have more support than you might think. Bo Zhongqi is a charismatic leader, and his influence and patronage networks are strong, especially with key factions in the military. The current government's hold on power is tenuous. If there's a crisis, a recession—if millions of laid-off workers and farmers take to the streets—many people believe Bo could rally the country behind him, consolidate power, and take China in an aggressively nationalistic direction."

"We need to act—and *soon*," Lin said. "The New Left Maoists are already conspiring with Middle East terrorist organizations to directly threaten the US. Their intent is to suck the US into a conflict that will tie us down while China 'breaks out' to become the dominant global power."

"Conspiring with Middle Eastern terrorists?" The specter of a nationalistic China aligning with the Middle East made me think of Samuel Huntington's *Clash of Civilizations*, which I'd studied in Professor Lin's class. "You mean these Maoists want to arm anti-American militants in the same way that we backed the mujahideen against the Soviets in Afghanistan?"

"Yes, but with much more far-reaching consequences," Lin said. "Think about what the US would do if terrorists smuggled nuclear devices onto cargo ships and set them off in Los Angeles or New York? China will soon be the largest operator of container ships and ports worldwide, and rogue factions in their military could easily make this happen. Or if they helped terrorists blow up dozens of US airliners simultaneously? If China could keep its role hidden and we were convinced that these acts were done by Islamic extremists, we'd send our whole army to occupy the Middle East and they'd be stuck there for years."

"That's hard to conceive."

"Not according to General Jiang," Ed said. "He says that elements in the Chengdu Military Region provided funding, training, and material to Egyptian Islamic Jihad and Al Qaeda to bomb our embassies in Kenya and Tanzania in August. And reliable sources say a Chinese military lab is trying to engineer a bioweapon—a virus—for Al Qaeda. We're investigating now."

I was stunned as I realized how easily China could carry out these plots—and how catastrophic they would be. "If the general and China's current leadership know about these plots, why don't they stop them?"

"Everyone's afraid to make a move right now," Ed explained. "Factions are competing for power in the run-up to the 2002 leadership transition, and everybody's trying to see which way the wind is blowing. Bo is ruthless—there are already rumors he's had rivals locked up or killed. If General Jiang sticks his neck out to try to stop him and the New Left, but they still win the power struggle…." Ed studied me, as if to take my measure. "It will be General Jiang's family's necks that are on the chopping block."

I faltered at the thought of Lily in danger, even as I wondered if bringing attention to her was an attempt to manipulate me.

"Bo already threatened the general after he began looking into the Kenya and Tanzania cases," Lin joined in. "And the general's guards observed a man tailing Lily."

Dark Suit?

Ed stood, stretched his back, and leaned against the wall, leaving me to digest the enormity of what he'd said.

"Wouldn't the defection of a top Chinese general just make a conflict between our two countries even more likely?"

"How would even a nationalistic, Maoist-led China fight us if we knew all their plots, their capabilities and weaknesses?" Lin answered.

"You really believe the general would give all that intelligence to America?"

"He wants what's best for his country," Ed replied, sitting back down. "Which is to keep it on a successful development path, integrated into the global community. And that's what we want, too. The general promises to turn over everything he knows on weapons development, espionage, terrorist connections, and dirt on Bo Zhongqi himself—if it can stop or deter these New Leftists and help shore up the position of the current leadership."

"He's already provided us with details on antisatellite capabilities, antiship ballistic missiles, germ warfare, and cyberattacks on American power and water systems," Lin said.

"The general is convinced that working with us is the only way to prevent Bo from bringing disaster to China, and, frankly, to America, too," Ed added.

I finally had the nerve to ask. "So where do I come in?"

Ed cleared his throat. "The general has agreed to defect during one of his regular trips to the US, on the condition that we can also simultaneously get his family out of China. As you know, whenever the general is overseas, his wife and daughter are closely guarded. You're the best-situated person to get Lily out of Beijing and then the country. You're a relative unknown and might be subject to less intense monitoring by state security. And the main thing is you have her trust."

I thought again about a future with Lily in America. But then dread set in. "What exactly do you need me to do?" I sounded more desperate than earnest.

"Don't worry. When the time's right, we'll brief you," Ed said. "We've done this before and we can do it again."

I was hardly convinced. I'd heard about plenty of CIA debacles. Was this some Bay of Pigs? "I don't know who you think I am. I'm an aspiring management consultant...not a goddamn Navy SEAL."

"But that's precisely why it could work. No one will suspect you," Lin said. "And we'll be helping you every step of the way."

Thinking again about Lily, I felt a hook settling deep in my belly. I told them what she had said about wanting to leave China, adding, "It seems she might already know about her father's plans."

"No, she doesn't," Ed replied. "But we expect that she'll cooperate if *you're* working with her. In our business, *rapport*—that's what we call trust—is the most important factor."

I nodded, relieved that Ed seemed to imply that Lily's feelings for me were genuine.

"Andrew, if General Jiang comes over to our side, it'll be the most significant defection ever by a Chinese national, the biggest intelligence coup of our time," Lin said. "Events are moving quickly, so we'll need your answer soon."

"One thing I don't understand," I said to Lin. "If you were recruiting me for the CIA, why did you encourage me to apply to W and M?"

Ed jumped in. "Everyone wants to be a banker or consultant. There isn't much interest in national service anymore. So your professor collaborates with W and M to recruit and screen candidates who wouldn't apply otherwise."

"Isn't that bait and switch?" Spy missions certainly weren't part of W&M's recruiting pitch.

"We all have blind spots," Lin said. "Abilities that others see but we don't. The CIA has found that many exceptional young people won't knowingly undergo the application process, background checks, and training for a career in national service—but might realize it's right for them if they unexpectedly find themselves already 'in the club,' so to speak."

"I'm guessing not everyone at W and M is with the CIA?"

"That's right," Ed said. "But a globetrotting management consultant is the perfect cover."

"You're proving even more skilled in the field than I had predicted." Lin grinned.

An allusion, I was sure, to my liaison with Lily. And an allowance, perhaps, that at least part of my life in China hadn't been scripted.

"We prefer to onboard people more gradually," Ed said. "But the urgency of this mission didn't give us that luxury."

Welcome to the land of smoke and mirrors.

The impeccably groomed professor smiled as he stood to leave. "I'd be playing a bigger role in this affair, but with my skin color I stand out too much in this country. Everyone thinks I'm Michael Jordan." He gave me a firm handshake. "Good luck. I've worked with Ed and his team for many years. You can trust them."

Ed got the door for him.

"How much time do I have to make a decision?" I asked.

"Not much, I'm sorry to say. We need an answer by tomorrow— this really is a fast-moving operation. And you need to know that, while we are confident about the plan, it's not without risks. If you get caught, we will deny all knowledge—you're just two lovebirds trying to elope. China executes spies. Or you could end up in a prison that would make Sing Sing look like the Ritz-Carlton—endless days sitting upright on a hard bench, looking straight ahead, no talking, just you and dozens of other zombie prisoners. So you should go into this confidently, but eyes wide open."

Ed had just described my worst nightmare. When I finally did reply, all I managed was, "How do I reach you?"

"You don't. We'll contact you. It would be too dangerous to give you any sort of secure communications hardware—you don't want to get caught with that."

"What if I say no?"

"We'll arrange for you to return to the US immediately. The embassy physician will report that you've been diagnosed with a serious health condition."

Leave immediately? That was the last thing I wanted to do. Could I refuse? And what would turning down Ed mean for the job offer with W&M—the "normal" W&M—which I'd *thought* I'd interviewed for.

"I know you've got a lot to think about," Ed said, "because once you start there's no turning back. While your relationship with Lily is very helpful, it needs to stay strong or it could jeopardize all our plans. And you also need to make sure your attachment to her doesn't cloud your judgment when the time comes for action."

Too late for that.

"One more thing," Ed paused to look me directly in the eye, "not a word of this to Lily. Not at this point. Her father hasn't spoken to her about this and you must not, either."

I nodded, which offered none of the uneasiness I felt.

"Now let's go back to that party and act like none of this happened—that's your first assignment, *China Hand*."

I looked back at him, confused. I knew the expression, used to describe diplomats, merchants, and journalists with deep experience in the country, but didn't know why he was mentioning it now.

"China Hand," Ed repeated. "Your code name at the Agency. Short, but easy to remember."

They have a code name for me...at the CIA? Despite myself, I was flattered.

Stepping back into the crowded room, Ed reverted to his role as genial host. I forced myself to appear at ease, pretending to enjoy the small talk with the various men and women he introduced me to.

I realized that I had to pretend with Lily, too. Our lives depended on it.

I made my exit. Down the block, I saw the white entrance to the three-star hotel Lily had found for us. I walked toward it, remembering her face, those welcoming eyes.

Ed might have thought he was giving me a choice, but that wasn't really true. I could never leave China without Lily, now that I knew the dangers she and her family were exposed to.

I loved her. I'd forge ahead with the task I was being asked to take on, despite the risks. That was as clear to me as Lily herself, waiting at the top of the stone stairs to the hotel.

CHAPTER 20

I climbed the final steps to Lily with another forced smile. More pretending, when what I wanted most was to spirit her away to a safe place and tell her the astounding secrets Ed and Lin had shared with me. But there was no safe place in China. I had to act as though nothing had changed—even as our world was flipped upside down.

Lily took my hand and pulled me toward the hotel lobby. My own desires came alive, but so did a deepening vigilance. I pulled my hand away from hers and whispered, "You go first. There could be cameras or someone watching."

I followed nearly ten feet behind, like a complete stranger. Head down, I massaged my brow as I walked, hoping to block the view of my face without appearing conspicuous.

The hotel itself felt deceptive to me. It looked too cheerful, with yellow and orange paper lanterns throwing light onto colorful graffiti and fantastical collages, which might have been started by one guest and continued by dozens of others. Every square inch of surface appeared touched by paint, pen, or pencil.

Two men on a stuffed couch in the reception area looked up and glared as I walked past. I kept massaging my brow, as though I had a migraine, hoping they weren't agents sent to trail us—or more thugs looking for a fight.

But they said nothing about the Westerner following the Chinese woman up the stairs.

The moment I pivoted toward the empty hallway on the second floor, Lily wheeled around and pulled me close for a kiss. "I couldn't wait," she said.

I didn't want to, either, but I backed away. "Let's get to the room." My restraint made me want her even more.

She opened the door with one hand and pulled me inside with the other before turning the lock.

"I missed you," I said, even as I scanned the room. Light streamed through a gauzy white curtain in front of double doors that opened onto a balcony, casting a soft glow on Lily's features.

"Me, too." She pulled off my shirt and pushed me back onto the bed, then ran her hands up over my thighs, squeezing them when she reached the tops of my legs. Her neckline gaped and I glimpsed her breasts. She saw me watching and slipped off her top.

"Better?" she asked.

"Better," I agreed, my voice husky with longing.

"*Bu gongping,*" she said with mock seriousness as she unbuckled my pants and pulled them down over my thighs. *Fair is fair.* Her wool skirt landed on the floor as well.

She stood smiling before me in her pale green panties. I sat up and kissed her bare stomach, feeling her flat abdomen and the firmness of her breasts. I took them in my mouth, one after the other.

I inched her panties down, the gusset moist, pulling free after the briefest resistance. My finger slid over her and she inhaled sharply, her eyes closed, hands in my hair. From her belly, my lips moved down until the enticing scents that belonged to her alone had me swirling with desire.

I eased myself off the bed until I was sitting on the carpet. Her legs began to shake, and she gripped my head as she pressed into my mouth.

"Yes, yes, yes," she whispered, shuddering, her back arched and head back, before collapsing onto my lap. Her eyelids looked heavy.

She held me tightly then rose to her feet as smoothly as a ballerina.

I sat back on the bed as she pulled off my underwear. Then she kneeled and held the length of me, still gazing up as she took me in her mouth, sucking hesitantly at first, then with an increasing rhythm.

Fearing my excitement would get the best of me, I drew her onto the bed and slid on a condom. She lay back and reached around me, first with her arms and then her legs. We merged and began to move together.

All my concerns—the obsessive caution from minutes ago—vanished in those intoxicating moments. Lily had arranged a rendezvous, and whatever light slipped through those curtains was a blessing, illuminating her body, the only thing I cared about now. But then I was gripped by a protective impulse and looked behind me. A figure on the balcony moved.

"Lily. Someone's there!"

She froze as a man vaulted over the wrought iron railing, clutching a small video camera. He moved so fast he was gone before I could rise from the bed.

I raced over, threw aside the curtains, and opened the door. A figure dressed in black sprinted down the street before disappearing into the shadows of a building.

Lily rushed up beside me. "Was someone—?"

"Yes—and he had a video camera. He was taping us."

She glanced at the bed the same instant I did, both of us realizing we'd been as exposed to that lens as we were to each other.

Lily covered her face, her shame palpable. "Oh, my God. They'll use this against my father." She began crying, shivering almost, as she retreated to the bed. I laid the cover over her and dressed, then stepped back onto the balcony to see how anyone could have jumped so easily from the second floor.

It wasn't far. No more than ten feet. Not difficult for someone well trained.

Who was out there? There were obviously people with a strong interest in scandalizing Lily and her father. Even if I was just collateral damage, Ed had made it clear that if our affair was exposed, everything could blow up and I could end up in the most awful prison— or executed.

I slipped back inside the room and closed the balcony door. I drew the blackout drapes that had been hanging at the sides of the window, then held her in my arms and stroked her back.

"My father will be so ashamed of me," she went on, shaking her head. "Even though he knows how much I care for you...." She looked into my eyes. "They're going to go after you."

I understood that better than she knew. And I needed to let Ed know before *he* was blindsided.

She sat on the high-backed armchair. Leaning forward, she wrapped her arms around her stomach. "I don't think I can talk to my father now. I feel sick."

As badly as I felt for Lily, her words came as a relief to me. I had no secure way to contact Ed—certainly not a phone call—but I could go to W&M's offices in the morning.

Lily returned to the bed, curling into a fetal position. I slipped into bed beside her.

I reviewed everything I had seen—the shadow moving, the male figure rising to grip the railing, the ease with which he cleared it even with a camera in hand. I wondered if we should leave right now, but where would we go? And flushing us from our nest might be part of their plan—whoever *they* were.

Lily's breathing deepened. I was glad. Tomorrow could prove the most harrowing day of our lives.

I was watching the outline of her body when she stirred and took my hand.

"It's dark in here," she whispered.

"I closed the blackout drapes."

She turned to me. "I'm so sorry. I didn't see them. I thought the light was so nice the way it was."

"It *was* nice, Lily."

She closed her eyes. I gently stroked her face. We kissed and made love again with desperate intensity. We'd been caught and knew this might be our last time together. Our fears whetted every kiss, every caress, every moment we shared.

When I whispered goodnight, she pulled me close one last time before falling asleep in my arms.

I stared into the darkness. That was all I could see.

CHAPTER 21

L ily was gone. I patted the covers in panic, then remembered that she needed to get back to the IAU before her absence was noticed.

The digital alarm clock on the bedside table said 6:55. I wished she'd woken me up. I'd wanted to hold her one last time before bad could turn to worse. The video of our lovemaking could foil the entire exfiltration and have explosive ramifications for Lily, her parents, and me. Although Chinese society had liberalized in many ways, it was still sexually rigid by Western standards, and with a strong nationalistic streak. If a top general's daughter was caught in the act with a Westerner like me, the New Left would have a field day.

Even worse, if they discovered that just before our rendezvous, I'd been conspiring with CIA operatives in W&M's SCIF, I would be treated as a foreign agent—without the protection of diplomatic cover. They could call this a capital crime and demand the execution of all of us—Lily, her mother and father, Ed Lee, Professor Lin and me. My mind was a frenzy of terrifying speculation.

I needed to see Lily, to confirm she was okay, but by the time I'd get back to the IAU the campus would be buzzing with people. Trying to meet her under all those watchful eyes would put us in even greater danger.

I need to talk to Ed Lee. In person. The consulting firm had a full-scale SCIF precisely for discussions like this. I would tell him about that video, and that I'd decided to do whatever it took to help Lily and her family escape—if the plan could still move ahead with me after last night. I was fully committed to helping Lily so we could be together, though another reason had come to mind as well. I'd heard people say that you're lucky if life gives you even one opportunity to make a real difference in the world. I'd never understood what that meant. Now I did. I had an opportunity to stand up not only for my love of Lily, but for a mission far greater than us. I wasn't without fear—or the potential for cowardice—but I hoped I could defy both.

I hurried to the bathroom to clean up. W&M didn't officially open until nine, so I had time.

A bare bulb burned above me, casting harsh light as I wet half the towel and used it on my face and armpits. In the mirror, I noticed my chest and abs, shoulders and arms, muscles standing out in shadowy relief. I'd always been fairly lean, but training had thickened my body in all the right places.

It had only been about a month since I started going to the Fight Club, and I doubted I'd have many more days there. That also went for the mixed martial arts lessons that Will had been teaching me in the weed-choked enclosure behind the Foreign Experts Building. Will was an efficient, systematic instructor. We'd progressed from fundamental strikes, holds, and submissions to escapes and reversals—repeating each until they became second nature. The biggest difference from the boxing sessions was Will's singular focus on *lethality.*

"In a real fight, if you're not ruthless, you die," he'd said. "Grab a brick, gouge somebody's eyes, headbutt."

That was the philosophy we trained with—and which had left my body peppered with scrapes, cuts, and welts. We'd only had about ten lessons so far, but my new skills were already raising my confidence.

Now, as I toweled off in the hotel bathroom, I caught myself in the mirror unconsciously lowering and swiveling my hips as if to execute a simple judo throw.

I threw on my shirt, shut off the light, and headed downstairs to the lobby. I peered around. None of the other guests were there. Before slipping out the door, I paused to look out. The street pulsed with people, but all of them appeared to be moving with purpose. I noticed nobody standing around smoking or staring at the hotel.

Why would they? They already got what they came for.

I checked my watch as I started down the white stone steps outside and hurried to my apartment. I wanted to grab a clean shirt to wear to W&M, but I also wanted to check for messages. What I wanted most was to find a note under my door saying I'd flunked the CIA's first field test by failing to spot the agent on the balcony before it was too late.

I wish.

I grabbed the shirt, listened to my voicemail—nothing—and headed back out, making it to the China World Trade Center by 8:15.

An empty elevator spirited me to the thirty-eighth floor. I stepped into W&M's lobby, where two burly men in suits were waiting by the receptionist's desk. One spoke into a headset and reported, "He's here."

A third man came out less than thirty seconds later, his face taut, his voice urgent. "This way."

Once more, I was led to the SCIF. And, once more, I was shocked by who would meet me there. My silent escort opened the door to reveal not just Ed, but also General Jiang.

What the hell is going on?

The general didn't offer me a greeting, or even a friendly nod. Ed rose, but only to lock the door after my guide had left.

"Can you give us a moment?" he asked the general, who nodded grudgingly.

Ed led me to the far side of the SCIF, opening a door set almost seamlessly into the wall. It led into a room as spartan and small as a prison cell. An overhead light came on automatically. Ed bolted the door and turned to me.

"We obviously have a mess to clean up." His words only confirmed what I already knew, adding to the chill I felt in that tightly confined space. "But first, I need to know. Are you in or not? If the answer is yes, we need to start moving forward right now with General Jiang."

"I'm in. But doesn't the general want to kill me now?"

"I don't know. But I'm glad you're joining us. We need you."

We headed back out to the general. Ed pointed to the chair across from him. "Take a seat."

The general didn't acknowledge me with so much as a glance. Then Ed stood at the head of the table and cleared his throat.

"General Jiang, Andrew, let's get started."

CHAPTER 22

Geneнеral Jiang leaned toward me and clasped his hands tightly together on the table, as if to stop himself from lunging across it to wring my neck.

"He's here to clean up last night's mess," Ed said to me.

"I'm sorry. I never—"

The general slammed his fist down.

"Gentlemen, please." Ed held a palm out to each of us, as though to break up a fight. I took the longest breath of my life. Lily's father put his own hands back together into a fierce grip.

Ed continued, "The general just briefed me. His security team was aware of a rumor, started by a housekeeper, that you and Lily were intimate. A couple New Leftists on campus heard about your liaison and hatched a plan—"

"To humiliate me," the military man interrupted. "Those radicals know I will stop them."

"Fortunately, the general's men followed Lily and were outside the hotel last night and grabbed them."

I sighed with relief. "So there's no video of—"

"None," Lily's father declared, cutting short what might have proved an awkward acknowledgment. "*I* destroyed it. And the two perpetrators have been *disappeared*."

I had heard that chilling expression used before in China but didn't dare ask exactly what it meant.

The general went on. "Their tongues are loosening up quickly. Those two 'boys,'" he said with obvious disdain, "are not military men. They will be reeducated."

"Lily knows about this," Ed said to me.

"I told her that my men captured a known blackmailer and the video was incinerated," the general added without sparing me a look. "That's all she needs to know right now."

"We think you and Lily need to lie low for a little while," Ed said.

The general grunted his agreement. "Keep your distance from my daughter until it is time to go. We cannot have a discussion like this again. We *will* not." His fist landed on the table a second time, so hard I flinched. "I will tell my daughter to stay away from you. I hate having to accept that her fate will end up in *your* hands," he added, with the same disgust that he'd shown when he spoke of "those boys."

"I won't let you down. I adore your daughter and will do anything to help her."

He shook his head, as if my feelings were an affliction, then stood and left without a word.

Ed locked up after him. "You realize we might have just dodged one helluva bullet?"

"*Might* have?"

Ed raised both hands in a "who knows?" gesture. "All we can be sure of is that any other man in his position would have had you in chains by now and washed himself of this mess."

"Isn't he in too deep to back out? He's already working with you—given you intelligence."

"Yes, but we know he's holding back on the really sensitive stuff until his family is safe. He could still be working with Beijing to entrap us all."

"I don't think Lily's lying to me about wanting to go to the US."

"And I don't think her father's lying to me, either. But I also know that none of us feels that way until a foreign operative you've put all your faith in slashes your throat. I'm just saying—caution has to be your top priority, Andrew. We can't let our guard down until all three of them are out of this country."

Ed's about-face made me dizzy. The day before, he was trying to convince me to support this critical operation. Now he's telling me it all might be a trap? "If this is a setup, either Lily's the world's best actress," the thought of which sickened me, "or he's been grooming her with a love of Western society since she was a little girl, just for an operation like this."

"KGB agents have had children born in the US and raised them to be American spies to gain any advantage over us," Ed said. "And General Jiang is very smart."

"If you really suspect this, we can't possibly go ahead, can we?"

"Look, in this business, if you don't think of every dire possibility, you could end up dead—or wishing you were."

Those last words made me worry again what the hell I'd gotten into, and who we were dealing with. "So what makes you want to give General Jiang the benefit of the doubt here?"

Ed looked away, slumping slightly for the first time. Silence seemed to hang from his shoulders like a funeral cloak. He turned back to me. "In for a penny, in for a pound."

"So when will we go?" I just wanted the mission over. I wanted to be safe with Lily in America.

"We need to wait until the time is right, and this close call with the video has obviously shaken the general. My gut says we're facing a delay, but you should prepare now and be ready to go when we give the word. Pack a bolt bag with a few very different looks."

"Meaning?"

"Make sure you bring a couple changes of clothing in sharply different styles, as well as some thick-framed glasses and a hat. Changing your outfit and grooming can throw people off without a fancy disguise. Oh, and hide some black hair dye in your shaving kit. Your passport photo will have digitally darkened hair."

"What about Lily?" I asked.

"She'll be prepared."

"I hope no one notices the bag," I told him. "Housekeeping's already busted me once."

"Keep the bag open in your room, like you're a sloppy guy living out of it, but close by so you can scoop it up and go when needed. Don't overdo it—just a light bag with basics. It'll get a little heavier soon, anyway."

"What does that mean?" *A gun?*

"We're working out critical details as we speak. We can brief you at another meeting tomorrow. I'll let you know where and when. In the meantime, keep your distance from Lily and don't do anything *else* stupid." He paused to let that sink in. "You'll hear from us after class tomorrow." Ed checked his watch. "Speaking of class, you better get going."

I left W&M feeling drained. I grabbed a taxi to campus and hurried into my classroom.

For the first time, most of my students had arrived before I did, including Rick. The sight of him made the hairs on the back of my neck come alive. He always seemed to be watching me. I wondered whether he knew the guys who'd "been disappeared."

I looked at the rest of my students. "Shall we get started?"

Several nodded and smiled. They'd never know how much I appreciated their friendliness after what I'd just been through.

And then I wondered how Lily was conducting herself around Dean Chen, and whether she was following the same advice that Ed and the general had given me.

Lie low.

CHAPTER 23

Rick pushed the audio-visual cart into the classroom, sending a sour look my way—disdain which I welcomed for its normalcy after hearing the gritty details of the impending mission. I guessed his scorn was rooted in what I planned to show his fellow students.

"Have any of you ever seen American television commercials?" I asked them.

No hands went up, though I realized that anyone who had seen American TV might not want to admit it publicly.

I'd brought tapes of commercials I'd recorded in the US as potential teaching aids because, in their own lowbrow manner, they spoke to the "distorted values of American society." That's how I pitched it to Dean Chen, in any case, which secured his quick approval.

After setting up the video player and screen, Rick handed me the remote. "Do you think you can operate this? Or do you need me to press 'play' for you, too?"

A couple students laughed, but a larger number frowned at Rick's sarcasm. Did that mean my efforts were generating at least some goodwill? I hoped so, but I also knew that whatever bonds I'd formed would be destroyed when I vanished with Lily, their assistant dean.

"The first commercial is for a breath mint."

"A breath mint?" Qianyi asked, her face wrinkling in disbelief.

"I know that sounds strange, but let's watch and then we can talk about it afterward."

Rick flicked off the light switch. I pressed the play button, hoping to God the tape would play because I didn't want to give him another shot at trying to humiliate me.

The screen came to life with blond female twins staring at each other. The one on the left said that Certs was a "candy." Her sister replied that it was a "breath mint." Then a booming male voice announced that they were both right and, over footage of a stream burbling past a snowbank, extolled Certs's ability to stop bad breath "in seconds" while also being the most delicious mint of all. The commercial ended with the young twins stepping into the arms of two handsome men who kissed them.

"That's stupid," said Rick without raising his hand. "Suck on candy and get a boyfriend."

"They do say 'sex sells,'" I added.

The others laughed.

"You're right, Rick, it *is* stupid, but apparently it works, because Certs sells millions of those mints."

He shook his head once more.

"Let's focus on the language used by the actors. Did you notice how the two women spoke to each other? Each made a distinct claim, arguing in black-and-white terms. That's the nature of commercials and dramas on American television. Good guys, bad guys, no in-between guys. Cowboys and Indians. Cops and robbers."

Even as I offered this mild critique of America, I thought about how Chinese history is taught and the government's blatant propaganda. The good-bad dichotomy was even more extreme there.

"American people believe that if they eat this candy, they'll have sex?" asked Dolly.

I was grateful she'd changed the subject. "Let me put it this way: they think they'll be sexier if their breath smells good."

"And they think that mountain stream smells good, too," Qianyi snorted. "It's probably full of animal poop," she said to even louder laughter. The Chinese generally enjoyed scatological references.

I gave up on Certs and played a Coke commercial. My students, like most American viewers, looked mesmerized by the long-legged women roller-skating in skimpy shorts, while tanned, well-muscled males swigged the soda.

"What are your observations about this ad?" I asked.

Qianyi jumped in again. "We have Coke in China, too, you know."

"It seems maybe Coke in America is *different,*" said Michael, the tall fan of US basketball. His eyes were still on the screen, where an attractive couple had been caught mid-cavort by the pause button.

Qianyi still didn't look convinced. Dolly checked her watch.

I gave up and asked Rick to put the lights back on.

"What about movie night?" asked Rose, typically the quietest woman in the class, though always ready with a smile for me.

I looked around and saw lots of nods. "Is there a movie you have in mind?"

"*Casablanca* with Henry Bogart," she replied.

"*Humphrey* Bogart. That's a good idea," I said, before worrying about the film's politics. *But Communists are anti-fascist, too, right?* All I recalled clearly about the movie was Bogart on the tarmac telling Bergman that they'd always have Paris.

I thought of Lily—*We'll always have Beijing*—as I glanced at the door, hoping she'd make an unannounced appearance.

We discussed other classic American movies. I mentioned *Citizen Kane,* thinking the story of a capitalist tycoon dying sad and alone might meet Dean Chen's approval, but a consensus emerged for *Casablanca*. Rick surprised me by volunteering to find a bootleg copy.

"Maybe I should clear it with Dean Chen first," I said.

Rick shook his head. "*I'll* do that, too."

I nodded, even as I knew I'd run it by Chen myself, to be safe. *Or his assistant.*

The class ended with smiles and tentative plans to get together at my apartment on Thursday night. I felt guilty knowing I might not even be in in Beijing by then.

Will was waiting in the hallway for me. Yet another person I needed to pretend with.

"Your girlfriend just went by," he said. "Didn't give me the time of day. Just letting you know she's not playing the field, even for me."

"Even for *you*? Wonders never cease."

"I made my play last year but she never warmed up to me, for what it was worth."

I didn't know why he suddenly felt compelled to tell me that. Jealousy? Could it affect the mission—or my friendship with him? I obviously couldn't ask any of this. "How'd your class go?" I asked as we started down the hall.

"Same ol' thing, man. Caught one of my students cheating on a quiz."

The pressure to score well on tests was immense. Will and other teachers often talked about intercepting crib sheets or other elaborate schemes, though I never noticed anything with my students. But as I listened to him explain what happened this time, it hit me that I'd probably never make the grade as a spy if I was blind to cheating going on right under my nose.

We crossed the quad to the mailroom, where all the foreign teachers shared a single mailbox. Our letters and packages had typically already been opened by government inspectors. No mail for me, but I grabbed a complimentary copy of the *China Daily*, full of the usual black-and-white Chinese propaganda. "Splittist Dalai Lama's Lies Exposed" attacked the Dalai Lama for supposedly fighting for Tibetan independence. Another article explained that while the rest of the world may have descended from Africans, the Chinese had evolved separately from Peking Man and were a distinct, superior race. But the headline that seized my attention was near the bottom of the page: "China and Middle-Eastern Friends Will Never Tolerate US Hegemony." *Christ!* Ed's description of a political coup and alliance with Middle Eastern terrorists might be edging toward reality.

"Fight Club or martial arts in the backyard?" Will asked as we headed toward the Foreign Experts Building.

"Martial arts." I wanted to stay nearby in case Ed sent a message about where tomorrow's meeting would take place.

"You okay?" he asked. "You don't seem yourself today."

I gave him the first excuse that came to mind. "Maybe just thinking too much about Lily."

"I'm telling you, man, a girl like that's trouble in a place like this. I sure hope you don't have to learn that the hard way."

I already have. But I nodded at Will.

"I'll take your mind off her once we get started over there."

He pointed to the back of the building, where the weeds were as brown as the sky was gray. "Go get your gear. I've already got mine." He tapped his bag. "I'll meet you down here."

I trudged toward the front entrance. As I turned the corner, I bumped into a middle-aged Chinese man. We both backed up, apologizing. Then he stepped closer and put his finger to his lips, whispering, "Metro Café, noon tomorrow."

I was still registering his words as I watched him duck out the North Gate and leave campus. He never looked back.

The same could be said for me. I'd made my commitment to Ed and a silent vow to Lily.

I entered my apartment, which now felt as fraught with international intrigue as a certain café featured so prominently in *Casablanca*.

CHAPTER 24

Will had been upping the intensity of our martial arts training, and that afternoon's session left me battered and exhausted. But despite my fatigue—and a cocktail of ibuprofen and Jack Daniel's—I lay in bed brooding over the upcoming meeting at the Metro Café, hardly sleeping. The next day, I would have called in sick but didn't want to arouse Dean Chen's suspicions. When I finally hobbled into class, several students looked at me with concern.

Fortunately, that morning's scripted lesson on "New York in the summer of 1977"—power outages, serial killer Son of Sam, widespread looting, violent police crackdowns—largely taught itself through photos and unflattering press clippings. I willed myself to hold it together just a few more hours until everything, hopefully, would become clear at the meeting with Ed.

Lonely Planet said the Metro Café was near the Workers' Stadium, a large sports and concert venue. I trudged past it under the dull gray sky, the massive curvilinear exterior looming over me like a ghost, no doubt the imagination of my sleep-deprived mind. My black and blue, throbbing bruises reflected my mood. I did not exactly feel prepared for *Mission Impossible*.

The café's faded red awning suddenly appeared by my side. Lifting my head, I straightened my shoulders and swung open the door. The savory smell of Italian food brightened my spirits, as did the serendipity of Simon & Garfunkel's "Scarborough Fair" playing softly in the background.

Ed waved at me from across the room. I weaved between tables crowded with pasta, bottles of wine, and baskets of bread. As he ushered me into a private room, I asked in a hushed voice if it was safe meeting in a crowded restaurant like this.

He patted my shoulder. "We ran surveillance detection on the way here and then swept the place for bugs."

The small room's only table was occupied by a ruddy man with thinning blond hair, who remained seated even as Ed introduced us. "Andrew, this is Owen Edwards from London," Ed said as I shook the Englishman's hand. "Owen, this is the young man I told you about."

"Delighted to meet you, Andrew." His accent was fit for the royal court.

"Owen is from British Intelligence," Ed said. "He's providing us with some help—"

"Forgive me, Ed," Owen interrupted as a waiter in white shirt and black vest opened the door, "but I could really go for a cheeky one. Gin and tonic with a slice of cucumber," he ordered as the waiter set a breadbasket and menus on the table.

"I'll have a San Pellegrino," Ed said.

"I'll have the sparkling water, too." I needed to stay focused.

Ed eyed the door as it closed, but still spoke in a lower voice. "For the exfil, Owen's team has a Canadian passport under the name Kevin O'Connor for you."

"Canadian?"

"Border agents here inspect American papers more closely," Owen explained. "Better to travel with documents from countries that face less Chinese hostility—Ireland, Canada, inoffensive places like that."

"We'll also give you a wallet with five thousand dollars cash and Canadian credit cards, a British Columbia driver's license, and business cards," Ed explained.

I nodded. Owen did, too—but at the waiter who was entering with our drinks.

"With gratitude, sir." Owen wagged his pointer at me. "The tortellini with aged asiago is divine."

"Sounds good to me." The pasta was the least of my worries.

The waiter left with our orders.

"So will you give me the documents now?" I was not looking forward to arranging yet another clandestine rendezvous.

"We will get you the documents and train you in some of the *craft* closer to the go date," Ed said. "The passports are a little tricky, since we don't know precisely when you'll be leaving. As a tourist in China, you can only stay for ninety days, so if we handed you a tourist visa right now, you would have a limited window to use the passport. And a longer-term business visa and Chinese Residence Permit come with their own complications."

I didn't need any more "complications." But ninety days? "I thought everything was happening soon."

"We hope so, but there are a lot of moving parts," he answered.

Owen leaned forward. His blue eyes looked watery enough to spill. "It would be awkward if we gave you the documents today and then the woman who cleans your apartment stumbled upon them. We might be forced to tidy her up, too."

"That's a joke, Andrew." Ed shot Owen a look.

"Yes, of course it is," the Brit replied, without a hint of regret.

The waiter delivered our plates of pasta. The familiar scents filled me with longing for the US.

Once we'd all taken a bite, Ed explained that Lily would carry a Taiwanese passport and a mix of other Taiwanese and Canadian documents, all under her assumed name, Yichi Chien.

"Once you have the documents, memorize the names, addresses, and other basic details," Owen advised. "We'll also provide you with a full backgrounder on your childhood."

"For you and Lily, once you're off campus, your high-level story is simple," Ed said. "You're recently married and have been backpacking through China on an adventurous honeymoon. You wanted to better understand Chinese culture, given that you married a 'Chinese' woman—any official here will love hearing you call your Taiwanese wife that. You're then taking a ferry to Korea before flying home. Pretty simple, right?"

"Sure. But why Korea?"

"I'll get to that in a minute. Once you have the documents, you only need to wait for the final signal that it's time to go. We will be training you in primary, alternate, and emergency communications channels."

Their thoroughness was scary but reassuring.

"Now, assuming the plan is a 'go'—"

"What if it's not?"

"If we abort, you and Lily need to burn all the documents, and you fly back with your real ones to the US right away—by yourself."

"Why?"

"Because everything's off."

My stomach rolled as I saw myself boarding a flight without her.

"But assuming the mission's on, you'll be facilitating Lily's exfiltration," Owen picked up. "Someone else will take care of her mother. And remember, the general will be outside China, so his family will be monitored even more closely than usual." I didn't like the sound of that at all.

By the time I got the "go" signal, Owen said that General Jiang would have already called Dean Chen and asked him to grant Lily and me permission to meet Lily's father at the Beidaihe government resort north of Beijing for an official event—a diversion from our true destination, and not suspicious given I'd already joined them for the Diaoyutai dinner, the night I first met him. "The general will ensure you have formal permission to leave campus."

"So once the dean tells us that the general wants Lily and me to meet him in Beidaihe, we head for Korea together?"

"Exactly," Owen confirmed. "Grab your bolt bags and go."

"So when do I tell Lily the truth—that we're headed to Korea and not Beidaihe?"

"As soon as you get her off campus," Ed said.

"What if she balks?"

"Her father says she's very eager to leave China…now more than ever, thanks to you," Ed continued. "All you and Lily have to do at that point is take one of the frequent trains from Beijing to Yantai and then catch the regular ferry to Incheon."

"If we have fake passports, wouldn't it be faster and safer just to fly out?"

"Security and customs at airports are much tighter. We've mapped Yantai's boarding procedures and believe we can get you through them undetected."

You believe *you can?*

"American agents will have the Incheon port under surveillance and meet you as soon as you dock," Ed assured me.

The only remaining question was *when*, such a daunting uncertainty that I didn't even notice that my bruises had stopped throbbing—proof that adrenaline is the most powerful analgesic of all.

CHAPTER 25

My students would arrive for movie night in minutes—along with, potentially, Dean Chen, whom I had invited out of courtesy and to demonstrate that any discussions about *Casablanca* would conform to the IAU's carefully prescribed guidelines.

My bolt bag! I darted into my bedroom and shoved the small internal frame pack under the bed. It was easy to imagine Chen inspecting the apartment.

I'd heard nothing from Ed since that lunch with Owen forty-eight hours earlier. Rationally, I knew that was to be expected but, like Lily's absence from my life, it had me on edge.

I had the living room set up and was wiping down my table when the irrepressible wonder Will burst into the apartment with a six-pack of beer. "Yo!" He gave me a gentle slap on the back. "I thought it'd be a great idea for us to get sloppy drunk in front of Dean Chen."

"Right," I laughed. "I'll drink if the dean does—but I don't see that happening."

Professor MacDonald walked in moments later. I had been enjoying my passing conversations with him—he had so much experience in Asia—and I worried about the blowback he and the other Americans at the IAU would suffer after I fled with Lily. The only teacher sure to escape unscathed would be the one who most deserved a comeuppance: Tom Blum, the modern-day Tokyo Rose, who would undoubtedly use my exit as an opportunity to take to the airwaves, denounce all his fellow compatriots, and gain even greater esteem in the eyes of his overlords.

As Will delivered his beer to the fridge, Paul MacDonald said he'd had coffee the day before with Ed Lee.

My ears perked up. He must have noticed.

"He's an old friend. I've known Ed since he first arrived in Beijing with that company of yours."

"How's he doing?"

"Great. Says you should stop by W and M tomorrow at five. Something about a start date."

"Thanks for letting me know."

"You're a lucky man. I had an opportunity to work for that firm years ago. Probably should have taken it."

Had Paul turned down W&M—or the CIA? Or both? I could hardly ask.

Will returned with a beer for each of us. I'd no sooner waved him off than there was a rat-a-tat at the door and a bustle in the hallway. My students were as punctual for movie night as they were for class—and far more ebullient than they appeared most mornings. Even Rose, the meek girl who'd suggested we watch *Casablanca*, all but shouted "Hello, Mr. Callahan," as she handed me a bag of dried plums. "This is my gift for you."

I thanked her and she blushed. *Does she have a crush on me?*

Tall Michael high-fived me as he entered, followed by Lily—a genuine surprise.

"Dean Chen asked me to represent him," she said with authority.

"That's great. I'm glad you could make it."

Rick arrived next, scarcely looking at me.

"You have the VCD?" I asked.

"I will take care of it." He was apparently determined to extend his audio-visual authority to my apartment.

"Everyone, help yourselves," I said, gesturing to the snacks. "And there are cold drinks in the fridge. Don't be shy."

As the group scurried about, I made a point of sitting next to Will on the couch, far away from where Lily was getting some rice crackers.

"Decent turnout," I said. "And I guess I can have that beer now after all." I took the one still unopened beside Will.

He nodded but looked past me as he waved Lily over. She appeared startled but eased her way past her fellow students. Will nudged me aside. "Make room for the assistant dean, Teach." He shifted so she could sit between us.

I wished he hadn't done this, but how could he have known about the mission and my need to stay away from her? From the look on Lily's face, she shared my discomfort.

She recovered enough to offer a smile as he chatted her up with his southern charm—tactfully avoiding any revealing references to me in the presence of others.

Qianyi, though, spoke up with her usual bluntness. "When will the movie start?"

Rick held up the VCD like it was an Olympic gold medal. "I have it right here."

"The switch is on the—"

"*I* know how these things work. Remember?" His tone could have stripped graffiti from a bathroom stall.

"I'd like to say a few words before we start." I rose from the couch while Rick rolled his eyes at the delay. "*Casablanca* was released in 1942, only a year after America entered the Second World War and before anyone knew how it would turn out. I always think about that when I watch this movie."

"China was already fighting Japan for many years by 1942," Rick said. "We didn't have the luxury of waiting until we could enter on the winning side."

"I think it is interesting that the writers didn't know which side would win when they were making it," Rose volunteered—bravely, I thought. Rick was glaring at her.

"Yes, that is very interesting," Michael agreed.

The class monitor shifted his grimace to Michael.

What's his problem?

When Rick's gaze fell to Lily, I had my answer. There was no mistaking the longing in his eyes, or the jealousy that replaced it when he returned his attention to me.

I can't believe I didn't notice this earlier. He could really fuck things up.

I asked Rick to start the movie. When I sat back down, Lily had clasped her arms across her chest. As the action began to heat up in Rick's Café, Will asked her quietly if she'd like a blanket. I felt guilty that it hadn't occurred to me she could be cold.

"Thank you, yes," she said.

"I'll get it." I started to rise, but Will said, "Stay there—I'll grab something."

Lily shifted an inch away from me as soon as he stood. It felt like a rebuke.

Will returned with a throw from my closet and spread it over Lily's lap. A flap of it fell over my leg as Bogart reminded Sam, the piano man, that he was never supposed to play "As Time Goes By."

Next came the moment when Bogie spots his old flame, Ingrid Bergman.

"I remember this," Lily said softly. Not to me or Will, but to the former lovers on the screen.

As Bogart's and Bergman's eyes met, Lily rested her hand on my leg under the blanket and gently squeezed my thigh.

I glanced down. No one, including me, could see that she'd touched me, but then I looked at Rick sitting stiffly on a straight-backed chair and saw that he was staring at me. In the same instant, he lowered his eyes to the blanket, only for a blink.

Defiantly, I slipped Lily's hand in mine and felt a wave of reassurance when she entwined our fingers together.

For the rest of the film, I delighted in simply touching her. I had Will to thank. Such a good friend—even as he was oblivious to the danger that his simple action may have exposed us to.

As the movie ended and the screen went black, I got up and flipped on the lights.

Rick retrieved the movie from the disc player as enthusiastic discussions broke out. Not all my students seemed pleased, though.

"Simple-minded American morality," Qianyi said. "And now that Europe is saved, America can turn its attention to starting wars with China and Korea."

I was sure I'd seen her wiping her eyes during the climactic airport scene, when Bogie gave up his ticket so his romantic rival could escape the Nazis with Bergman, leaving him behind to fight the good fight.

"No one even says that China won the war by defeating Japan," Rick piled on.

I wanted to reply that maybe the studio could add that historical gem to its notes for the sixtieth anniversary edition of the film, but I clamped my mouth shut.

Rick wouldn't let up. "When China is stronger, we will make movie studios teach the correct history."

I remained silent. Better to give Rick the last word, which seemed to satisfy him.

Fortunately, even that uncomfortable conclusion didn't smother the smiles of appreciation from the others, who made a point of thanking me for hosting them.

"We'll always have movie night," Rose said as she looked me in the eye, putting her empty Yanjing bottle on my end table. Had the beer emboldened her? Not enough to keep her from blushing again.

Right in front of me, Rick asked Lily if he could "escort" her to her dorm. To my knowledge, this was his first overture to her. *Good luck, asshole.*

"A dean's assistant does not need to be escorted by a student," she said, then thanked me and headed out on her own.

Rick turned to me and held up the disc. "I will keep this."

"Of course. Thank you for bringing the movie."

Will closed the door and laughed. "What a creep."

"He sure is."

But as class monitor and the dean's nephew, Rick was not a run-of-the-mill creep any more than I was now just another teacher at the IAU. We were facing off in the unspoken language of espionage. My restraint in choosing silence over sarcasm told me that I might be more suited than I thought for the role that Ed and Lin and unknown others had cast for me.

CHAPTER 26

The next evening, I didn't feel nearly as confident as I pressed the elevator button to ascend to W&M's office in the China World Trade Center. Was it really a non-official CIA station in the heart of Beijing? Or a giant trap by China's counterintelligence agencies to snare American spies, which would now include me?

Ed himself greeted me at the reception. He didn't offer his customary smile as he ushered me to the SCIF. He closed the door and gestured for me to take a seat.

Owen Edwards slouched in a conference chair across from me. One of his long arms engulfed the back of the seat next to him. But his eyes maintained a steely focus, scrutinizing me as though searching for a loose thread in a Savile Row suit.

"Hello, Andrew." He leaned aggressively across the conference table. "We're about to educate you in re-dun-dan-cy." He hit all four syllables with a hammer's force. "Do you know what that means in your new line of work?"

"Like, backups?"

"Correct. Putting reinforcing systems into place to ensure mission continuity, control, and security." He pushed even closer to me. "It's not something we felt comfortable going into at the café. And to be frank, I wanted to meet you in person first."

I flinched, feeling uncomfortable at his assessing me.

"You shouldn't do that. It's unbecoming and could cost you your life. The point is, I liked what I saw. Since this is a joint operation with our cousins here," Owen glanced at Ed, "that meeting was necessary. We rarely veto each other's candidates, but it does happen."

Ed took over. "We're both glad to have you. We're going to explain how we'll communicate from now on, because it's not safe to keep meeting in person."

"This will be our primary means of communication." Owen pushed a beat-up *Lonely Planet China* guidebook over to me—a seemingly identical version to the one I had brought to Beijing. He appeared to be holding back laughter.

"What?" I asked.

"Here we are in the age of the information superhighway, and we are about to explain one of the oldest forms of secret messaging. Sometimes life really is too rich for words." Ed picked up where the amused Owen had left off: "This special edition of the *Lonely Planet China* includes twenty tearaway inserts which look like innocuous 'top ten' lists of things to do in various cities. Hidden in invisible ink on the right side of each 'activity,' in what look like blank spaces for taking notes, are small 'one-time pads.' These are single-use cipher keys—rows of letters in groups of five—each accompanied by a table to help encrypt and decrypt messages. Pull your chair over."

I scooted beside Ed. Using a practice pad, he showed me how to reveal the hidden type by brushing the paper with a diluted iodine solution.

"Reminds me of a children's spy kit," I mumbled.

"It works," Ed said.

"It does, indeed." Owen nodded.

"We will give you a bottle of iodine," Ed told me. "Keep it in your shaving kit. If you lose it, you can get more at any pharmacy. If questioned, say it's an antiseptic for first aid."

He taught me how to encrypt and decrypt messages by using the random letters from the one-time pads and the reciprocal alphabet tables included alongside. "What's this message say?" Ed tested me with a new one.

"Help!" Owen laughed.

"Let the man concentrate." The chill in Ed's voice could have frosted Owen's grin.

"Arrived," I answered, after decoding it moments later.

"Nice." Ed took me through several more examples. "Every Monday, Wednesday, and Friday, so long as you're still on campus, we will communicate a simple 'hold,' 'abort,' or 'go' message and other critical details in code over short-wave radio at seven fifteen a.m."

Professor Lin's "necessities for China" had now taken a new significance.

Ed went on. "The coded letters will be communicated using phonetic alphabet—Alpha, Bravo, Charlie, and so on. You follow?" I nodded. "Good. We operate on several frequencies between 18.864 and 21.866 megahertz. Listen on headphones to avoid surveillance. You'll know the message is for you because it will always start with the shorthand for your code name: Charlie-November-Hotel. Chi-Na Hand."

This suddenly felt much more personal.

"You'll use the one-time pads one after the other, in order. And every time you decode a message," Owen tapped the guidebook, "rip out that one-time pad as if you've completed that tourist activity, then burn or otherwise destroy it and any other notes you made." He handed me a Bic lighter. "Eat the papers if you have to."

"Eat them?" It was hard to know when to take him seriously. "That's—"

"Old-school?" Owen asked. "Absolutely. A gin chaser helps," he added, deadpan.

They both smiled.

"What if I miss the transmission?" I imagined myself oversleeping, ruining everything.

"We will know if you receive the instructions to act," Ed started, "because you will wear a red tie to class that day to confirm you received an 'abort' signal and a green tie for a 'go' signal. And, from now on, red and green ties are not to be worn at any other time."

Ed had made it clear they were watching me, but I didn't realize it was this closely.

"But what if I'm not on campus? Shouldn't I have a cell phone or beeper—"

"Mobile devices make it too easy for Chinese counter-intelligence to track you, unless you follow proper protocol," Owen said with lordly impatience. "We try to avoid them."

"But we are prepared for contingencies," Ed continued. "If for some reason the short-wave radio signal is jammed or you do not pick it up and it's time to act, you will receive a phone call on your landline from your 'Uncle Gary' in Cleveland."

I actually had an Uncle Gary in Cleveland.

Ed ran me through the procedures for confirming the caller and conveying the signal to move to the execution phase, or to abort. I thought about how "abort" meant leaving Lily behind, a point they had made painfully clear at the Metro Café.

"In a real emergency," Ed said. "Someone will find you in person. He will identify himself by asking, 'Have you ever done the night hike at Simatai?' You'll say 'No, I've only been to Jiankou.' Our agent will then confirm the exchange by saying 'I hear that's a tough section.'"

"Simatai and Jiankou, the Great Wall sections?"

Ed nodded. "It's like your Uncle Gary calling. It won't sound unusual if anyone's listening but, seriously, has anyone asked you about a night hike at Simatai?"

They took me through additional eventualities, testing me over and over to ensure I remembered each detail. If I needed them to contact me urgently, I could lower my kitchen blinds—the ones I had never used—or call a phone number scribbled into the *Lonely Planet*, say nothing, and then, after exactly fifteen seconds, hang up. Or, in an absolute emergency on the road, I could use the last two one-time pad sheets to send an encrypted message to ejl888@hotmail.com from a newly created email account of my own—Hotmail, Yahoo mail, whatever wasn't blocked by the Great Firewall.

"Email?" It sounded vulnerable.

"Yes," Ed said. "The Chinese closely monitor all traffic to and from official US government email addresses. We don't want them to notice the anomaly of your sending an email there from a random Chinese internet café, or wherever you might find yourself. So we'll both use harmless-looking email addresses. Even in the unlikely event that it's hacked, you'll be using a one-time pad, so no one except us will be able to understand your message."

"And to confirm that it's you and the pad hasn't been compromised," Owen added, "you should end each message with 'China Hand,' your code name, which only we know."

Ed handed me the iodine and battered *Lonely Planet*. "Be *very* careful with this. Possessing one-time pads is *prima facie* evidence of espionage."

My pulse—already about twenty beats a minute faster than usual—must have doubled as I took in what Ed had just told me.

I gave him my own copy of the book to dispose of. He promised to arrange delivery of the fake passports and other documents closer to our departure.

"We're very good at what we do. We think you will be, too."

Suggesting my untested skills might be in the same league as the Agency's made me question *their* competency.

The two of them walked me out of the SCIF.

With every departure from W&M, I felt more vulnerable than before. Now I was carrying a *Lonely Planet* guide with tables of encryption keys written in invisible ink and a bottle of iodine to make them appear. Ed had made the potential consequences crystal clear. How would I ever explain these away to hard-nosed Chinese counter-intelligence officers? And who else would be compromised if I were caught with this incriminating evidence?

The answer—brief and terrifying—was everybody.

CHAPTER 27

I attempted the breezy demeanor of a confident spy as I walked out of the China World Trade Center. My performance was shaken, however, as I thought of my parents and worried about how they would feel if they knew that I was involved in my first spy mission.

First mission?

I realized I *liked* becoming the "China Hand." The prospect of earning and keeping that handle sparked more pride than hesitation. And as I hailed a cab, pretending to be nothing more than a teacher, I found myself assuming a much more dangerous persona—like one I'd taken on for a high school play.

But this was not a role I could abandon by stepping off the stage. History itself was eyeing me. A bad performance would have horrendous consequences. I needed to look no further than the incriminating evidence in my hand.

Yet the thrill was irrefutable.

I all but dashed up to my apartment, placing the *Lonely Planet* in plain sight on my living room bookcase, where my previous edition had been. The iodine and lighter went straight into my shaving kit.

As days and then weeks passed, I dutifully listened to the short-wave radio transmissions. All I decoded each time was "Hold, China Hand," before incinerating the one-time pads and notes as instructed. My speed at transcribing the messages was improving and my confidence growing. This new routine—and the guidebook that was a fixed reminder of my upcoming mission—brought an edgy awareness to my life that was both frightening and exhilarating, distancing me from the now seemingly trivial concerns of teaching and hosting student movie nights.

Although I thought about Lily a lot, I only had a few opportunities to speak with her on campus. Once, when I ran into her in line at the cafeteria, we had lunch. Although any outward signs of intimacy were clearly off limits, her gaze—and mine—lingered in the few passing moments that felt safe.

The only behavior that might raise eyebrows was Rose's increasingly open adoration of me in class, and her repeated small gifts. I kept my appreciation to thank-yous.

With December approaching, we experienced little to mark the Western holiday season. Chinese New Year would not come until February 16, 1999, so we found ourselves in the classroom straight through Christmas and New Year's Day. But we foreign teachers, including the great communist Tom Blum, tried to celebrate.

We ordered "Christmas chickens"—there were no turkeys in China—from a nearby restaurant for another lively dinner in Will's apartment, then ended the evening with a stroll outside the gates, singing Christmas carols. It almost felt like home as the familiar songs echoed in the wintry air. Confused onlookers halted in their tracks, and the bewildered police didn't even stop us—maybe the holiday cheer was contagious. We paused only at a hotel to laugh raucously at a nativity scene featuring Snow White and the seven dwarfs.

We needed the comic relief. I felt the homesickness that expats often experienced when they were away for the holidays. International events were also starting to weigh on us. In mid-December, President Clinton and British prime minister Tony Blair had launched bombing missions of Iraqi military installations and enforced "no-fly zones" to punish Saddam Hussein for refusing to comply with various UN resolutions on weapons inspections. Those actions triggered an anti-Western backlash in the Chinese media. Because of its own problems with secessionist movements in the northwestern territory of Xinjiang, neighboring Tibet, and of course Taiwan, the Chinese government was especially sensitive to what it viewed as the United States' meddling in other countries' internal affairs. Chinese officials argued that if the US could interfere in a civil war or domestic dispute in another nation, it could also intervene in Taiwan.

Will warned me to keep my eyes open. "This anti-American hysteria is coming at a bad time," he said as we climbed the stairs of the Foreign Experts Building. Lowering his voice, he added, "The economy's slowing, and the natives are getting restless. The US is giving Beijing just the bogeyman they need, and that includes you and me and everyone else from the States."

"When in doubt, blame the foreigners."

"That's about the size of it, my man."

I turned on CCTV, where a grim-faced news anchor called the "hegemonic" US the "number one threat to China's future." A report from the Foreign Ministry urged the Chinese to "sacrifice now so we can someday stand up to the United States." The BBC World Service was reporting Westerners regularly being attacked in restaurants and bars.

The uproar over the bombing of Iraq even reached into my classroom. Qianyi criticized me outright: "You are a poisonous element of American cultural imperialism."

And that's not all, I told myself in the voice of a game-show host.

Dean Chen himself walked in minutes later to offer his own criticism, in front of the class. "You must stop injecting political color and American values into the classroom. And no more movie nights."

That week we'd seen *Butch Cassidy and the Sundance Kid.*

At a school assembly, Communist Party speakers railed against the United States. Dean Chen ended the gathering by urging students to work hard so they could study in the US, gain employment with American companies, and bring back coveted technologies. *Steal them*, in other words. He was hardly subtle, glaring at his American faculty with undisguised contempt. "Technology will allow China to exact revenge for historical humiliation at the hands of foreigners, especially the United States." Sneering openly, he quoted Deng Xiaoping, China's leader during the "reform and opening" period of the 1980s. "We need to 'hide our brightness and bide our time,' gradually building our collective strength so that we can destroy America when the time is right."

In the meantime, his American faculty could serve as a punching bag.

His tirade was cheered wildly by students and Blum. And why not? My communist colleague was in the papers constantly, ranting about how the United States was bent on holding China down. With the dean's nodding approval, he had announced at a faculty meeting that he'd been invited to the China People's Congress to advise officials on how best to deal with America's "imperialist aggression."

The pressure only got worse. In February, Lily told me that her father would be shuttling back and forth to Washington in the months ahead for the next round of high-stakes economic and military negotiations, so I tensely awaited the go signal at any moment. When she was away for Chinese New Year that same month, all I could think about was the idyllic time we'd had Shanghai, and I longed to be with her again. Instead, I was holed up on campus with Will and the other foreign teachers.

A US-led NATO bombing campaign against Yugoslavia, Operation Allied Force, started in late March, aimed at stopping the ethnic cleansing of Kosovar Albanians by Slobodan Milošević's government.

The Chinese strongly opposed those bombing raids. Anger continued to throb at the IAU. I saw it spelled out in black and white when Professor MacDonald pointed to the blackboard in his empty classroom. In large, chalked letters someone had revealed the depths of ugliness on campus. "Professor MacDonald = USA; USA = Nazi murderer; therefore, Professor MacDonald = Nazi murderer."

In my own class later that morning, Rick shouted at me, "How can the US claim to stand up for human rights when you are bombing all those innocent people in Yugoslavia?"

"Doesn't killing people violate *their* human rights?" Qianyi piled on.

Hostility from those two was predictable. But then Michael stood up. "How can you claim to defend minorities in other countries when you made Black people into slaves and committed genocide against American Indians? You and all Americans are just hypocrites."

I couldn't defend those past American actions, or the current bombing of Yugoslavia, but after months of interacting with my students I'd thought that even at a time like this they would be able to see me as a human being, a friend perhaps, not just an ugly American. I found it all so disheartening.

If the rage had remained in the classroom, that might have become a learning experience for all of us. But Beijing was starting to feel downright unsafe. Strangers on the street were giving me horrid glances and murmuring "hegemonist" as if it were a mantra. Then on the morning of Saturday, May 8, I heard furious voices outside the Foreign Experts Building. I looked out to see dozens of protestors vehemently chanting, "NATO equals Nazi American Terrorist Organization!"

What the hell's going on? I'd never felt so cornered. And the next short-wave radio communication wouldn't come until Monday morning.

The phone rang.

Uncle Gary?

But it was Will. "Have you heard?"

"No...I mean...yes, I can hear them outside. What's happening?"

"NATO bombed China's embassy in Belgrade. Three dead, twenty injured, some critically. All hell's breaking loose."

"Oh, fuck."

"You have no idea, buddy."

America and NATO representatives insisted the bombing was an accident. They said they were aiming at a nearby Serbian government building, an explanation roundly rejected by Chinese officials who branded the incident a "gross violation of the United Nations' charter."

I believed the US. Why would the United States deliberately bomb the Chinese Embassy and risk General Jiang's defection? Getting him and his family out were far more important to US interests than the operation in the Balkans. But that was hardly an argument I could make publicly.

The Chinese government propaganda machine—already in full gear—turned it up to eleven, inciting scores of protests across the country. The IAU administration summoned the entire student body to a meeting in the main auditorium, riling them up with more jingoistic speeches. Faces taut, students vehemently chanted, "Revenge! Revenge!"

It was unnerving to watch them.

The students were instructed to protest the bombing at the American Embassy. Twenty official anti-American slogans were approved for banners and chanting. "Blood for Blood" and "NATO = Nazi" were among the favorites. As the IAU students all descended on the American Embassy in Beijing that very day—along with tens of thousands of their brick-hurling compatriots—we foreign teachers laid low in our apartments.

When the students returned, the situation on campus grew more frantic. Those of us in the Foreign Experts Building became hostages to hundreds of raging students outside.

"This is tenser than some war zones I've been in," Will said.

"You think they'll break in here?"

"If they do, don't try to rationalize with them or fight them off. It's like a riptide—just gotta ride it out and hope for the best."

So all of us foreign teachers huddled inside, except for Tom Blum, who moved freely through the throng, a clearly favored foreigner. It was easy to see why. On China Central Television, a party official declared, "We welcome all foreign friends as long as they adopt the correct view." Blum certainly had. Within hours of the news from Belgrade, he'd appeared on every TV channel, claiming the bombing was intentional and that "top American scholars"—like him, I supposed—"recognize the US's barbaric violence, its flagrant violation of international law, and its brutal desire for hegemony."

As evening neared, I sat alone in my apartment wondering what this madness meant for my mission—or if it was still on at all. I had no idea where Lily was and knew even less about her father. Phones and the internet in my building had mysteriously stopped working. "Uncle Gary" couldn't reach me, and I couldn't email the CIA address even if I wanted to. I considered lowering my kitchen blinds, but there was little chance they could get someone onto the IAU campus under these circumstances. *So much for their vaunted redundancy.* China was exploding with anger and I was trapped.

There was a knock on the door.

I opened it and saw Tom Blum standing there in his annoying Chinese army surplus jacket. *Are you kidding me?* He was smiling, looking overjoyed. I wanted to punch that smile right off his face.

"Hey, I'm glad you're in," he said.

"Where the hell else would I be with that mob out there?"

"I've got to say, they are pretty worked up. Did—"

"I wonder why, Tom. Do you think you had anything to do with that?"

"Oh, I might have helped." He was smirking, *enjoying* this exchange.

"Get the fuck out of here." I tried to slam the door in his face.

He stopped it with his foot. "Actually, it's quite a beautiful night out. Made me wonder if you've ever done the night hike at Simatai?"

I froze. Stared at him.

His smile vanished.

CHAPTER 28

*T*he night hike at Simatai?

That was my cue. But I couldn't remember how to respond. I just stood there in the doorway, frozen. I wanted to tell Tom, *I don't remember what I'm supposed to—*

And then I did. "No, I've only been to Jiankou."

"I hear that's a tough section." His chest slumped as he exhaled deeply, his relief so palpable that in an instant it put to rest my questions about his loyalties. His decades of living under an elaborately crafted identify had all come down to this.

"I'm going over to the store. Want to come?" The bombastic communist professor had vanished under the crushing pressure of a life-or-death exfiltration.

"Sounds good. Yeah."

"Bring an empty backpack—that one you take to the boxing club. And keep your wits about you," he whispered.

I followed him down the stairs and across the lobby. The *fuwuyuan*, always attentive to our comings and goings, waved at Tom, no doubt in appreciation of his latest anti-US diatribe on China Central Television.

Then I heard the mob right outside the building chanting "Blood for blood!" and "Death to the Americans!" I elbowed Tom. "They want to kill us."

"We'll be fine." Tom's voice barely rose above the chanting. "I'm a fucking hero in this country. Relax—and don't panic under *any* circumstances."

We stepped outside to the latest chant—"USA equals Ugly Stupid Americans"—as furious young men and women unfurled a "Blood for Blood!" banner directly in front of us.

"Blood for blood!" Tom shouted, raising his fist to urge them on. "Shout it," he said to me in a lower register. I raised my fist and bellowed.

While the crowd roared its approval, he grabbed my arm and led me toward the back of the main classroom building. His eyes were constantly moving, showing an alertness I'd never seen in him before. There was no one in sight when we stopped.

"Look, we don't have much time," he said. "Remember your discussions with Ed Lee?"

"Yes, of course."

"We need you to do exactly what you and Ed talked about—and do it tonight. Lily's father is back in Washington right now for more WTO talks, but he could be recalled any moment because of the embassy bombing. And he won't be able to refuse that order. So you need to act fast. We've already sent someone to get her mother."

He tore off his Chinese army surplus jacket. "Put that in your backpack. Wear it when you leave. From a distance, at least, you'll look Chinese." I stuffed his jacket into my pack. "In the right inside pocket, you'll find the passports and other stuff Ed told you about. Just follow the plan."

But months had passed since those discussions with Ed, and with all these events hitting me at once, I feared I would forget critical elements.

"There's a cap and a phone in the left outside pocket," he went on. "And a map. Do you still have the black hair dye?"

"Yeah."

"Use it before you leave." Tom pulled out a black watchman's cap. In a fisherman's sweater, he still looked dressed for the weather. "Now let's keep moving to the campus store. We want everything to look routine."

He kept briefing me as we hurried along. "The guards lock the campus gate at ten. Once they've retired to the guardhouse, you two can hop the fence and get out of here."

"But with her father out of the country, won't they have someone watching her?" Ed had been explicit about how closely she would be surveilled when her father was abroad, and I'd already witnessed that firsthand.

"Yes, but no one will be in her room. They'll be watching from the hall or lobby and monitoring those cameras. If she can get out of the bathroom window, like she did for your rendezvous, no one should see."

How did he know about that? I didn't even bother to ask. "Won't the protestors see her?"

"That's working in our favor. All their attention's focused on the foreigners in our building. Besides, the students have been ordered to end the demonstrations and be back in their dorms by ten. The administration doesn't want them getting out of control."

"Wouldn't it be easier to just walk off tomorrow? Why tonight?"

"Because there's talk about troop movements in and around the city starting tomorrow. Nobody's going to be allowed to leave the campus except to go to the American Embassy for the official protests. And Lily will be expected to help out by taking student roll call every two hours."

"Whoa...." I shook my head.

"'Whoa' is right. So, Lily's going to try to sneak out of a window at ten-thirty, then she'll meet you in the garden behind our building."

"Where Will and I train?" I figured Tom knew everything else, he'd know that.

"That's right. But if she's a little late, don't panic. By the time you head out together, with any luck at all the guards will be asleep."

Loud chanting in the distance had us both looking around. I turned back to Tom quickly.

"So Lily knows?"

"Yes, I just had the same talk with her. She also knows her father is defecting and wants you to help her get out, and that you've been prepped very carefully."

"How'd she react?"

"Not as surprised, frankly, as I would have thought, which makes me think her father might have let on more than we thought advisable."

Or the whole thing's a trap.

"Don't overthink this," Tom said, as though reading my mind. "Her father's in the US. Her mother's in flight, or will be at any moment. Nobody's playing games here. This is *real*. But here comes the hard part."

There's a harder part?

"You can't walk out of our building on your own. The *fuwuyuan* will see you and report it, and they'll also catch you on the lobby camera. So," he took a breath, "you'll need to leave from your balcony."

"My balcony? I'm on the sixth floor, for Christ's sake. How about I leave from *yours*?" Blum lived on two.

"What do you think's going to happen when you're spotted on camera walking to my room with a backpack and a Chinese army coat?" He didn't wait for an answer. "You've got climbing gear. You can rappel, like you did with Lily in Shanghai."

Of course he would know about that.

"You gotta be kidding." I pictured myself dangling sixty feet above the ground. A simple train and ferry trip out of the country—with the general telling Chen that he wanted Lily and me to leave campus—was turning into a multitude of horrors. "Back then I was on a climbing wall and she was belaying me. I'll be six stories up—on my own."

177

"The principles are the same," Tom said. "You can and will do it. Double-check your knots and just focus on what you're doing every moment of the way. Then get your girlfriend away from campus as quickly as possible. If you do need to spend the night in the city—if routes are blocked—I've included the location of a safe house. It's in the jacket pocket, too."

Safe house? "Do I need a key?"

"Knock eight times. When they ask who's there, say nothing, just knock eight times again."

Eight was the lucky number in China. Easy for me to remember.

"Last thing," he went on, "I mentioned the mobile phone in the—"

"Ed said not to make any phone calls...that I should use the one-time pad."

"That's generally right, but it's safe to use this clean, prepaid phone *once* if you follow my instructions. To keep us informed, call a number that's taped to the back of the phone tonight. Don't say a word. If you make it out of Beijing, wait five seconds after it's answered, and hang up. If you have to use the safehouse, do the same but wait ten seconds. Then throw that phone away. Do *not* use it again."

"Understood."

"All you and Lily have to do at that point is hire a driver to take you from Beijing to Yantai and then catch the regular ferry to Incheon." He held up his index and middle fingers. "Two days. That's all. It'll be simple. Just get a car to Yantai."

I'd been prepared to take a train out of Beijing, but with the city in turmoil I didn't question the change of plans. The only worry I had now was about Yantai. "It's about five hundred miles away. Isn't there anything out of, like, Tianjin?" Two hours by car.

"It shouldn't be hard for you to get a driver for Yantai, and once you have one, we want to get you far from Beijing. A couple thousand RMB should be more than enough to hire someone for that. You've got the cash and those bank and credit cards. Use them. Tip generously, and if the driver has the radio on, tell him to shut it off—say Lily has a headache. You don't want him hearing news updates about you two. If you have to, take control of the vehicle."

"What?"

"Think about what's at stake," Tom said as we hurried along. "Do what you have to."

I looked at him. He was staring straight ahead. I didn't think I had it in me to kill an innocent man. But then I imagined being in a car with Lily, the driver suddenly recognizing us and threatening to turn us in—everything that was at stake.

I tried to visualize applying a chokehold Will had taught me. I shook my head. Tom must have noticed. "Trust your instincts, Andrew. You'll know what you need to do. You already do."

We arrived at the campus store. The shelves were nearly empty, but I grabbed two of the last bottles of water, some crackers, and a few bags of peanuts—enough to tide us over if we wouldn't be able to stop at another store or restaurant for a while.

"So what about you?" I asked as we headed back toward our apartment building. "Are you getting out?"

"I'll be right where I've always been, here in Beijing."

"But people saw us leave together just now."

"Before we met up, I made a point of checking in on Paul and Will, and even our French and Japanese colleagues. Now I'm doing it with you. I'm the foreign faculty president, so it's nothing out of the ordinary, under the circumstances."

"And Lily."

"That wasn't in the open, I assure you."

"You had me totally fooled, Tom."

"That's why they pay me the big bucks."

I knew that wasn't true. He had been putting his life on the line and playing this humiliating anti-American character for so many years for the love of his country. I might not have considered myself a super patriot, but I was suddenly a huge fan of Tom Blum. The man had been tested repeatedly. He had courage.

Enough, I hoped, to rub off on me.

CHAPTER 29

My heart was jackhammering as I rushed up six flights of stairs to my apartment. Tom's decades of astonishing courage *had* rubbed off. I felt emboldened—until I entered my apartment, looked down from my balcony, and weighed rappelling into the blackness below.

I tried to catch my breath as I backed away from the railing. Pivoting, I dashed into my bedroom, eyed my internal frame pack— the bolt bag—on the floor, and transferred the items Tom had given me into it. Pausing, I considered which other IAU mementos to bring.

None.

And I didn't dare do any more packing while the lights were still on, given the likely surveillance *inside* my room.

I glanced at my watch. It was already three minutes past ten. Ten thirty loomed impossibly close, and I still had to dye my hair black, not to mention rig and test the equipment so critical to my escape.

I switched off my living and bedroom lights, then went into the bathroom and closed the door. If there was one place in my apartment that wouldn't have a camera, it was in there—at least I hoped. Not so much because of propriety, but rather, the difficulty of concealing a lens in such a small and seamless room.

I'd read the dyeing instructions carefully, so I was well prepared to color my hair...if not to step off my balcony at the end of a rope.

Forcing aside self-sabotaging fears, I stripped off my rugby shirt and wet my hair in the mineral-stained sink. I put on the thin plastic gloves, squeezed dark globs of gel onto my trembling hands, and worked the dye into my blond hair. Then the waiting began: ten minutes to let the dye set. An excruciating delay, considering the strict time frame.

When I finally rinsed the gel from my hair, I spotted black streaks on the edge of my scalp. Dabbing did nothing; I had to scrub furiously to remove them. Then I combed my hair straight down, the way I'd seen it worn by Chinese men my age.

I pulled my shirt back on, shut off the bathroom light, and opened the door. Moving swiftly—making the best of a few rays of moonlight piercing the overcast sky—I grabbed my bolt bag and added a few remaining items, including the guidebook and black-framed glasses for my disguise, before finally confronting the climbing gear in my closet. It was barely visible, and looked as foreign to me as I must have to most Beijing residents.

Creeping quietly, I carried the gear and backpack out to the balcony, wincing as a carabiner dropped to the floor and clattered across the tiles. I worried it would draw the attention of whoever was monitoring the listening devices, assuming they were still paying attention in the aftermath of the uproar on campus. But no one came. Yet.

It was 10:21.

I rushed to put on my climbing harness when another cautionary thought gripped me: *That's a fifty-foot drop. Do not hurry.* I looked over the balcony railing. In seconds my eyes adjusted to the darkness and I spied the cold hard ground, unforgiving as concrete.

I'd never loved heights. It had been all right when Lily held the rope at the climbing gym. But now I was on my own. I forced myself to put on the waist harness, which I inspected twice to make sure my legs were, in fact, in the correct openings.

Check.

I tied the rope first to the steel radiator just inside my apartment and then to the iron balcony railing. I reexamined both knots before tugging on the rope as hard as I could to make sure it would hold.

Check.

I attached the carabiner to my waist harness, aware that I was betting my life on a tiny aluminum-alloy device, which seemed insane. But I persevered, connecting the figure-eight descender.

Check.

Then I ran the other end of the rope through the descender and began to visualize leaning back into the blackness with my feet up against the building and walking my way down. With my backpack strapped on, I took a deep breath and warned myself not to look down again. I did anyway.

I'm going to fucking die.

I imagined Lily, waiting for me just out of sight, hearing a lurid scream and a dull *thump*.

I took three deep breaths—procrastination as much as an attempt to steady myself—then swung my gelatin legs over the railing, sucked in another breath, and threw the long line of slack into the blackness below. I listened for the rope to hit the ground but heard only a breeze rustling the trees.

Keep moving.

I jerked the tied-up rope and leaned back slightly, testing the radiator and railing again. I leaned more. The balcony creaked, but the line held tight even as I applied most of my weight. Leaning back even farther, I worked up enough courage to launch myself out as I'd done on the climbing wall.

It felt just like it had with Lily—until it didn't. I'd descended no more than three feet when I swung right and my ribs hit hard against the balcony's concrete floor, knocking the wind out of me.

I gasped in pain and shock—and then in sudden relief. *I didn't fall.* The rope had held. The carabiner hadn't failed. A miracle.

That was the good news, but I was still dangling in relative darkness some fifty feet above the ground with sweat-slick hands and only a vague idea of what I was doing.

I gave up any fanciful notion of smoothly walking backward down the side of the building in favor of trying to descend vertically, like a piano lowered by a pulley from a high-rise apartment. It wasn't pretty, but who was watching?

Maybe stragglers from the protest.

The same stingy moonlight that had helped me pack might now leave me silhouetted against the building, like the lamest Spider-Man ever, ready to be grabbed by campus security before the mission was even properly underway. I looked down but saw no one.

And that was the moment a real miracle happened: I stopped fretting and went to work, loosening the friction on the descender so I could feed the rope slowly through it. My muscles seemed to understand what my mind scarcely could: survival.

Without gloves, the rope was rubbing my hands raw, but I moved steadily down past darkened windows, one after the other until a gust of wind banged me into a balcony, the wrought iron railing reverberating as I bounced off it. *Jesus Christ.* I looked down to see which floor it was, having been so preoccupied feeding the rope through the descender that I'd lost track. Third floor.

I was still swearing under my breath when the lights went on behind the curtain just a few feet in front of me. I could hear talking from inside the room. Then footsteps.

Oh, Christ.

I let out more slack, desperate to get my body out of sight. Then I grabbed the bottom of the railings that had just abused me and dragged myself to the side so the rope would be less conspicuous. I peeked over the ledge. Makoto, my Japanese colleague, was looking out from a slit in the curtain, which sent a beam of light across the concrete. A puzzled expression filled his face, but then he shrugged and drew the curtains back into place.

Relieved beyond words, I slid back over to the center of the balcony and continued my descent.

I came to the end of the rope about six feet from the ground. *Close enough, thank God.* I dropped, landing on my feet, fully amazed that I'd made it down. I unhooked the webbing from around my waist and stuffed it into my pack, hoping never to have to use it again.

The rope, however, still hung a foot in front my face, like a giant pointer leading right up to my apartment. The first glimmerings of daylight would bring it into full view.

My impulse was to contact Tom to have it removed. But then I realized that with both Lily and me suddenly absent from the IAU, the rope would be the least of the evidence against me.

The time was now 10:32. Eleven minutes on that wall had felt like an eternity.

I ducked behind some bushes in the garden to hide. I peeked my head up to see her scurrying toward me along the side of the path, hunched over, carrying a small backpack.

Staying low, I waited until she was only about ten feet away before whispering her name.

Lily startled and looked around, then beamed when she recognized me. "Andrew!" she whispered as we rushed toward each other. The fierceness of our embrace eased only so that we could kiss so deeply that we might have been melting into each other.

She still cares. That's what I had wanted to know most of all, even under those distressing circumstances.

She took hold of my face. "Andrew," she said again with the greatest urgency.

"What?" I feared the worst—that she was backing out, that she couldn't—

"I love you. I don't know what's going to happen to us, but I had to tell you. Every day I wanted to, but I knew I couldn't."

I felt the world sway in my favor. "I love you, too, Lily. It's been killing me to see you around campus but to have to keep so much distance." I kissed her again. "But we've got to get moving."

We crept around the Foreign Experts Building and headed north toward the fence that surrounded the campus. It looked as daunting as the Great Wall of China.

And, with its guardhouses, it was.

CHAPTER 30

A light burned in the guardhouse about a hundred feet from Lily and me. The ten o'clock curfew had ended the demonstrations. The night was now eerily quiet. Her absence could be noted at any second.

The clock was ticking.

We scanned the area around us. The guards started talking, a murmur at this distance. But if we could hear them, then they could hear anything louder than a whisper from us.

With no one in sight—and without another word—we inched diagonally toward the far corner of the fence. I figured it would be easier to climb the railings where the two sides came together. The night sky left only those dim glimpses of moonlight to help us on our way. The fear of being caught made our careful footsteps sound as loud as a parade.

We came to a copse of leafless linden trees and took meager cover behind their trunks. I reminded myself to be careful—that where there were trees, and gusts of wind, there might be broken limbs on the ground.

A snapping branch made a loud *crack*.

It wasn't us.

Who's there? Lily and I couldn't see anyone. But we must have been spotted. If it was the guards, I hoped they'd at least fire a warning shot before taking aim at the two dark figures prowling around their campus in the midst of a national emergency.

We stayed motionless. I could hear my rapid heartbeat. A full minute must have passed before I realized that a guard wouldn't hide. He—or *they*—would be ordering us to stop at gunpoint.

Who, then?

"Do you see anyone?" I whispered to Lily.

She shook her head.

I bent close to her ear. "We should keep moving."

What else could we do?

We crept out of the trees, with little but the darkness to shield us. As we drew nearer to the corner of the fence, the guardhouse door flew open, spilling light that fell threateningly close to us.

A tall man in a guard's uniform was silhouetted in the doorway staring into the night.

We froze only a few feet from the fence. If he or his partner did start toward us, we would be cornered in every possible way.

But the big guard headed for the group of linden trees we'd just left.

Lily and I lowered ourselves to the ground to reduce our profiles. Lying on our sides, we watched the guard. He started running, as though he'd spotted someone. His rush flushed his quarry from the trees—a person who must have been following us. Why would they be doing that? Or was it coincidence?

No way.

"Look." Lily pointed to the dark outline of a person running toward the student dormitory.

The guard shouted, *"Zhan zhu!" Don't move!*

His partner bolted from the guardhouse and ran after the tall man, clutching a flashlight. The first guard tackled a woman. We heard her cry out. The second guard was sprinting up to them.

Light appeared in the window of a nearby student dormitory. Then a second and third came to life. Backlit faces were watching as the guards dragged the woman to her feet. The second guard turned his flashlight on her face.

"It's Rose," Lily said.

"Rose from my class?" I peered closely. "What's she doing?"

"I don't know. Maybe she followed me. She was watching me the other day in the courtyard, too—and it wasn't the first time. When I asked her what she was doing, she just walked away."

"She's been stalking you?"

"Maybe, but I don't think it's about me. She's crazy about you. Haven't you noticed?"

I *had* noticed the gifts, the open flirting at movie nights, and her growing boldness in class, but I hadn't taken it seriously. And I hadn't been aware of this business with Lily. How could I? We'd been forced to keep our distance from each other for months.

"She probably realized we were running off together from the second she saw our backpacks," Lily said.

We are so fucked. Every detail was supposed to be covered, and now we were getting exposed by *Rose*?

She would be hailed as a national hero once she pointed us out to the guards. While they were still distracted, we needed to at least try to make a break for it—throw our packs over the fence, then climb it, jump down, and run like hell. It was the only option. I lifted myself to one knee and grabbed a wrought iron rail.

Lily gripped my arm. "Stay still," she whispered. "Let's see what Rose does."

Lily was right. Fleeing could be a death sentence if it drew the guards' attention.

They began to question Rose right in the open. "*Ni shi shei?*" *Who are you?* The tall guard's voice carried clearly through the stillness.

The second guard held Rose by the shoulder before losing patience with her silence. He started shaking her hard. "*Kuai shuo!*" *Answer the question!* He sounded as though he might be the one in charge.

Rose gave her Chinese name.

"What are you doing out at this hour?" the tall guard continued in Mandarin. "There is a curfew, you know."

Lily squeezed my hand, as if to say, *Here it comes.*

Rose didn't answer, but she looked in our direction, beyond the glare of the flashlight. I thought the guards would follow her gaze, but they must have thought she was trying to avoid their questions.

"Answer him!" The shorter man demanded again.

Rose started to cry. "My boyfriend left me. I had to go for a walk. When I saw you, I was scared, so I ran. I'm so sorry," she finished, still staring right at us.

The two guards looked at each other as in, *Are you kidding me?* The guard who had tackled her brushed leaves off her sleeve.

"Go home," the shorter guard said, pointing to the dormitory. "It's been a hard day for everyone. Maybe your boyfriend will come to his senses. You seem like a nice girl."

Rose whimpered, "I don't think he's ever coming back."

The taller guard patted her on the shoulder and nudged her toward the dorm. "You just need some sleep."

She put her head down and trudged away. She looked meeker than ever, but she'd saved us from immediate arrest—or worse. I wondered why—was it really feelings for me, or some deeper sense that it was the right thing to do? I owed her, yet I hardly knew her. Didn't she realize that by not speaking up about us, she might soon fall under suspicion, too? Unless, once the news of our escape got out, the guards decided to keep this incident to themselves to cover up for their own inaction tonight.

We remained absolutely still until the two men retreated to the guardhouse and closed the door behind them. Then I helped Lily up onto the wrought iron fence.

She climbed it easily. I studied her hand and footholds as carefully as I had in the gym in Shanghai, then lofted the packs over to her. They were heavy, but she caught them easily, making little noise.

I climbed less nimbly but found it much more manageable than the descent from the balcony.

We scurried down a nearby alley, just east of campus, where Lily leaned back against a brick wall, cushioned by her pack. "What now? Tom said you would know what to do."

I certainly knew the overall plan, but I confessed that we had not expected to escape while the country was in turmoil. With the state of emergency, the streets were unnervingly quiet. There was no traffic at all and not a cab in sight. That's when I understood why Tom had given me the address of a safe house that hadn't been mentioned in the original plan. *Just in case.* Well, just in case had now come to pass.

I showed Lily the address, which was unfamiliar to me.

"Qianmen District. That's at least an hour and a half by foot."

Too much exposure. "A twenty- or thirty-minute bike ride?"

"Yeah."

My bike was parked on the street not more than a hundred yards away, but in precisely the wrong direction—back toward campus. Far worse, it was in open view of the guardhouse at the IAU North Gate. By now, officials at the school could have been rousing everyone to track down Lily.

It's your only chance.

"I'm going to get my bike. Stay here. Watch my pack."

Lily looked intensely into my eyes. "Be careful."

I hurried back to the main street, checking that no one was there. With a deep breath, I walked as nonchalantly as possible toward the IAU North Gate. As I neared it, I could see that the lights in the guardhouse were on, but it looked empty. The door had been left wide open.

Glancing up at the Foreign Experts Building, I saw the lights in Tom's and the Japanese couple's apartments, but the other teachers appeared to be asleep.

I continued to the row of bicycles parked alongside the road, about twenty feet past the guardhouse. There were dozens of them, almost all identical black Forever bikes with racks on the back, just like mine. *Which one is it?* I couldn't remember the last time I rode mine, much less where I'd parked it. I grew increasingly frantic as I searched for the one with the combination cable lock I'd brought from home, rather than the more common U-locks. I finally found my bike.

As I began to roll it out of the rack, footsteps pounded down the path toward the main quad. I was completely exposed. If I ran back toward Lily, I would be seen for sure.

What the hell?

I rested my bike against the one beside it, laid down, and rolled up against the rear tire.

The footsteps grew louder. I peered up through a gap in the bicycles and saw the two guards who'd questioned Rose.

"You take the east side of the fence, and I'll watch this side until backup arrives," the shorter one said in his gruff Mandarin. The tall guard turned and strode toward the part of the fence we had climbed—and toward the alley where Lily was now crouching not more than fifty yards away.

There was no way I could get up, much less go back to her. The shorter guard was standing post right at the North Gate, alternately looking inside and outside campus.

Sirens blared from the east, getting louder as they approached. The headlights bore down on me. I faced away from the police car, hoping to be dismissed as a passed-out college student—an irrelevancy when a general's daughter has gone missing.

The cruiser raced past me, tires screeching as it rounded the corner of the next intersection. Then it turned left, toward the front gate of campus.

The phone inside the guardhouse rang loudly.

"*Wo kao*," the guard muttered as he hurried inside. *Damn it.*

I could hear him on the phone. "*Ming bai, ming bai*," he said. *Understood, understood.* I didn't know how long this conversation would last, but it might be my only chance.

I stood quickly and pulled my bike from the rack, knowing I couldn't ride directly to Lily, not with the tall guard in the way.

Just go.

I sped after the police car, away from her. As I turned left at the intersection, I saw the People's Armed Police cruiser parked at the IAU main gate, its red and blue lights still whirling. At least a dozen people were speaking with the cops.

Head down, I rolled to the opposite side of the street and pedaled hard as I looped around campus until I re-entered the alley where I'd left Lily. I braked as I approached her, crouched beside a trashcan. She jumped up.

"Did you see the police?"

"Yes. And guards, too—that's why I had to go around. Hop on the back."

"Can you ride with me on it?" We both had heavy packs.

I nodded, not knowing if I had the strength. But it was do or die.

CHAPTER 31

I pedaled furiously, fueled by panic and the pressing need to get away from the IAU as fast as possible. I wasn't sure we were on the best course toward the safe house in Qianmen, but the arrival of that People's Armed Police car at the university's gate told me loud and clear that an alert about Lily's disappearance must have been issued.

My own absence would be noted as soon as the door-pounding started at the Foreign Experts Building. I was sure that security protocols for the missing daughter of a high-ranking official were firmly established and would be put into action immediately.

"Keep your face pressed against me and your hat pulled down," I said as a car came toward us, its headlights momentarily blinding me. I wanted her to look sleepy, while hoping that with my dyed hair combed straight down, Tom's Chinese army surplus jacket, and the black-framed glasses, I just might appear Chinese at a distance. If we came across a roadblock, though, it would mean certain arrest and the most serious charges possible.

"I need you to help me navigate to the safe house," I said. "I'm going to stop at that canal up ahead." I'd spotted it thanks to those otherwise threatening headlights. "I bet there's a footpath under the bridge where we can get some cover."

I braked hard as soon as we arrived at the canal, spotting steps leading to the footpath. "You go first," I said to Lily, who hopped off and scampered down. I picked up the heavy bike and carried it with me, breathing hard. The beams of moonlight that had alternately helped and hindered us vanished as we stepped into the dark shadows under the bridge.

We dug out a flashlight and the map, which noted the safe house.

"You know the way?" I asked Lily.

"Give me a second." She peered at the map.

"I want to get off this main road."

She nodded, still studying the possible routes. "Okay, I know this area. Let's get back on the road, then you'll take the next left."

The most direct route would have followed busy Chang'an Avenue, but Lily led us into a dimly-lit *hutong*, a traditional Beijing neighborhood with narrow roads and two- and three-story buildings with flat exteriors that extended almost to the pavement. Our zigzagging progress on these tight, roughly paved streets was slower but seemed safer.

I wanted to ask Lily so many questions—*Are you scared? Happy to be going to America? Worried about your parents?*—but all I could manage as I rode over a pothole that bounced me off my seat was, "You all right back there?"

She tightened her grip around my waist. "I'm okay."

I pedaled on, north of the Palace Museum toward Dongzhimen and the Beijing Fight Club.

"Turn right at this one," she said.

I did, but our circuitous path was now leading us near the American Embassy and the site of the protests. I gripped the handlebars tightly as the distinctive rumble of large troop transport trucks grew louder.

They sounded just a few blocks away. So did the shouts of an angry crowd spewing ugly anti-American slogans.

I slowed down, unsure if we should go farther. Before I could speak, Lily jumped off and rubbed her bottom.

"This way seems risky. They're so close we can hear them," I said.

"The protestors?"

"The army trucks, too. If anyone looks closely, we're in trouble."

"You did bomb our embassy. People have a right to be angry."

"Jesus, stop," I said, louder than I should have. "I didn't bomb anything. I'm here with you, trying to get you out of the country." I lowered my voice. "Is there another way to get to that safe house without going past that mess over there?" I looked toward the sound of the chanting and saw red lights reflecting off low-hanging clouds.

To my relief, she dropped the embassy bombing debate. "We could go farther east, across the Second Ring Road," one of Beijing's most distinctive thoroughfares. "Then we could head south. We can't avoid Jianguomen Wai, which is always busy, but there will still be fewer people than up ahead."

"Do you think it'll be barricaded?"

"I don't know, but we should be able to see from a block away at least."

Warily, I pedaled on. Lily was right—we spotted the well-lit thoroughfare from what I hoped was a safe distance. Soldiers were stationed every twenty or thirty feet along the sidewalk, but traffic was passing through without being stopped. If we'd had a car, we could have driven right through, too. On a bike, I had my doubts, which I shared with Lily.

She asked me to stop, climbed off, and looked me over closely. She reached for my face, flattening my dyed bangs before shaking her head. "You're right, this isn't going to work."

I was relieved. The prospect of trying to cross a line of armed soldiers on a well-lit road horrified me, though I didn't know what else we could do.

She did. "If we go a little farther, past Guomao," where White and McInerney's office was located, "it shouldn't be so busy. It'll take longer but—"

"That's okay."

As Lily predicted, we didn't encounter soldiers and were finally able to veer west toward Qianmen. I was riding so intently, head down, that Lily startled me when she said, "There it is."

The safe house. A six-floor walkup, like the Foreign Experts Building, but considerably older and more run down. After the challenge of getting there, it looked like a citadel to me.

We parked the bike among similar models on the street, then made our way up to the fourth floor, encountering no one.

I knocked eight times on apartment 412, then repeated after a soft voice asked who was there.

A small, wizened woman opened the door. You could tell at a glance that she'd lived through the Civil War, Mao, the Cultural Revolution, Deng Xiaoping's reforms, Tiananmen Square, and now this. She studied me, then pulled me in with shockingly strong bony arms, snapping at Lily in Mandarin to close the door.

We dropped our backpacks in the entryway, drained by nerves and exertion. The woman led us to a small living room, where she chatted quietly with Lily. Then, as I settled on the couch, I remembered that I was supposed to call the number Tom had given me.

Lily looked over as I got back up and retrieved the mobile phone. I dialed the number and heard someone pick up. Then I waited out the ten seconds of silence to signal that we were in the safe house. The empty line felt haunting.

I hung up and looked at Lily.

"What's next?" she asked.

"Sleep, I guess." I called to the old woman, who was in the kitchen, "Where should we sleep?" I asked in Mandarin.

"No sleep." She walked in with a tray. "Black tea. Stay awake. Wait." She returned to the kitchen.

Lily fell asleep anyway, with her head on my shoulder as I sipped tea, wondering nervously what came next.

About fifteen minutes later there were eight knocks on the door. "Who's there?" the old woman asked again without getting out of her chair. Another eight knocks. She pointed to the door, as much as saying, "Answer it."

Lily blinked awake when I eased from her side and stood up. She sat forward on the couch, looking petrified.

I held my hand against the door as I unbolted it, prepared to slam it shut again if needed. I opened it just a crack and peeked out.

"How ya doin', brother?"

I would have known that Carolina lilt anywhere. I threw open the door. "*You?*"

"The one and only," Will said. "And I brought company." He stepped aside so I could see the diminutive woman behind him.

"Mama!" Lily exclaimed as she ran up and hugged her mother. I could see her shoulders shaking as she began to cry.

I was surprised but not shocked that Will was involved. More than once I'd been tempted to fish around in our conversations to see if he'd bite. But then there had been other times, like that first movie night, when he'd seemed utterly clueless in calling Lily over to sit with us. All part of the performance, I guessed.

With his duffel bag in hand, Will herded the women into the apartment, where Lily re-introduced me to her mother.

She bowed her head slightly, then looked in my eyes. "Thank you, Mr. Callahan, for bringing me my daughter." She sounded as formal as she had at the dinner for her husband back in the fall.

"It's my honor," I replied, wanting to say, *You might want to save it till we get you two out of here.*

"And *you?*" Lily said to Will.

"You just can't get rid of me."

"I'm glad." She looked at me. "For both of you."

"It's one thirty," Will said, glancing around. "That leaves us only a few more hours of mostly empty streets."

"Aren't we taking the train?" My schedule said the first train wasn't until 7:00 a.m.

"Definitely not," Will replied. "We can't go to the station with this chaos. There's a car downstairs. Shall we get moving?"

With General Jiang's wife and daughter in our care, that wasn't really a question—not with the threat of a bullet in the head or a noose around our necks.

CHAPTER 32

W e bade goodbye to the old woman and followed Will down to the street, where he waved at a "bread loaf" car—a microvan—idling about fifty feet away. As the vehicle rolled slowly toward us, Will turned to me. "The driver's an old friend of mine and one of your new ones."

"Who?"

"Wu from the Fight Club. He's driven for us before."

Yet another of Will's secrets. "You sure that's a good idea? Does he know what we're doing?"

"The only thing he knows is he needs to drive. He's smart enough not to ask questions. We pay him good cash money, and he needs it to take care of his sick pop. Besides, he's the only guy I could get on short notice with the city going haywire."

So much for our perfect plan.

SCOTT SPACEK

"You take the front seat, Mrs. Jiang—it's more comfortable," Will said, as bull-necked Wu jumped out and walked around the car to greet us.

"Andrew! I didn't recognize you in that Chinese army jacket and those glasses!" He gave me a thumbs-up. "He beat me up the last time we boxed—that's why it was the last time." He laughed as we all piled in. Lily took a lone seat protruding from the side wall, while Will and I shared the rear bench.

"So where are we headed?" I asked Will as Wu walked around the front of the van.

"Shijiazhuang."

"What? I was told Yantai, and Shijiazhuang's west."

"Right, but all the roads heading east either have armed checkpoints or they will shortly."

I leaned closer as Wu opened the driver's door. "Two hundred miles in the wrong direction?"

"Right now, we just need to get the fuck out of Dodge." He said to Wu. "*Zou ba.*" *Let's go.*

As Wu put the rickety old vehicle in gear, Will turned back to me. "Shijiazhuang's a transit hub—we can keep our options open from there."

"He doesn't seem to know who they are," I whispered, glancing at Lily and her mom, both of whom were quietly gazing out the window.

"I doubt he does," Will replied. "They don't exactly travel in the same social circles."

I mentioned the warning about the car radio.

"With Wu, the biggest danger is having to put up with Leon Lai on a loop," Will said, referring to the Chinese pop singer.

"But don't you think with everything going on, he'd at least want to turn on the news?"

"If he does, I'll tell him he *really* doesn't want to listen. Or I'll pay him more."

As we approached Jianguomen Wai from the south, I remembered Tom's phone, which he'd said to ditch. I asked Wu to stop momentarily and tossed it down a storm drain. Climbing back into the car, I heard the roar of diesel engines, then saw a column of military vehicles pass in front of us, heading east toward the US Embassy. The lead car was an open-air jeep filled with soldiers, antennae sprouting from the hood, giving it an insectoid appearance. Canvas-covered troop transports followed closely behind. Through the open backs, I saw more soldiers with rifles. A pair of armored personnel carriers brought up the rear, making me worry about manned checkpoints.

Will and I exchanged looks. He appeared as uneasy as I felt. Lily grabbed her mom's shoulder in reassurance.

"Shouldn't we stay off Jianguomen Wai?" I asked as we turned onto it.

"It's the fastest way onto the Second Ring Road and out of town," Will said.

I could do nothing but trust his judgment. I lowered my voice. "So, how long have you been involved?"

"I can't tell you everything, and it's better you don't know, but I've been part of this operation for over a year." Then he whispered in my ear, "I couldn't believe how well things worked out between you and Lily."

"That's one way to put it."

Keeping his eye on the road ahead, Will continued quietly, "A certain somebody asked me what I thought of you. I said—"

"What somebody? Ed Lee?"

Will smiled. "It's on a 'need to know' basis. We keep information compartmentalized—just in case. But I can tell you that I said you seemed to have potential." His devilish grin took over his face. "I guess you can blame me for nudging you along, and you can blame love for the rest." He nodded at Lily, who was still vigilantly looking out the vehicle. "Why do you think I've been training you so hard? For barfights?" He glanced at Wu. "I needed to teach you to take care of yourself. That was an order from on high."

"I gotta know something. Did Wu take a dive when he ended up on his knees in the ring? Was that part of my training, or was that legit?"

Will laughed. "Totally legit. He told me later he was getting too old to take on guys like you."

"How did you manage to get Lily's mother?"

"Yesterday, we had our regular dance class—"

"Dance class?"

"I'm her instructor. I had to put my skills to some good use. Last year, she started taking dancing lessons, so I applied for a part-time job and next thing you know, I'm guiding her around a ballroom."

Now it was my turn to laugh. *Unbelievable.* "Another tile in the mosaic?"

"Exactly." Will winked. "Anyway, yesterday, I showed her a letter from her husband that explained part of the plan, then I filled her in on the rest. She stared at it and said, 'He's really doing it.' So she must have known something. More than I did until a couple of days ago."

"Lily's reaction was kind of like her mom's."

"Mrs. Jiang wanted to call her husband, but I told her it was too dangerous. So she went home right after class to get ready. I swung by with Wu about an hour before I met you at the safe house. That was the diciest part of this evening. I can't tell you how relieved I was to drive away from there with her."

"Have you—"

"Checkpoint!" Lily said sharply. It was three long blocks away.

"Turn right," Will ordered.

Wu complied, but not without throwing a concerned look back at Will, who then directed, "Take the on-ramp from Beijing Station Road."

No one said a word for several minutes, until we were safely on the 2nd Ring Road.

I nudged Will. "So now picking up Lily's mom was the *second* diciest part of your evening?"

"Things certainly would've gotten interesting if we'd driven straight into that roadblock. I think it's fair to assume, now, that they're looking for these two." His eyes were back on Lily and her mom, both of whom appeared fully alert. "Probably us, as well."

We soon reached Changxindian, past the 5th Ring Road, and Will leaned back. "Should be smooth sailing from here."

Lily, her mom, and I settled back, too. I felt like a deflated balloon. That image was my last thought before I nodded off.

I awoke, suddenly, to the sound of the radio—a news broadcast, no less, about 50,000 protestors who'd descended on the American Embassy in Beijing. It was light outside.

How long has that radio been on?

I looked at Will, Lily, and her mom, all still sleeping. At that moment—with the news blaring—I wished I could have said the same about Wu at the wheel, irrational as that was. The next bulletin might report the missing wife and daughter of the great General Jiang— along with two American instructors from the IAU.

"Could you please shut that off?" I asked Wu.

He replied by shaking his big round head. I noted his thick neck again, remembering how I might have to "take care of the problem," as Tom had so delicately put it. But this was Wu, not some stranger.

"Big news. I must listen," Wu said, interrupting my thoughts of choking the life out of him, which had been so vivid that I was appalled with myself. "You people bombed my embassy."

Not that again.

"Will and I didn't bomb your embassy," I said.

"Americans are always bombing everyone—Vietnam, Cambodia, Laos, Iraq, Serbia, and now China!"

"Wu, we're friends, and I'm tired. We need to sleep. I promise I won't bomb you. Please turn it off." I slipped him a hundred renminbi note, which had the desired effect. Silence wasn't golden—but it did have a price.

I soon passed out again.

I came back to consciousness about an hour later. *We must be getting close.* I saw two military transport trucks whiz by in the opposite lane—toward the capital.

Will stirred and looked out the window. "Shijiazhuang has a big army base."

I closed my eyes and started laughing. This all felt like the worst possible joke.

"I know it's not perfect," Will admitted, "but we didn't have much choice, with Beijing on the verge of lockdown and rumors of checkpoints on major roads to the coast. You do notice that all these trucks—"

Another military truck sped by, as though cued.

"—are *leaving* the base. Hold on."

He reached forward and tapped Wu on the shoulder, asking him to turn on some music. "No news, just music."

Wu nodded and turned on the radio. Cover for our conversation, which Wu undoubtedly understood. Lily and her mother were still asleep, resting their heads on their jackets, bunched up against the windows.

Will went on. "We should figure out our next move. Given this is a major train junction, we should have a lot of options."

I reached into my pack and pulled out a train schedule along with my *Lonely Planet*. "Let's see."

Will and I studied the timetable. "We could either head south, farther into the center of China," he started. "Or go back up through Dezhou or Beijing on our way to Yantai, where we could catch a ferry as planned."

"Beijing? Are you kidding?"

"It would be relatively safe if we're already on a train."

That seemed like pushing our luck. I had no idea what Dezhou would be like.

"Why can't we just fly?" I asked. "As long as we're flying domestic, there shouldn't be any customs agents, right? And they'd never expect us to be flying around *within* China. They'd be worried about the opposite."

"Maybe," Will replied, sounding uneasy at the prospect of air travel.

I found a spiderweb map of domestic flights in the *Lonely Planet*. "According to this, we could fly from Shijiazhuang to Dalian. That might work." It was in northeast China and relatively close to South Korea.

"What's the schedule?" he asked.

I dug that out, too. "It says China Southern has flights on Wednesday—in three days." Then I checked the ferry schedule from Dalian and groaned. "If we land Wednesday, we'd have to wait until *Friday* for the next ferry."

Will shook his head. "Is there anywhere we could fly and still make it to Dalian for the Tuesday ferry? What about Shenyang?" An industrial city north of Dalian, notorious for being the most polluted urban area on the planet.

I scanned the schedule. "There's a flight every Monday at noon. So tomorrow."

"Sounds like the answer."

I hoped Will was right, though I had a bad feeling about Shenyang, and it wasn't just the thought of inhaling the most polluted air of any city on Earth. It was the lack of other Westerners. Shenyang didn't attract tourists; it repelled them. Amid a toxic anti-American climate, we'd stand out when we most needed to blend in. But I didn't have a better idea.

We'd made it out of Beijing, but I feared those troop transport trucks were merely a preview of what was to come.

CHAPTER 33

The Taichung Mountains were shrouded by low-lying clouds as Wu drove swiftly into Shijiazhuang early that morning.

"Reminds me of the Smoky Mountains back home," Will said.

His comment made me imagine hiking the Appalachian Trail with Lily, surrounded by nothing but forest. Then Wu hit a pothole, plunging me back into the reality of a cramped microvan and waking up the two women.

"Where are we now?" Mrs. Jiang asked.

"Shijiazhuang," Wu announced as he pulled up to the city's central bus station. A state-owned travel agency was right next door, the military base less than a mile away.

I slipped off Tom's army surplus coat and the fake glasses. Up close they wouldn't fool the authorities or even security-conscious citizens. My black hair *might* suffice if anyone were looking for a blond foreigner. I combed it into a side part and put on my own jacket. Will nodded his approval of my transformation.

"Where'd you get the jacket?" he asked.

"It's on a 'need to know' basis," I joked.

"Ha ha," Will said straight-faced.

"You taught me well."

Lily turned and looked at me. I smiled. She didn't, which I attributed to her fatigue and stress, not the exchange I'd just had with Will, who was now tipping Wu generously. We thanked him for driving us and said goodbye as we climbed out.

"Give me your passports and I'll go get the plane tickets," Will said. "There's a noodle restaurant right over there." He pointed to it. "Go make yourselves inconspicuous."

Easier said than done. No other Westerners were visible at the busy station.

Lily and I handed over our fake passports. Mrs. Jiang hesitated.

"Don't worry about it," Will told her. "I have yours."

She nodded. Maybe it wasn't the first time she'd traveled on a forged document.

"And order me some beef noodles," Will added as he walked off.

The Jiangs and I walked into the restaurant. I glanced around, relieved at the absence of televisions or radios. Lily's eyes landed on a public computer in the corner.

"Grab it," I said. If our names and faces were now plastered across the internet, it was better we see it before the other patrons.

Mrs. Jiang and I took the table next to the computer. I asked a waitress if we could get online.

"*Dangran keyi*," she shot back. *Of course you can.* "Fifteen RMB per hour."

"Perfect," I replied. "We'll use it." I asked what the Jiangs would like, then ordered four bowls of beef noodles.

The waitress grunted her approval and turned back toward the kitchen.

Mrs. Jiang and I crowded close to Lily, who was clicking onto *The Washington Post* website. As the page rendered, she bit her lip, easing up when there was no mention of us. She scrolled down to an article titled "American Consulate in Wuhan Attacked with Molotov Cocktails."

This surge in anti-Americanism was exactly what Lily's father had said the New Leftists wanted. The next headline, though, read like a counterpoint: "Chinese Vice-President Hu Warns Against Extreme Acts." His comments were directed at the protestors and demonstrated that establishment figures in Beijing were urging a more pragmatic approach to the US.

Still, no reference to us.

Thank God.

The waitress arrived with our food and set it down on the table. She glanced at the screen, but Lily had already clicked to the *Post's* arts and entertainment section.

Will rejoined us as we turned to the Chinese news sites. The top story in the *Global Times* reported "President Clinton's Dishonest and Insincere Apologies." The *People's Daily* declared "China Not Afraid of War."

We ate and scanned more articles in silence. Lily was about to close the browser when Will leaned forward and pointed at a developing story in the *People's Daily*: "Senior Chinese General Jiang Guangkai Missing from Talks."

Oh, shit.

Will reached past Lily and clicked on the link. A short paragraph stated only that "American sources" expressed surprise that General Jiang, who was known to be in Washington, failed to appear at high-level talks scheduled with the US State Department, and that "relevant organs" in China were investigating. Still no reference to us, but I was certain the disappearance of his wife and daughter would soon go public.

I could feel the noose closing around our necks.

So, evidently, could Will and Lily, who closed the browser. We immediately stood and glanced around. Of the dozen other patrons, only one bothered to look up. The rest continued slurping their noodles and reading their papers.

Mrs. Jiang remained seated, staring at the now empty screen. How many surges of raw panic had she been forced to suppress in her life? Enough, it appeared, to inure her to even our desperate situation.

"Sit," she said quietly in Mandarin. "What kind of person leaves a half-eaten bowl of noodles behind?"

A guilty one, I thought, embarrassed at my lack of composure.

We silently finished our noodles. Will distributed our passports and tickets. "Beautiful day for a plane ride," he said, reclaiming his calm demeanor with a smile.

We headed for the door and our path back across the plaza.

"What do you think of that story about General Jiang?" I whispered to Will as we moved ahead of the two women.

"It's an intentional leak. A cover for the fact we just granted him political asylum. So, we've got the prize. But now we've got to get these two the hell out of here to keep them from turning into trade bait."

"At least *we* haven't made headlines yet. I was about to run a search."

"I would have stopped you," Will said. "With tens of thousands of Chinese bureaucrats monitoring internet traffic, checking for suspicious keywords, that could have been a serious mistake."

I nodded, chastened, before worrying aloud about our colleagues at the IAU. "You think they're getting interrogated already?"

"Maybe some rather *enhanced* interrogation," Will replied.

I was stunned by how casually Will dismissed the ordeal the other faculty members might be enduring, which only reinforced my own determination to avoid a similar fate.

"We should get to the airport," Will said, looking at his watch. "Our flight leaves in ninety minutes."

He hailed a cab and grabbed the front seat. I squeezed into the back with Lily and her mother. The cabbie's radio blared news of demonstrations and denunciations, along with sounds of furious chanting and shouting. The streets were clearly coming back to life all around China.

"Please shut that off," Will asked the driver in Mandarin.

The cabbie looked askance at him. Will handed him a hundred *yuan* then personally reached over and turned it off just as the broadcaster said, "At the IAU this morning, a report that—"

"The airport," Will said without reacting to what we'd heard and the mystery of what we'd missed. "We're tired," he explained to the driver. "They want to relax," he glanced over his shoulder at the three of us. We dutifully closed our eyes. "We've got a long day ahead of us."

That much was true. Our escape was beginning to feel endless, even though it had barely begun.

CHAPTER 34

Cameras stared down at us from the roof of the crowded terminal at the Shijiazhuang airport as the four of us waited in the chilly air for the tinted automatic door to open. My eyes darted side to side in search of any security officers sent to capture us—only to step in and find myself face to face with an armed guard standing next to an X-ray machine.

"*Huzhao!*" he barked. *Passport.*

I held up the phony document emblazoned with Canada's official coat of arms, hoping like hell the CIA counterfeiters knew what they were doing. The guard took it but continued staring at me. I could sense Will, Lily, and Mrs. Jiang stiffening behind me.

Security at transportation hubs had already been tightened in response to terrorist attacks and hijack attempts by Uyghurs, but I knew he wouldn't mistake me—a light-skinned Westerner—for one of them. As the guard looked back and forth between my face and the passport, I worried I'd overlooked a revealing smudge of dye along my hairline.

He turned to my China visa and paused. "You need to go there," he said sternly, thumb crooked over his shoulder, not taking his eyes off mine.

"Go where? Why?" My scalp steamed. I feared my brow would soon be streaked with black sweat.

The guard now turned and pointed to a kiosk forty feet away. "To pay the airport tax." He shoved my passport back into my hand.

"Yes, sir," I said, more pleased than ever before to be handing money over to a government.

I swung my backpack over my shoulder and walked with Will to pay up, the Jiangs about ten feet behind us. *Be cool*, I reminded myself as I casually wiped my brow—*clear* sweat, thank God.

I paid the ninety-yuan levy, then returned to the guard, who grunted his approval as I held up the receipt for him to see.

"Everything in the machine for inspection," he ordered.

An inventory of my bag was running through my head as I threw it on the belt. The first thing he would find would be the Chinese Army surplus jacket.

I prepared myself for worst-case scenarios, the number of which seemed to multiply with every step of our escape. *Should I say it's a souvenir?* I wished I'd tossed Tom's jacket, as I had his phone.

My bag rolled out of the X-ray machine, and another guard picked it up. My stomach sank, but all he did was wrap it in red tape to show that it had been checked. Then he grabbed Lily's bag and said he needed to look inside.

"Yes, I understand," she replied in Mandarin. "*Wei le anquan.*" For security.

Mrs. Jiang followed, though not so volubly as her daughter.

Then the guard took one look at Will and grabbed his bag. I tried to take my cues from Lily and her mother, who affected the air of weary but bored travelers, but that was hard because I knew a wallet with our real documents was hidden under the false bottom of Will's bag. Feeling tense, I glanced at him, but he was smiling sheepishly as the guard opened his pack.

"Sorry, man, but it's a little stinky," he said with a laugh.

"Ugh," the guard groaned in disgust at some strategically placed dirty underwear. "*Nimen qu ba*," he said. *Just get going.*

"An old trick," Mrs. Jiang said moments later.

Will agreed. "But it worked."

At the China Southern Airlines counter, a young woman took our tickets and asked if we were enjoying our visit to China.

"Oh, we're having a great time." I tried for hearty, but feared my words sounded no more genuine than my passport.

"I'm so happy to hear that." She appeared to mean it. "Have a *great* flight," she added as she waved us toward the gate. Apparently, she hadn't received the memo that courtesy to Westerners had been suspended.

The four of us collapsed in the boarding area, carefully maintaining our distance to avoid drawing attention. We were too spent to say much, anyway. Loudspeakers soon filled the silence, blaring that China had officially protested the US bombing at the UN: "The Chinese government today demanded a formal apology and compensation from the United States for its flagrant violations of Chinese sovereignty and international law."

A few passengers gave Will and me the evil eye. One in a dark-brimmed hat snarled "NATO!" A younger couple shook their heads. But no one appeared to notice Lily and her mother.

I turned away and looked out of the gate's floor-to-ceiling window at our plane to Shenyang. It looked a little like a Boeing 727, but it had two engines mounted on the tail fin and one suspended on the vertical stabilizer.

"A Tupolev-154," Will said. "Russian for 'piece of shit.'"

"If the Public Security Bureau doesn't kill us, China Southern will," Mrs. Jiang deadpanned.

Will, Lily, and I all laughed.

We took our assigned seats, Lily and her mother next to each other, directly in front of Will and me. We were near the wings, reputedly the safest part of a jet. I had no idea if that held true for a "piece of shit."

The plane was only about twenty percent full. I mentioned this to Will. He looked around and said, "Well, at least eighty percent will survive."

We took off at a steep angle. Once in the air, my adrenaline ebbed; the most dangerous part of the flight was over—until the landing. I watched my companions nod off.

I tried to sleep, too, but couldn't. The drone of the engines kept me awake, along with the creaking of the fuselage, which shook like a trampoline in the frequent turbulence.

I couldn't stop thinking about the number of close calls we'd already had—it wasn't supposed to be this way. From Shenyang, we still needed to get to Dalian before we could shove off for Korea. I tried to remember the ferry schedule. But when I couldn't, and was too lazy to dig it out, I finally closed my eyes and drifted off.

I was dreaming of a rugged coastline pounded by ceaseless waves when I was jolted awake by my chest slamming down into my knees, the seatbelt strangling my waist, and my head whipsawing back into the seat.

"Jesus Christ." I was suddenly wide awake. "I thought we crashed."

"Crashing's a whole different feeling, brother," Will said.

"You've crashed?"

"In one of these." He glanced around. "Long story. Not now."

Lily and her mom looked rattled, too. We rolled to the gate with frightening speed. My watch said it was 1:30 p.m., but the air outside was battleship gray. I wondered what the conversion rate was between breathing the Shenyang air and packs of Marlboro Reds. Even inside the plane, the air tasted bitter, metallic, sour.

"We made it," I said to Lily.

"To Shenyang." She had sleep lines from the sweater she'd used as a pillow.

We hurried through the bland airport. Even the usually bright red and white propaganda banners looked faded. Will and I kept our distance behind Lily and her mom. No one appeared to notice them, but several travelers murmured their hit parade of insults at Will and me: "NATO!" "Americans!" "Hegemony!"

"Fuck off!" Will replied under his breath. When we regathered near the terminal entrance, he spoke more audibly, "We need to find out when and where we can catch that train to Dalian."

"I'll go check." Lily motioned toward a travel agency. She sounded refreshed by her nap.

Her mother took her arm. "Be careful. They may be looking for you."

They absolutely are looking for her.

"I can't wait to be on that goddamn ferry," Will whispered to me.

Mrs. Jiang slumped against a wall but never complained. No doubt she'd known worse.

Lily hurried back to us. "There are trains every couple hours to Dalian from both Shenyang Station and Shenyang North. The trip takes about four hours. What time does the ferry leave tomorrow?"

"Hold on." I dug out the schedule, hoping it was still up to date. "Eight in the morning."

"And the last train out is at what time?" Will asked.

"About seven p.m., from Shenyang North."

"Let's take the last train out," Will said. "I don't like traveling during the day. People are too alert. We take that seven o'clock train tonight, find a place to crash in Dalian, and then have plenty of time to get that morning ferry. Let's get rooms here and lie low for a few hours."

We cabbed slowly into the city, past dreary farmland and a semi-urban wasteland before we hit the smoggy heart of Shenyang, where the upper floors of modern high-rises vanished into soot and exhaust. Otherwise, the city's core consisted of Soviet-inspired concrete facades, much like the ones I'd seen in photos of other Chinese cities. Only a few landmarks dotted the downtown. Through pollution thick enough to carve, I spied a pink-and-blue-domed structure that housed God knows what, a large arena, and a soaring space needle that vaguely resembled Seattle's, save one major difference: the top was engulfed in a toxic cloud.

From *Lonely Planet*, we picked out the Youzhen Dasha, the Postal Hotel right off the main square southwest of Shenyang North Station. It seemed big and anonymous enough to hide out in.

The cab dropped us off at 2:30. A weathered awning with "China Post" hung over the entrance of the concrete building. After what we'd been through, it looked better than the Taj Mahal.

Will told Lily that she and her mother should check in separately from us. "It'll be safer that way."

"But we arrived together," Lily said.

"They might not have noticed us pulling up, and even if they did, we could have shared a cab from the airport to save money."

Mother and daughter strode into the hotel with an air of confidence. We followed a good twenty feet behind them, pausing to roll our eyes at the eclectically appointed lobby, its wood carvings and antique replica vases no older than last week's factory shipment. Our reflections appeared many times over in huge Vegas-style mirrors beaming under gaudy chandeliers. A spotless yellow Ferrari shared center stage with a life-size cardboard cutout of a Korean Air flight attendant.

My eyes settled on the stewardess, Will's on the Ferrari, until the Jiangs made it to the elevator.

We got our rooms without incident, despite the unflinching stare of the receptionist, Miss Zhang. *She's just not accustomed to seeing Westerners here*, I tried to tell myself, before suggesting to Will that I could go buy our train tickets before the Public Security Bureau widened its search and posted our faces in interior cities like Shenyang.

"Good idea."

After calling the hotel operator and tracking down Lily and her mother for their passports, I hiked over to the massive train station. The ticket booths were on the third floor. Four escalators marched side by side up from the broad lobby, but only one was working. I rode it while gazing at the glass roof, which revealed only Shenyang's dismal gray sky.

I walked to the closest booth and asked for four tickets. The sales agent's eyes widened when he saw me. *Or was that my nerves?* He glanced to his left.

My eyes followed his to the wall nearest him. I swore furiously to myself. Our four faces jumped out at me from a board full of black-and-white headshots. My dyed hair wouldn't have fooled anyone, surely not the sales agent, whose gaze shifted from the wall to me as though to further verify my identity. Beside each photo was our name and physical description. Under Will's and my photos, large, black letters all but blared:

WANTED!

It was written in English and Mandarin, and accompanied by the Chinese characters "通缉令", *order for arrest,* and "Reward: RMB100,000."

Oh fuck....

"I need all four passports." The agent tapped the counter with his index finger. "Do you understand?"

Did I ever. I imagined him pressing an emergency call button, like bank tellers use on bandits.

"I'm so sorry. I only have mine. I'll be right back."

By the time I began to retreat from the booth, two other sales agents were also gaping at me.

I felt dizzy from fright, like I'd just taken a knockout punch and was melting onto the mat, down for a ten-count. The ref was staring at me, like those sales agents. Like the whole goddamn country now.

One...two...three...

CHAPTER 35

Reeling, I fixated on the nearest escalator, resisting the impulse to race away. The ticket agent must have recognized me. He could have been watching a ping-pong championship the way his eyes bounced back and forth between that poster and me.

Our pictures must be everywhere.

I had no idea how we could survive this exposure. I headed for the exit as calmly as I could, then broke into a jog the instant I stepped outside. Head down, I entered the Postal Hotel, passing the front desk and Miss Zhang, who looked as severe as a prison guard as she eyed her screen.

I hoped she kept her focus as I made my way onto the elevator and punched floor seven. I took a deep breath as the doors started to shut—but then a hand reached in and stopped them.

"Sorry," an Asian man said in lightly accented English when he noticed me.

"No problem," I answered in Mandarin.

I should have stuck to my native tongue. He did a double-take. "*Yi ge hui shuo Zhongwen de laowai!*" *A Chinese speaking foreigner!* He continued in his own language. "You should meet my son. He'd get a kick out of you!"

"I'm sorry, I really don't have time."

"Speaking Chinese, you must have many opportunities to make money here." He smiled and pushed the button for the fourth floor then switched back to Mandarin. "*Meiguo ren?*" *American?*

"Canadian."

He studied me with open curiosity as we started to ascend. *He will definitely recognize me when he gets to his room, turns on the TV, and my mug flashes in front of him.*

"Have a nice day!" he chirped as he got off.

"You as well."

As soon as the elevator opened on seven, I ran down the hall and pounded on our door.

"*Shei a?*" Will asked, seemingly unperturbed. *Who is it?*

"It's me. Hurry the fu—," He pulled it open. I brushed past him. "They know. They know everything."

"What're you talking about? Who knows what?" He shut the door.

"Our faces are on posters—all four of us." I told him about the encounter with the ticket agent.

"Wanted posters?"

"Yes. With a one hundred thousand *kuai* reward."

"Are you shitting—"

"No—I wish like hell I was."

Will turned pale. I'd never see him do that. It scared me.

"Where's Lily and her mom?" I asked.

"They said they'd go grab some toiletries."

"Christ, I hope they haven't left their rooms yet." I could feel myself freaking out. "We've got to get out of here. I'll—"

Someone knocked on the door.

I froze—Will too. We looked at each other.

Whoever it was knocked more firmly a second time.

"*Na wei?*" I asked.

"*Fuwuyuan,*" said a female voice. "I've got your hot water bottle." In mid-grade hotels, maids periodically stopped by to refill a room's hot water thermos.

"Answer it," Will said in a hushed voice.

I stepped toward the door. My hand shook as I turned the handle. A squad of police officers could be waiting to charge past the maid, who could be a ruse.

"Hot water?" She stood next to her cart.

"No thanks." *We're already in it.*

I locked the door and turned back to Will, who'd already started repacking some of his things. "I'm calling Lily." I picked up the phone. God, I hoped they were still in their room.

Will grabbed the receiver from my hand and cradled it. "The hotel could be monitoring calls by now. I'll go right now and tell them in person."

"What about your shirt and pants?" I pointed them out, draped over a chair.

He was already opening the door. "I'm leaving that stuff and tooth-paste here on purpose. It'll make it look like we're coming back—and it'll lighten my load. You should do the same." He started out again, then stopped. "Give me the flight schedule."

I dug it out and handed it over. He underlined a flight departing later that evening for Chongqing and set it on the nightstand, adding to the false trail, then left to warn Lily and Mrs. Jiang.

I collected my own things and tossed some funky underwear, pants, and a Chicago Cubs T-shirt into the staged disarray, the whole time hoping Lily and Mrs. Jiang hadn't left the hotel. They could have been picked up by the police by now.

After ten minutes of waiting and pacing, I was sure Will and the Jiangs had been apprehended. I cracked the door and peered down the hall. The three were rushing toward me. Lily looked petrified. I stepped aside to let them in.

"They're looking for us?" Lily asked as I deadbolted the door. "You saw posters?"

"Big ones. Right by the ticket booths. No way we can take a train out of here. Where were you guys?"

"Downstairs, picking up some stuff."

"We need you two to find an unmarked cab *now*," Will said to Lily and her mother.

They nodded. Illegal taxis were usually parked by exit ramps at train stations and airports.

"We may be the only two white guys in Shenyang," Will continued, "so we can't move around out there together. Even with our black hair." He ran his hand through his mop.

"*Meiyou wenti*," Mrs. Jiang said. *No problem.*

"Don't worry about the cost." I handed her 2,000 RMB. "We need to get to Dalian." I also handed back their fake passports. "Take these."

"Get a car with tinted windows if you can," Will added.

"Should we come back and pick you up here?" Lily asked.

"No, not here," Will said. "If they've got our photos posted, someone may have already put two and two together, meaning you two and us. They could be coming for us already. I noticed a school that we passed on the way here. Did you see it?"

"Yes, there's an alley next to it, right?" Mrs. Jiang replied.

"Yes, that's it. Let's meet there in twenty minutes," Will said. "Andrew and I will leave separately and split up—we won't be such easy prey that way. Now let's keep our heads down and not panic."

Lily took my hand, her first sign of affection in front of her mother. Then she kissed me.

She touched my cheek in parting and ushered Mrs. Jiang out the door. "Be careful," I said as they left. I threw the lock, wondering if I'd see Lily again. I didn't even know if I'd live to see the sun go down.

Will had no time for sentimentality. "I need my passport back." I gave him the forged document. "I'll head out first," he continued. "There's a row of shops down the main street about a hundred feet toward the station. I'll wait in a seedy-looking tea house I saw on our way here and keep a lookout. Give me a two-minute head start."

"You want me to follow you toward the station and *away* from the school?"

"Yes. A little misdirection in case anyone's tailing you. Don't rush. Just walk past that tea house and casually look in. If there's anything suspicious—if I see someone tailing you, or if someone's onto me—I'll have my hands on my temples, like *I have a big fucking headache*. If I do that, just keep walking straight, away from the school to protect Lily and her mom. Don't circle back until you know you've lost any tail and are in the clear. But if I don't give that signal," he continued, "double back toward the alley next to the school." He handed me a pack of cigarettes. Another prop, I presumed. "Light up when you get there so you'll look like someone taking a break from one of the nearby businesses."

"Maybe from a hundred feet away."

"Sometimes that's all the margin you need. And I'll follow a little behind to keep an eye out."

"OK. You take care of yourself," I said. Each of these partings felt painfully permanent.

"You, too, brother. You're ready for this, and from what I just saw with Lily, you've got a lot to live for."

Then Will slipped away, duffel in hand.

I double-locked the door behind him, wishing I could do the same to all my fears and misgivings. The two people I cared about most in this country had just stepped into unknown and terrifying territory.

And I was about to follow.

CHAPTER 36

I sat on the edge of the bed, foot jiggling, and waited for the two minutes to pass. Our scattered clothes and the conspicuous flight schedule might trick security forces into believing the room was still occupied, if they didn't look too closely—and if they hadn't already rounded up Will, Lily, and Mrs. Jiang and were coming for me right then.

After forcing myself to hang tight, I cracked the door. The hallway was empty, though that did little to ease my fears. The Korean coastline I'd dreamed about on the flight felt as distant as Mars.

I rushed to the elevator, listening intently as it came alive. My groin tightened as the door creaked open—a sound straight out of a horror film.

No one was inside. *Thank God.*

As I started down, I pictured sharpshooters waiting in the lobby, hands on triggers, eyes on the lights that tracked my movement from floor to floor: 7, 6, 5...

Another killer countdown.

The narrow elevator felt like a casket sinking into darkened earth, shuddering as it came to an abrupt halt, hopefully at the ground floor. But they could have thrown a switch and left me dangling like some animal in a snare, ready to be seized by armed men rappelling down the shaft.

I was still looking up when the door creaked open again.

The lobby. *Thank God.*

It looked empty—as if they'd cleared it.

I forced myself forward, the area silent except for the tinkle of Chinese music. Even slimmed down, my backpack felt enormous, blatantly compromising. We'd just checked in—and now I was obviously leaving.

Looking left, I was relieved to see Miss Zhang on the phone, listening, her eyes glued to her screen, maintaining the same stern, mannequin-like expression.

But now as she turned away from her computer and toward me, I ducked behind a garish replica of the famous Greek sculpture of a baby in the arms of a woman, hiding my legs behind the blanket falling from the infant, my body behind his mother.

I pulled out my *Lonely Planet* so anyone seeing me from a different angle might take me for a befuddled tourist. When I looked up, as if considering a choice of destinations, I saw a cubicle in the corner with a sign showing an image of a computer. I glanced at my watch. Time was precious, but we needed any intel we could get—what was being said about us, where they were looking.

I checked on Zhang. She was shaking her head. She looked agitated. She was typing on her keyboard with the phone snugged under her jaw.

Go! I strode across to the cubicle.

Whatever composure I'd mustered was fleeting. When I sat at the computer my fingers shook so badly that I couldn't string together a simple web address.

Frustrated, I resorted to hunt-and-peck, finally managing to access *The Washington Post*. I raced through every bulletin about China. The bombing and subsequent protests still dominated coverage. Nothing, thankfully, about us.

A news brief reported that China had started to fund Al Qaeda. The account came from the *Post's* Pentagon sources, who said the White House was concerned about China's increasing influence in the Middle East and its ties to the terrorists responsible for the bombings of US Embassies in Africa that had killed more than two hundred people, including a dozen Americans.

It sounded remarkably similar to what Ed had told me. It was only a matter of time before those same sources could be talking about us. I needed to keep checking.

I'd been warned by Will that using any suspicious keywords in China was dangerous, but that was then and this was now—we *needed* to know if our names were out there. I started with a few variations on the obvious: "American spies."

I worked my way through the list and didn't see anything about us.

I went to Sina.net, an internet portal, scanning the main page's headlines in Chinese. Nothing there, either. I searched General Jiang Guangkai's name in characters—江光凯. Thousands of entries appeared, but nothing from the past few days. Pushing all my chips to the center of the table, I entered "Andrew Callahan" into the search bar, then my own Chinese name—高安祝.

Fuck!

Blazoned on the screen were my passport photo *and* stills that appeared to be lifted from security cams that had caught Will and me in the jackets we had on now—the same ones we were wearing on the wanted posters. In my panic at the ticket booth, the clothing hadn't registered. Christ, it did now.

You moron. I took off my jacket and shoved it into my bag.

Not that hiding it solved much. We were still conspicuous Westerners in northern China.

I turned off the computer without reading any further. We needed to get out of the country and every second counted. But first I had to make it out of the Postal Hotel.

I peered over the top of the partition. No sign of Miss Zhang.

Did she go get help? I wasn't about to wait for the answer.

With my pack firmly in hand, I made a beeline for the front door. I put my shoulder to the glass and slammed against it with a thud.

They've locked me in.

"*Zenme hui shi?*" Miss Zhang shouted as she rose from behind the counter, glaring at me. *What's going on?*

I answered by trying a second time to shove the door open.

"*Youbian!*" *The other side.*

I pushed the door to the right and it opened.

Heading out, the large clock on the railway station tower told me that barely an hour had passed since we'd first checked in—and we were already late to meet Lily and her mom.

I anxiously looked for Will's signal as I approached the row of small shops, but he gave me only a scowl from inside the tea house. I doubled back toward the school. "You're late," he said, bursting out of the door and falling in step behind me.

"That's the least of it," I muttered over my shoulder. "We're on the internet. There's a photo of you in that jacket."

He yanked it off and bundled it into his backpack.

We walked in line toward the agreed rendezvous point. Lily and her mother were nowhere in sight.

After a few more steps, we spotted a black Volkswagen Santana with tinted windows in the narrow, lightly concealed alley beside the school. A hand emerged from the rear window, frantically waving us over.

"You think it's them?" I asked Will.

"Gotta be."

We veered toward them and broke into a trot.

Then we heard a gunshot behind us.

I turned around instinctively and saw a policeman beside the road with his pistol pointed to the sky. A warning shot.

The only one we're gonna get.

Will froze. I did too.

"*Zhanzhu!*" the man with the gun shouted in a harsh voice. *Don't move!*

"Stay where you are!" ordered a second officer beside him, in Mandarin.

"We *will* shoot!" a third officer yelled in Chinese, though the threat would have been clear in any language.

Oh my God. I couldn't breathe.

The three Public Security officers raced toward us. Two had their semi-automatics drawn. The third, trailing slightly behind, was speaking into his walkie-talkie. The VW with what we hoped were the Jiangs was only a hundred feet away, but we'd never make it—and we'd jeopardize their lives if we tried.

Will grabbed me and we sprinted toward the main square, darting past an open-air police stand before we realized it was even there. A young officer looked up, wild-eyed, fumbling to draw his gun as we bolted by.

"Where are they?" I gasped to Will, finding my voice.

He glanced back. "Falling behind, and that kid cop isn't moving at all."

"Stop!" An older officer, some thirty yards ahead, moved with his partner to hem us in.

We were trapped.

CHAPTER 37

"**T**here!" I pointed to a subway entrance on the other side of a four-lane road. At a slight break in traffic, Will and I raced ahead.

Tires screeched as a vehicle on our left skidded to a stop. The stench of burning rubber swept over us as we darted across the next lane and vaulted the concrete and wrought iron road divider—then stopped right before a six-wheeled truck barreled by.

Jesus Christ!

Wheezing heavily, I looked back, scarcely aware of the pack on my back. One of the officers was stepping into the first lane of traffic, raising his hand to try to halt it, but the cars and trucks whizzed by him.

"Now!" Will yelled as he grabbed my arm and pulled me into the next lane.

The driver of a small van charging toward us slammed on the brakes. His alignment must have been off because the van lurched to the right as it smoked to a stop within a foot of smashing into us. We saw the driver's head fall to the steering wheel in relief as we dashed across the remaining lane, just before a passenger car rear-ended the van so hard it accordioned and leapt to the spot where we'd been a second earlier.

On the sidewalk ahead of us, we heard another command to stop, this time from three officers about a hundred feet to our right. We broke left—away from the subway—and scrambled down concrete steps into an underground shopping mall. I heard the clatter of the cops behind us as we sprinted along a crowded corridor. We spied another set of stairs leading back aboveground and bolted toward them, pushing people out of the way. We were already halfway up them when two more officers opened a door at street level and started descending toward us, pinning us in yet again.

We turned and dashed back down. People were hurling them-selves out of our way and yelling. So was Will. "There!" His eyes were on another down staircase farther along the corridor.

We swung our hips over the railing and jumped to the floor some ten feet below. I nearly stumbled into the opposite wall before catching my balance and running after Will, who was already bounding down the stairs ahead. The two new officers pointed at us from above and shouted to the ones who had chased us into the mall. I took four stairs at a time trying to catch up with Will.

The mall's second underground level was much larger. To our left, a pair of escalators led back up. To our right was another, wider hallway, painted yellow and jammed with people. Red streamers hung from the ceiling, drawing my attention to a security camera high on a wall—undoubtedly one of many documenting our flight.

We plunged into the mass of shoppers, zigzagging through nearly at full speed. I struggled to keep up with Will, lactic acid burning in my legs as we sprinted another few hundred feet. We slowed to a jog as the hall forked at two exit ramps.

"Right," he grunted, not breaking stride.

We hurried up, past a garage entrance, both of us brushing by delivery vans parked on either side of the ramp to avoid the torrent of cars coming down. Will, several paces ahead, dashed up a flight of stairs on the left. Trying to stay with him, I ran right in front of a Volvo van, coming so close to getting hit that I could hear the driver swearing inside the closed cab.

I caught up with Will as we emerged at ground level beside another four-lane road. Old men were playing Chinese chess on the sidewalk. They barely looked up as we hurried by.

The train station was now a couple of hundred yards to our left. A large roundabout appeared to our right. Without speaking, we took off toward it, following the roadway past two arteries feeding in—only to be met by a Public Security van roaring against the traffic, emergency lights on but siren off. It screeched to a halt no more than twenty feet in front of us.

"Don't move!" blared a megaphone mounted on the roof. The driver and the officer in the passenger seat threw their shoulders into the doors.

"This way!" Will backtracked along the curving roundabout, keeping us out of easy gunshot range behind all the bunched-up cars, then raced down the street toward a Bank of China branch, me close behind.

We almost made it into the maze of alleyways behind the bank when the police started shooting, no warning this time. A bullet whizzed by my head, the deafening crack reverberating in the air. More shots chipped the pavement and scarred the bank's marble cladding. I saw Will fall, clutching his thigh. The echo of two more bullets sounded close enough to kill.

"Keep going!" he yelled over the screams of bystanders.

"No!" Instinct had me dragging him from behind. Hunkering as low as I could, I made it around the corner of the bank, terrified that I'd be shot any second. I propped him against the wall of a shabby apartment building next door.

"I'm ordering you to go." Sweat spilled down his face.

I was shaking. I didn't know anything about bullet wounds, but his pants were turning crimson fast. *An artery.* "Clamp your hands on it to stop the blood. I'm gonna carry you."

"Like hell you are. Run! Now!" He unbuckled his belt.

"Can you walk at all?"

"Fuck you!" Will tied his belt tightly around his thigh, just above the wound. "This all depends on *you* now. Go! And take this." He tossed me a phone. "Call the others from the Agency. You've got to warn them that the mission's blown. Call anyone you've spoken to."

"Is this safe?" I stared at the phone.

"Christ, man, of course it's safe. It's Agency issue. Go!"

I peeked around the corner of the building. The police were creeping forward as though they thought we'd holed up and might be armed and desperate enough to ambush them. I looked back at Will.

"Go, goddamn it!" He closed his eyes and shook his head.

I ran down the narrow street. Seconds later, I entered a labyrinth of lanes and smaller buildings. I followed one alley to the next before running into another thoroughfare, where I stopped at a nearby public bathroom.

Too obvious a hiding place.

Electric megaphones blared in the distance. A terrible thought hit me: *Helicopters?* I looked at the blue-gray sky. None that I could see.

I took the road to the right, walking with my eyes straight ahead as cars and people passed me. I tried to look like a tourist or foreign student with all my belongings on my back, not an escapee, even though fear was boiling me alive. I glanced down to see if I had Will's blood on me. I didn't. I was relieved—but then racked with guilt for leaving him.

I was running out of options in a foreign city. All I knew was I had to keep moving, away from the police who could not be far behind, and make those calls. I prayed Lily and her mother had gotten away safely.

To my side was another run-down apartment building. The front door hung open on a single bottom hinge. I didn't see anyone so I hurried inside, carefully easing the door up an inch to close it as quietly as I could.

The entryway looked like so many Chinese apartments, including mine at the IAU and the safe house where Lily and I had found a brief respite—a concrete floor and staircase, the country's ubiquitous bicycles clustered underneath. I considered squeezing myself back there among them but thought better of it. I'd be too vulnerable, not just to the police but also to anyone retrieving a bike.

I started up the stairs. The building felt at once oddly familiar and dangerous, a potential informant behind every door. As I reached the second-floor landing, I heard footsteps inside an apartment a few feet away. My impulse was to retreat, but then I'd be trapped if another person entered the building. I clearly didn't belong there, and most likely radio alerts had already gone out about a violent foreigner on the loose.

I scampered up to the third floor, where thankfully the light was dimmer. I heard a man enter the stairwell below, shouting in Mandarin that he was going to the store. "I'll be back in an hour."

I hoped to God I'd be long gone by then.

The third floor, like the second, offered no reprieve. The same for the fourth and fifth. I was losing hope. I worried about Will and resigned myself to an awful, inevitable fate as I dragged myself up to the sixth level. That landing was even darker than the last, but in the shadows I noticed another staircase to my right. I crept toward it and saw that it led up to a black door.

The roof?

I expected it to be locked, the end of the line, but it scraped open loudly. I stepped out, bathed in the late afternoon light. Junk lay strewn all about the rooftop. Rusted bikes, broken tables and chairs, old appliances, and televisions, their picture tubes smashed, perhaps in frustration. But it was as good a refuge as I would find. I closed the door behind me.

A large metal storage shed stood about halfway along the near wall. Ducking low to avoid being seen from neighboring buildings, I inched toward it, then peered inside at a loosely organized jumble of tools, replacement fuses, and spools of electrical wiring. The shed was large enough for me to hide in.

No, too obvious.

I continued toward a dense cluster of items near the far edge and wedged myself beneath a three-legged table leaning at an awkward angle. I pulled a wheel-less child's wagon over my head and torso. Falling rust flakes tickled my exposed neck. Hunkered down, using my pack as a pillow, I listened. I didn't need to wait long. As I reached to pull out Will's phone, the door to the roof suddenly burst open, as if a bomb had gone off.

A man swore in disgust. "Search!" he shouted.

I counted three pairs of footsteps. The officers began kicking the refuse, sending it flying, working their way closer with a thoroughness that I knew would not spare me.

CHAPTER 38

A police radio crackled sharply. Sweat streamed down my back. The officers paused. I couldn't make out the words, only the forceful tone. Much clearer was the voice of the commander on the rooftop ordering one of his men to finish the search while the other joined him going door to door inside the building. "I want everything on this roof turned inside out."

I swallowed and hoped that the remaining man would light up a cigarette and take a break the moment his boss was out of sight, but I should have known better. They didn't sound like undisciplined *cheng-guan*, local cops on the prowl for illegal street vendors to harass. No, these guys were almost certainly Ministry of State Security, China's equivalent of the CIA and FBI rolled into one. He began picking up junk and tossing it aside.

At first, he concentrated near the rooftop door. Then he moved to the shed and peered inside, before walking along the edge of the rooftop toward me. I felt around silently for something hard or pointed, any potential weapon. My right hand landed on a cylindrical length of wood, the missing table leg maybe. I gripped it tightly and eased it aside to make sure it was loose.

The cop was lifting and tossing things no more than a few feet away now. All I could do was hope that he was using both hands to paw through the piles, leaving his sidearm holstered. He grunted, as if hefting a heavy object—perhaps the washing machine tumbler I'd noticed a few feet from the clutter that I'd burrowed into.

Now or never!

Fighting a strong instinct to just curl up and pray, I leapt to my feet, spilling the wagon off my chest. He dropped the tumbler and fumbled with his holster. I cocked my arm with the wooden object—it *was* the missing table leg—and swung it wildly at his head. He blocked it with his forearm, crying out in pain but still groping for his gun with his other hand.

I tackled him immediately, wrapping him up like an opponent on the rugby field and driving him to the floor. He punched at my head, but I was on top of him, straddling his chest, so his blows lacked power. With my legs blocking him from grabbing his pistol, I pounded his face. Knuckles struck bone and an ache pierced my left hand, but I didn't quit. He squirmed, managing to turn his head and body. I latched onto him from behind with a chokehold, my arms flexed around his neck and my legs now trapping his torso.

I could hear him gasping for air, yet he was still struggling to get his gun. I needed to stop him, but to do that I'd have to free one of my arms and relax my grip. *Or you can hold on tight and finish him off.*

I remembered what Tom had said to do if I had trouble with a taxi driver: *Take care of it.*

I was tempted. With his last ounces of energy, the cop stretched his fingers toward the pistol grip.

I choked him as hard as I could. The instant he began to go limp, his hand flopping to the floor, I snatched his pistol out of the holster, a basic semi-automatic like I'd fired at my grandparents' farm many times growing up. Then I stood and backed away before he could recover.

Seconds later, he turned his head slowly, his eyes focusing on me.

"Do you have any kids?" I asked quietly in Mandarin.

"A boy," he answered, coughing.

"Do you want to see him again?"

"Yes."

"Then you do exactly what I say." I wiggled the gun.

He nodded.

"Get up, slowly," I said, tracking him carefully with the muzzle. "Stand next to the shed."

With him in full view, I pulled out the coil of rubberized wire and old rags. Then I marched him back to my hiding place, where I hog-tied him and shoved a rag into his mouth. Then I dumped the wagon on top of him and pushed the table back onto its side. They'd find him, just as he'd been about to find me, but I'd take whatever seconds or minutes I could buy.

I grabbed my pack, tiptoed over to the rooftop door, pulled it open a crack, and listened for the other two cops combing the building. Nothing. Cocking the hammer of the gun, I started down the stairs, pointing the muzzle into the shadows that soon swallowed me.

On the sixth floor I heard only the hum of radios or TVs. *Where are those cops?* I tried to imagine how they would have checked the building—top to bottom, or did they split up?—but then realized it didn't matter. I needed to be on the lookout either way.

I was about to descend to the fifth floor when I heard a door open just below me. Peering over the rail, I watched an older woman close the door and head downstairs with a string bag to go shopping. She hadn't used a key. Maybe she left it unlocked. But if she did, was it because someone else was home?

I gave her enough time to get to the ground floor and outside before I walked swiftly downstairs to her door and tried the knob.

Locked, after all.

I put my ear against the door but heard nothing. After checking up and down the stairwell, I jammed my shoulder into the old door, which gave way with a dull metallic sound. Through a two-inch opening, I looked inside and saw no one. Then I shoved it wider and stepped into a poorly lit room with a single bed, two-burner stove, and a tiny table with one chair.

She lives alone.

I closed the door quickly and, with the lock housing busted, slid the door chain in place—it could hold the cops off for a few critical seconds, if it came to that. Then I went to the window, hoping to find a fire escape. They weren't common, but some older buildings had them. No such luck. Only an eight-inch ledge several feet below the window. In the twilight, I saw that I was in an L-shaped complex. A roof-high drainage pipe ran down from the corner, where the two wings met.

That pipe might be my only hope—if I could shimmy down.

I knew that if I thought about it for too long, I'd be too scared to move, so I uncocked the pistol and stuck it into my belt. Then I called Tom Blum. I had to try to save him and the others in the CIA. Tom's was the only number I had with me. When he answered, I tried my damnedest to be oblique: "Hey, Tom, the trail to Jiankou is closed so I won't be able to hike it after all."

"I'm so sorry to hear that," he replied, no hint of alarm. "But maybe you can take it next time you get to the Great Wall."

"Do you think you could let the other hikers know? I don't have their numbers with me."

"Sure. Take care." And he hung up.

I was relieved to have gotten word to him—and grateful to Will for trying to protect Tom and the others.

I opened the apartment window and climbed onto the ledge, my belly to the building. After closing the window quietly, I carefully removed my backpack so I could wear it across my chest, then turned around. The front part of my shoes hung over the ledge, a dizzying sixty-foot drop.

With both hands against the wall—and my head still clearly visible through the window—I shuffled sideways toward the drainpipe, which was about forty feet away. I kept the flat of my hands against the smooth concrete, as though that contact could ensure my safety. In reality, I was clinging only to hope.

Slowly, I made progress. Each time I passed a window, I winced at the thought of someone looking out. All the windows in the other wing had a direct view, but thankfully, at least half the apartments were dark. I hoped the bleakness of the courtyard view meant the residents confined their attention to their own apartments. I heard a news report that could have been airing on a radio or television in one of the units around me, but I forced myself not to listen closely. It was all I could do to keep moving. Ten agonizing minutes later, I made it to the pipe, a four-inch affair with rusty bands bolting it to the two buildings every few feet. Holding firm, I slid my pack onto my back, then tested the pipe by pushing and pulling on it. It felt firm, and the bands gave my hands and feet purchase—as long as they held.

The first few steps down felt like descending a ladder with big gaps between the rungs. My long legs helped, and I gained speed as I made it to the top of the third floor, where I spotted a two-inch crack in an unbolted portion of the pipe. I feared it would break away from the corner when I put weight on it, but I had no choice.

I placed my left foot on the next band, weighting it slowly, then my right. The narrow strip of rusty metal held. *Thank God.* I lowered my hands below the crack to make my next move. That's when the untethered length started bending away from the walls. I reached twenty-five feet above the ground, then twenty, as the drain slowly bent to a ninety-degree angle. I clung to the pipe like a panda to a stalk of bamboo.

The pipe started to split apart with a low nauseating sound. I'd hoped like hell it would bend slowly all the way to the ground, but it snapped off. I managed to fall, feet first, onto a patch of dirt and weeds, rolling to the side to try to absorb the impact. The pipe thumped down inches from my head.

Thankfully, the gun remained in my belt. I looked around and listened intently. All I saw were shadows. But then from above I heard, "Li Wei! Li Wei!" The other two cops were back on the roof, calling out to their comrade. They would find him in no time.

Go!

But where? Night was falling. I knew nothing of the city or Will or Lily and her mom.

Most of all, I wasn't sure of myself in these horrifying circumstances half a world away from home.

I'd never felt more alone.

CHAPTER 39

I edged away from their voices, sticking close to the wall of the building I'd just escaped. I hoped it would be harder for them to see me directly below.

When I turned the corner, I bolted to an alley across the street and kept running, finding refuge—I hoped—behind a dumpster about a hundred feet in. The smell of rotten garbage was awful, but I needed to catch my breath and get my bearings.

With five- and six-story buildings on either side, darkness had already claimed the alley. The moon hovered behind clouds, casting little light. Only the city's glow reflecting off the haze above made it possible to see at all.

I imagined the officers untying their colleague, the guy I'd threatened with death, and learning that I had his gun. That might slow them down—or infuriate them. I needed to get far away, and fast. *But where?*

As I tried to figure out what to do next, I worried that Will was dead. Or strapped into a chair wishing he were, as torturers tried to extract every last shred of intelligence from him.

My concerns quickly switched to Lily and her mom. I hoped like hell they'd told their driver to speed away from the gunshots—a natural reaction for anyone in that situation. I suspected Mrs. Jiang, a survivor of the Cultural Revolution, had plenty of practice keeping her wits in grim circumstances.

Then I was back in motion. My legs were tight, still tense from balancing for so long on that narrow ledge. As I passed overflowing rubbish bins, I reached back and felt the shocking comfort of the gun in my belt, then reminded myself that if I used it, they'd definitely execute me. China had no qualms about capital punishment.

At that dark moment, I considered just using the gun on myself. Suicide would certainly be preferable to decades of persecution in a Chinese prison. I'd never considered it before, but I was starting to see it as a real option. Fear, I realized, had quickly drilled down to my second-worst outcome.

Cars whizzed by on the street at the far end of the alley. I slowed to a walk and listened intently, catching voices filtering through the night. As I passed another apartment building, the enticing aromas of cooking awakened my hunger. I told myself that was the least of my problems. I needed to escape Shenyang, but how? Police would be watching bus terminals, train stations, and the airport. The only way out of town might be a cab.

For the next quarter hour, I stuck to a series of alleys, encountering nobody, but seeing dozens of garbage bins. I came to three overturned rubber ones minutes later. As disgusting as they looked and smelled, I stashed my backpack behind two of them before sitting down, drawing my knees to my chest, and pulling the largest one over me. I wanted night to fall fully before venturing onto the main boulevard in search of a cab. The stench of rotten food all but suffocated me. I did my best to put aside thoughts of maggots and rats, and strained my ears for any hint of my pursuers. I heard only three women talking as they walked by. I found courage in how oblivious they were to my presence just feet away.

I glanced at my watch. *Eleven thirty.* Slowly, I lifted the bin off me. The alley was black as pitch. Hearing nothing but my own efforts, I stood and straightened my legs slowly and painfully, taking full breaths of the now seemingly pure Shenyang air. I swore I'd never again spend time in a garbage can.

But it worked.

I retrieved my pack and headed toward the sound of traffic, pulling my Chinese cap down over my dyed hair. When I reached the street, I saw that it was the busy one that Will and I had raced down before he was shot near the bank. I moved in the opposite direction. There would be no returning to the scene of the crime for me.

I did my best not to appear in any hurry and kept my eyes on the shop windows. The glass reflected the passing cars and people around me. Nobody seemed to take note of me. Up on my right, half a dozen men were drinking beer outside a restaurant. A convivial scene with lots of laughter. I tensed up as I passed, but they paid me no mind. Then I noticed a boisterous crowd half a block away on the other side of the street. A breeze, I thought, compared to walking right beside those beer-drinkers. I meandered along opposite them until I saw what captured their interest: two women in negligees gyrating in a massage parlor window.

That's when I also spotted cabs lined up near the parlor. I waved the first one over. He hung a tight U-turn and pulled up alongside me. Keeping my head down, I climbed into the back seat.

"Where to?" the short man asked in Mandarin, his eyes on the rearview mirror.

I hesitated. "Dalian."

"Dalian!" he exclaimed, his pitch rising as if it were the craziest thing he'd ever heard. He shook his head, then turned and did a double-take. I knew that he knew. I pointed the gun right at his face, surprised at my own response, my survival instincts fully engaged.

"It's you!" he said.

"Shut the fuck up and I won't kill you."

He froze and stared at me speechless.

"I don't want to use this, but I will, unless you do exactly what I say. Understand?"

He nodded slowly.

"Drive away from here like you always do."

He closed his eyes and turned away, as if expecting to be murdered. Then he put the car in gear.

I leaned forward, my head inches from the back of his neck. "You do exactly what I say and you'll not only live, but you'll make a thousand *yuan*. Sound good?"

He nodded again, maybe still too scared to talk. A perfect reflection of my own fear.

"I need gas for Dalian," he said finally, his voice trembling like his hands on the steering wheel.

I looked at the gauge. A quarter tank, enough to at least get us outside the city. I said so.

"It's late. Some stations might be closed." He still sounded scared, but he was probably right. "I have an account at one near here."

"Not that one. I'll pick the station."

I had him drive about two miles before nudging his neck with the muzzle. "There, see that one up ahead?"

We slowed as we came closer. I spotted a weary-looking woman by the pump. *Even better.* She'd probably been on her shift for twelve or more hours, too tired to care about the news or random customers. A rush of probabilities filled my thoughts, but that's what my life had become—a constant roll of the dice.

"Know her?" I asked.

"No."

I slouched into the corner of the back seat with my cap tilted down, the gun hidden by my side. "*Zuihao shi zheyang*," I said as she walked up to fill the tank. *That better be true.*

The driver paid and accelerated slowly away.

Sitting forward, I told him he'd done a good job. "I'm not out for blood, no matter what you might have heard." I pointed to pictures on the dash with the gun. "Is that your family?"

He nodded.

"Your wife is very pretty, and your children look happy." I patted his shoulder with the barrel. "Let's keep it that way."

I'd stick to my word, as long as he didn't try to be a national hero, immortalized on some socialist realist propaganda poster. I'd already experienced enough violence. God only knew what cruelty Will, Lily, and Mrs. Jiang might be suffering right now. I did my best to push aside those thoughts and focus on my own few remaining options, but my mind was shot. Hunger added to my light-headedness. To stay awake, I stared at the barren land sliding by in our headlights, broken only by low red-brick buildings and towering coal stacks.

Some five hours later, the driver entered Dalian city limits. It was 5:30, the sun still below the horizon. "Go to Zhongshan Square," I said, referring to what my *Lonely Planet* showed as a landmark less than a mile from the harbor terminal. "Then I'll tell you where." I was improvising but wanted to sound in control.

We lapped a roundabout as I tried to get my bearings and look for the right place to ditch him and the car. "Take that one," I said at the last minute, pointing to a road heading away from the terminal. Then I told him to turn into an alley. I spied no one as we drove another hundred meters.

"Back the cab in there." I pointed the gun to a narrow passageway between two concrete-block buildings.

He blanched with fear in the rearview as he ground the gears and put the car in reverse. Carefully, he wedged it into the opening.

"Now shut it off and give me the keys."

His hands started shaking again. The keys jingled. When I reached for them, he held onto the key ring for a second too long. I jammed the gun under his chin.

"Don't be stupid or you're dead."

He surrendered the keys, then twisted around in his seat, eyes wide with fear. Mine probably were, too. I did not want to pull the trigger.

"Here's what we're going to do." I was terminally exhausted but had to maintain control. "We are going to get out and go to the trunk. I will open it. You will get inside quickly. Don't shake your head!"

"You're going to shoot me."

"Not if you do what I say. I have a wife and baby, too. I know how you feel about your family. I don't want them to lose you."

I must have lied convincingly because he asked, "Then what?"

"You'll take off your shirt and socks and belt because I'm going to tie you up with them. You won't make a sound or the last one you'll ever hear will be this gun. Do you understand? No fucking around."

He nodded.

"I promise that once I get to the next town, I'll make sure they find you. It's going to be a long day, but at the end of it you'll still be alive."

He kept shaking, but he lay down in the trunk next to a towing chain, used engine belts, a box of wrenches, and a blanket.

"Give me your shirt." I thought I heard a car. Looking up, I saw a helicopter in the distance. "Hurry up."

Lying on his back, he took it off. I set it on the ground.

"Now your socks and belt."

He left them by his side.

With my gun on the bumper—and in easy reach—I twisted one of the engine belts around his wrists until it was as tight as a sphincter behind his back. Far tighter than if I had used his shirt, which, along with his jacket, would now give me a change of clothes. I used another engine belt on his ankles. They were hard as hell to get on, but he'd never get them off. I kept looking around, but the buildings around us remained shadowy and quiet.

I forced the chain between his calves and forearms and hogtied him, as I had the officer on the roof. I didn't want him kicking or roll-ing around and drawing attention to the car before I was long gone.

"Here's your money," I said, peeling off a thousand renminbi.

"No!" He was shaking his head. "They will think I did it for money. No!"

He sounded frantic, and I realized that he was right. Paying him might get him thrown in prison, or even killed. Nodding, I shoved the money back into my pocket and his socks into his mouth. Then I wrapped his belt around his head, cinching it behind to make sure he stayed quiet. I finished by tucking the blanket around him. It was chilly.

"You'll be okay. When they find you, tell them the truth—that I threatened to kill you. You've done nothing wrong."

He closed his eyes, as if in prayer.

I slammed the trunk and pocketed the keys, then stripped off my rugby shirt, picked up the cabbie's synthetic button-down, and put it on. A little snug, but I wasn't expecting a custom fit. Same for his jacket, which I retrieved from the front seat. I stuffed my own clothes into my pack, then hurried back down the alley, noting the location of the cab.

I'd keep my word to him—if I could.

CHAPTER 40

My legs felt heavy but my mind was alert as I checked repeatedly to see if anyone was following me toward the Dalian ferry terminal. All I noticed were dockworkers sleepwalking to their six a.m. shifts. I wanted nothing more than to lie down right there and crash, but I knew the authorities could be right behind me.

I just needed to get my ferry ticket and keep my head down for two hours. Then I could sleep as much as I wanted on the cruise to Incheon. But when I double-checked my travel documents, I remembered that I'd used my fake Canadian passport to buy our plane tickets and check into the hotel in Shenyang—a fact the Public Security Bureau would undoubtedly have uncovered by now. Using that same phony passport to buy the ferry ticket would be game over. I stopped in my tracks and just stared at the starless sky, wondering what the hell I was going to do.

I've gotta get hold of Ed Lee.

My handler. Those words carried a corrosive tone. I couldn't help it—I wasn't feeling good about the guy who'd thrown me into this disaster, with Lily and Will and Mrs. Jiang missing, me now trapped in—

It wasn't him. It was you. I was the one who'd fallen in love with Lily and *I* was the one who'd made the decision to help get her out of the country—wherever she might be now.

I needed to get a grip. Ed was my best hope.

But how could I reach him in time for today's ferry? The idea of holing up for two days until the next boat gutted me. I took a deep breath and asked myself what Will would do.

Find a computer.

I knew little about Dalian beside the fact that it was on the water and had a few good universities and a lot of foreign students, which augured well for finding an internet café and maybe even blending in—though it also ran the risk that those same web surfers would be looking at my face in the headlines.

I started searching with a newfound urgency, turning onto a busy commercial street with a bunch of brightly lit signs. After hurrying along for a few more blocks, I found a place near the Dalian Harbor Passenger terminal.

It was a dingy, twenty-four-hour joint that looked like it catered to Chinese videogame junkies. I paid an indifferent clerk for a Coke and a terminal, choosing one as far as possible from prying eyes. For once I was glad to cloak myself in the cigarette smoke clouding the dark room. Fortunately, the other patrons appeared to be in a collective gamer trance, staring at screens filled with first-person shooter mayhem.

Leaving my jacket and Coke at the terminal to save my seat, I took my guidebook and pack into the small restroom, which was almost as foul as the garbage can I'd hidden under in Shenyang.

What to say? The less the better.

Under a bare ceiling bulb—on a piece of paper I was careful to place on the hard steel sink to avoid leaving any imprinted grooves of letters—I drafted a simple message: "At agreed ferry site alone.

Separated from others. Passport compromised repeat compromised. Need new one. Please provide guidance. Urgent. China Hand."

To make the eventual transition into code easier, I grouped the letters into blocks of five, Xs between sentences. I now needed to methodically translate it into the cipher text.

I placed my *Lonely Planet* on the edge of the sink, then tore out the one-time pad I was supposed to use and revealed the hidden type by applying the diluted iodine solution. Next, I converted my message into a new, undecipherable string of letters to be transmitted as Ed and Owen had instructed.

I thanked them silently for the dry runs they'd put me through at the café, then the practice I had with the short-wave radio transmissions. This felt like one of the few actions over the last twenty-four hours that I at least knew how to do right.

Someone pounded on the bathroom door, startling me. Had the cabbie found a way to bang his head against the hood of the trunk, get help, and alert the authorities?

"One minute," I managed in Mandarin, trying harder than usual to make my accent sound authentic, even as I crumpled the small paper with the handwritten note and put it in my mouth, ready to swallow if need be.

I reached behind and clutched the pistol that was still in my pants as I opened the door slowly, then peeked out at a short, emaciated-looking guy whose gaze never rose from the floor. I brushed past him, returned to my seat, and retrieved the paper from my cheek so I could send my mayday plea.

Hotmail was blocked by the Great Firewall, but I managed to get on Yahoo and created an account under Kevin_Sheehan14@yahoo.com, a name I made up on the spot. Then I banged out the random sequence of letters from the cipher text into the body of the email, left the subject line blank, and sent it to ej1888@hotmail.com. With my distress signal in the ether, I ripped my handwritten message into more easily digestible pieces then swallowed it and the one-time pad, chasing it all down with the Coke.

I hit refresh over and over, hoping for an immediate response, but there was no reply.

With nothing to do but wait, I turned to headlines in *The Washington Post*. General Jiang's disappearance was now news, though there were few details—only that he hadn't shown up at a scheduled World Trade Organization negotiation in Washington with his American counterpart.

The *People's Daily* story we had seen earlier about him disappearing from those talks had been taken down, which didn't surprise me. Chinese officials were probably trying to determine exactly what had happened—or they knew and were now busy distorting the story by concealing key details, reordering the chronology, and inventing new "facts" that fit their chosen narrative.

Remembering Will's warning, I didn't want to type in our names, so I searched for "missing Americans." The browser returned an alarmingly large number of photos and stories of Lily, her mom, and me on Chinese sites, but none in the US media—and nothing about him anywhere. Skimming the Chinese text, I saw that I was wanted for abducting the Jiangs. I sickened at the thought that the only reason they weren't also looking for Will now was that he'd bled to death, alone, next to that bank.

I should have stayed with him.

I was so shaken that it took me several moments to realize that the news reports suggested the authorities didn't know that the Jiangs had fled on their own—or maybe the Chinese leadership was keeping their options open about how to play this.

My brain was swimming with all this information—none of it good. I felt dizzy from hunger. Even though I felt wretched about Will, I had to eat to keep my strength. I gathered up my jacket, pack, and *Lonely Planet*, and went looking for a quick bite. I didn't have much time if I was going to catch that ferry.

As soon as I stepped onto the street, though, the sight of the concrete triggered flashbacks of Will, pants soaked in blood, ordering me to leave.

Was there anything more I could have done?

A Scandinavian-looking guy bumped into me, startling me out of my daze. Up ahead, I saw some Westerners stepping into an eatery. I should stick near them. I might be able to melt into that crowd. Easing past the busy doorway, I was relieved to find there were no TVs, just background music heisted from the old Broadway musical *South Pacific*. "Some Enchanted Evening."

Indeed.

Despite the hour, I passed on the breakfast fare, ordering cashew chicken and *riben dofu,* Japanese tofu. "*Kuai dianr,*" I implored. *Make it fast.*

I all but inhaled the meal, paid my bill, and hurried back to the internet café to check my email.

Settling back at the same terminal in the back row, I logged on and sipped on another Coke, terrified that I might pass out from exhaustion. But I woke the hell up when I saw a message.

Holy shit it worked!

I sat forward and opened it:

YEMAP QLGJN EOWJG NYXSB EOTIY QZHAL
FKGNQ PFKYI SJUWH TJAFL GOWJR IVMDK
SLEOA HGVYQ DJBXC YRTMQ PROMX UQLEK
UWISM JQPFE MALGY

I forced myself to walk calmly back to the bathroom, locked the door, and followed the decryption process. Partly through, I felt a rush of adrenaline. The initial phrase read:

IWVQE MESSA GEREC EIVED XPROC EEDTO
FERRY

"Message received. Proceed to ferry."

But first I had to finish the message, hoping against all odds that it would contain good news about Will.

IWVQE MESSA GEREC EIVED XPROC EEDTO
FERRY TERMI NALRP TPROC EEDTO FERRY
TERMI NALXO URMAN WILLF INDYO UXGOO
DLUCK CHINA HANDX

There wasn't a word about Will, but a man would find me at the terminal. It ended with "Good luck, China Hand."

Good luck? How about, the cavalry's coming to save your sorry ass?

With a deeply resigned breath, I logged off and headed toward the ferry, casually dumping the pistol into a trash bin on a quiet street along the way. I hated to give up the weapon, but it would never get through security, and if I got into a shoot-out at a major transportation hub I was doomed anyway.

A crowd of a couple hundred passengers was lined up outside the terminal building, waiting to buy tickets and board. Two police cars were also parked near the entrance, with another pulling up as I arrived.

Please, God.

Officers quickly fanned out through the crowd. Who would find me first? And what did it matter, anyway?

I arrived at the end of the line. Which is how I felt in every sense.

"Your passport," an officer demanded.

I considered running, but where? I was in the middle of an open square, with cops and people all around me.

I reached into my pocket and handed over the fake Canadian passport, the one they had to know about by now.

"I thought so," he said, looking over his shoulder. "It *is* you."

CHAPTER 41

The officer's stare was so intimidating, and he spoke such precise English, that I assumed he was from the Ministry of State Security in Beijing, despite his local policeman's uniform. Those around me must have thought so, too, based on the way they looked at anything but him.

He thrust the passport back into my hands, shaking his head. He smirked, maybe pleased to have planted the evidence back on me just in time for the dramatic arrest photo.

"I made a mistake," he said. "I'm sorry." His eyes fell to what he'd handed me.

It wasn't the passport I'd given him. Its cover said, "*Éire*," And below that, "Ireland."

You're the guy they sent to meet me?

I was too stunned to talk—not that I would have been so foolish as to utter a single word, even to thank him. He probably wouldn't have

noticed, anyway, because he was already shaking his head at his commander, who was waving him over.

With my heart still drumming, I shuffled a few steps forward as
the police cars pulled away. I waited several minutes before casually
opening the Irish passport. There was my photo with my darkened
hair. My new name was James Boyle. And my new ferry ticket was
waiting for me between the pages.

As I slowly moved forward in line, I had time to admire the CIA's
fast response—and also to worry that their efforts would fail me in
the end. I still had to pass inspection with the border agent, who was
probably staring at a computer screen with my face on it beside the
Chinese version of "Wanted: Dead or Alive."

And then what?

The lines disintegrated into a single crowd as we neared the six
border agents. "A mountain of people, a sea of people" was an old
Chinese expression, which described almost every public space I'd
seen in the country. Still, I stood out in that mass of people like a sea-
shell on a sidewalk—and I could be as easily crushed.

The roar of a nearby locomotive briefly distracted me. I smelled
diesel and saltwater, looked up, and through an open corridor spotted
the ferry for the first time. It was much bigger than I expected—maybe
five hundred feet long and several stories high.

My stomach roiled as the woman behind the counter beckoned me
forward with her curled finger, studying me openly as I approached.
She was middle-aged and appeared deadly serious—far more so than
her sleepy-looking male colleagues in the other lanes. An armed guard
stood motionless against a wall behind her. He suddenly shifted his
cold gaze toward me and I struggled not to flinch.

The woman gestured for my passport with another slight movement of her hand. I slid it across the counter, exactly as the other
passengers had done. She stared at me for a couple of seconds, and
I feared she was on to my dyed hair and Chinese cap. But then as I
observed her flipping through the stamped passport pages, I realized

I had another, potentially bigger problem: I had no idea where I had supposedly traveled. *Why didn't I check my backstory? Espionage 101!*

"Why do you come to China?" she asked in heavily accented English.

"I'm a tourist," I replied. "My friends flew out of Beijing, but I wanted to try the ferry."

You sound defensive—suspicious. Keep it simple.

"Your friends are also from…Ireland?"

"Yes." I was suddenly conscious of how little I knew about the country. God, I hoped the same held true for her. I didn't want to find out that she'd just visited a daughter studying in Dublin, and then get quizzed about the city's highlights.

"How many friends were you traveling with?"

You idiot—why did you mention friends?

"Three."

"Three other men? Or was there a woman?"

"Men."

"*Only* men?" she asked again, sounding sterner by the second.

"Yes."

Don't ask me their names. Don't—

"Names?"

Panic froze my mind. I couldn't just make up names—she would cross-check them in the system. I must have looked guilty, and I was painfully aware there was no way out—not through the solid wall of people behind me and that armed guard staring at me from the front.

Checkmate.

The phone on the counter rang, startling me. Jesus. *Someone else must have spotted me, too—maybe on a surveillance camera.*

The agent picked it up.

"*Wei,*" she said. *Hello.* She listened for a moment, then mumbled, "He's here."

Me?

"Just a moment," she said to me as she rose from her stool and began to walk away, leaving me riddled with fear.

Before she took more than a few steps, though, a younger customs official rushed up to her and apologized for being late. Scowling, she waved him toward me.

He hurried over and stamped my passport quickly, as if to make amends for his tardiness.

I suppressed my overwhelming relief and walked down a corridor to the gangway. I took my place at the end of a short line. No one seemed to take note of me. I longed for a bunk, where I could shut my eyes to the world.

As I waited to board, though, I knew putting everything behind me wouldn't be so easy. I'd left a trail of disaster across China—Will bleeding on a sidewalk, probably dead, all in an effort to get Lily and her mother out of the country. And where were they? The whole point of the mission now seemed lost on me. I felt guilty about the innocent bystanders, like that taxi driver I'd left in the trunk. But what, really, could I do? Leaving a note or telling anyone risked giving myself away. I promised to ensure he was found once I got to Incheon.

I showed my ticket to an attendant. She glanced at it and said my berth was on the B deck, near the bow.

I hurried up the stairs, eager to hide from public view, counting my blessings even as I doubted them. I planned to stay in that cabin for the whole voyage.

My head was still down as I turned the knob to open the door to the stateroom.

"*Shei*?" a voice called from within.

I double-checked my ticket. The number of the cabin matched. I pushed the door open.

"Andrew? You made it!"

Lily! I was so shocked I couldn't say her name. But I grabbed her, picked her up, whirled her around. We kissed as survivors do, drunk with gratitude for the forces that had saved us. But I should have known better.

"How did you get here?" I asked.

"Tom gave me a cell phone with a prepaid SIM card just like you had, in case anything happened."

"You had a phone?"

She nodded. "Tom said to keep it to myself. Strictly need to know basis." She raised her lovely eyebrows to me in playful reproof.

I laughed hard, a reaction fueled by the relief still surging through me. I was still holding her when the ferry's horn bellowed. It was quarter to eight. In fifteen minutes, we'd be gone.

"Where's your mother?" I finally thought to ask.

She motioned toward the restroom. "Where's Will? We saw police chasing you guys. Thank God you got away." She paused when my hands fell to my sides. "Andrew?"

"I don't know. He..." I stuttered, struggling to get the words out, "got shot in Shenyang."

"*What?*"

"The police got him. I don't even know if he's alive. His leg was bleeding badly. I dragged him out of the line of fire, then he ordered me to go."

I still couldn't believe I'd left him behind—but I didn't know what I could have done differently. I must have looked a wreck. Lily's eyes pooled. We stood in silence until I took her hand and asked how they'd made it aboard.

She wiped her eyes, solemn in response. "When I called the number Ed gave me, I was told to come to the ferry terminal. I didn't know what to expect, but a Japanese woman walked up to us and asked about the ferry schedule. I thought she was a tourist. She pulled out a guidebook and pointed to a pair of tickets. I took them. Then she flipped the page and pointed to two Korean passports." Lily motioned how she'd palmed them and slipped them into her pocket. "She thanked *me* and walked away."

Lily buried her face in my chest as the latch on the bathroom sounded. Her mom stepped out. Mrs. Jiang looked exhausted but rallied to greet me.

"Andrew, I thought I heard you." She smiled until she looked around. "Where's Will?"

I told her about the shooting.

"I am so sorry." Mrs. Jiang looked stricken. She'd known Will longer than I had, first as her dance instructor. "Is he alive at least?"

"I…I don't know."

"You know if he's alive, they'll make him talk," Mrs. Jiang said, shaking her head. "We all talk eventually."

I felt disgusted with myself, realizing I was hoping that my best friend—if he was even alive—would be holding out under torture at least long enough for us to get away. Yet another countdown had potentially begun. There was just so much I didn't know.

The ferry's horn blew once more. It was eight o'clock. We might make it. I sat on a straight-backed chair. None of us said a word, each of us grieving Will.

The huge diesel engines rumbled. The floor shook. I looked out the portal at the gray morning skies.

"I'm going up on deck," Mrs. Jiang said. "It may be the last time I will ever see China."

"Maybe you shouldn't," I said, "until we get a long way from shore." I was thinking of international waters, but I didn't say that.

Mrs. Jiang wrapped a woolen scarf around her head and chin and put on dark glasses. "I can handle this, Andrew."

I felt sheepish. Of course she could. She'd dealt with far worse in her life, and even I wouldn't have recognized her now.

As Mrs. Jiang closed the door, I felt the boat moving away from the dock. I looked out the portal to see men rolling up the hawsers.

I sat back down, drained of any remaining energy. Lily sat on my lap, facing me. I wondered if her mother had left to give us privacy. We held each other close, then pulled away to look into each other's eyes.

"It's so good to see you." My voice finally relaxed.

We leaned our foreheads together. She smiled.

Someone banged on the door. We both stiffened.

"*Na wei*?" Lily called out. *Who is it?*

"Ticket check," a man said.

I looked at Lily. She shrugged.

"I'll get it," I whispered.

"No, you stand out too much."

"Open up!" the man demanded. He pounded the door again. He didn't sound like a ticket agent.

"I'll answer it," I insisted. "Get into the bathroom and lock the door." She rushed in and threw the latch.

I looked around frantically for anything to use as a weapon. As Will had taught me, a real fight is not a boxing match. All I could see were Lily's mom's platform shoes beside the entrance to the stateroom. Thick soles, thicker heels. They might do. I grabbed one by the toe and held it by my side like a hammer.

"Open the door."

I peered through the peephole. The man on the other side looked tall, at least through the fisheye lens. His muscular frame was apparent under his dark gray shirt.

It took me another second to realize that he wasn't wearing a crew uniform.

I had no choice, no escape. I tried to brace myself as I unlocked the door—but he slammed it into me so hard that he sent me reeling.

Before I could gain my balance, he grabbed me by the throat and growled, "Where are they?"

CHAPTER 42

H is tense face was inches from mine, his hands so tight around my neck I was sure he was about to crush my larynx. I couldn't talk or think clearly, but I reacted instinctively with a move drilled into me by Will—I lifted my right arm straight up, twisted, then slammed my elbow down onto his forearm, breaking his hold. With my hand right by his face, I drove my fingers toward his eyes.

He turned his head aside violently. Not fast enough, though, as I stabbed my thumb into his socket. He gasped and shook and stumbled backwards, hand over his wounded eye. I grabbed the platform shoe and bashed him across the face. Blood burst from his nose and upper lip as he tried to steady himself. Madness tightened his lopsided glare. For a second, I thought he looked familiar, but I couldn't be sure.

That's when he managed to pull a knife from under his belt, the edge flashing under the ceiling light.

I felt sick as I looked at the shoe in my hand.

He lunged at me, but I jumped back and he came up short. I swung the shoe to try to dislodge the knife from his hand, but he jerked it away—then slashed at my face. It was almost an eye for an eye, but I raised my right arm quickly. I thought the shoe would block the blade, until a hot sensation pierced my forearm. He'd sliced me from my wrist to my elbow.

I retreated toward the bathroom door, startled at the amount of blood already splattering onto the cabin floor. I was tempted to yell at Lily to let me in—to chance getting inside and throwing the latch. But I knew the door was too flimsy, the man too determined. He was repeatedly switching the grip on the knife, holding it like an ice pick one moment, a hammer the next. Blood continued to ooze out of my right arm as I raised my hand, brandishing the shoe. Adrenaline was neutralizing the pain, but nothing could lessen the threat before me.

Suddenly, he thrust the knife toward my chest. I spun to the right. He shifted his body sideways, like a fencer, and lunged at me. I grabbed his wrist with my left hand, held it tight, and cracked the side of his skull with the shoe. On my second attempt, he put his arm up to block me. At the last moment, I swung the shoe in a narrow arc across my body and smacked his knife hand squarely enough to send the blade skittering toward the cabin door, equidistant from us.

He launched a big right at my head. Ducking punches was second nature to me now. His fist sailed overhead, and his momentum carried him to the side. I exploded with a hard left to his liver. He grunted and doubled over as I swung at his head with the shoe. The thick wooden heel glanced off the top of his skull.

Squinting through his injured eye, his face twisted in pain, he charged me. His full-throttled lunge took me by surprise, and as he drove me into the bulkhead, I dropped the shoe. I avoided going down, but then he pressed his forearm against my throat, pinning me against the wall. Snarling, he landed several shots on the top of my head before I could tie him up in a bear hug. The struggle quickly turned into a hockey fight, each of us clutching the other's shirt with our left hands while pummeling the other with the right. My sole advantage was his injured eye, which left him partially blinded as he tried to fend off my swings.

My edge didn't last long—he caught me hard on the left cheekbone. My face rattled from the impact, but I didn't feel any bones break. A few months earlier that shot might have done me in, but a lot had changed. I was now fighting not just for myself but for Lily and her mother and America and—if the general was right—even China. I kept swinging.

We were both weary now, breathing heavily. With our faces only inches apart, I seized an opening and grabbed him by both collars and tried to head-butt him. He jerked back before I could nail him, but that threw him off balance, leaving me just enough room to swivel my hips for a judo throw. It was slower and uglier than any I'd practiced, but it landed him hard onto the small of his back.

I came down on top of him with all my weight. He wheezed loudly. I sat up slightly, tried to pound him left and right, but he rammed his goddamn knee up into my ribs, spilling me to the side.

Clawing his way onto my back, he grabbed me in a choke hold. I'd learned enough to keep my chin tucked tight to my neck to stop him from crushing my windpipe, but that was about all I could do. I elbowed his torso with all my might—to no effect. I tried to lift him up for another judo throw, but he was yanking me backwards so hard I couldn't gain any leverage, and my failure opened my neck to his forearm. The pressure was agonizing. I couldn't breathe. I whipped my entire body forward to shake him loose, but that didn't work, either. He had me as tight as a vise, and my exertions were costing me precious air.

"Help!" I finally croaked to Lily. I had no choice. I was losing consciousness. It was only a matter of time.

Lily burst from the bathroom with the steel rod that she'd pried from the towel rack. She charged at the man with murder in her eyes. Then she stopped.

"Xiong?"

"Leilei," he gasped, easing his grip slightly.

I sucked air.

"*Gan ma?*" she asked. *What the hell are you doing here?*

"Your father sent me!"

Lily's arm dropped to her side. "What? Why?"

"We've been trying to find you."

"Let him go," Lily told him, pointing the rod at me.

For several seconds, Xiong kept his hold before pushing me away.

"Who's he?" I asked hoarsely. With his face and shirt so covered in blood—much of it from my arm—I was surprised even Lily could recognize him.

"My father's bodyguard. I have known him since I was a little girl."

That's where I'd seen him. The formal dinner honoring the general.

"And *he's* your kidnapper," Xiong said. "The IAU teacher!"

"What? No, he is not kidnapping me." Lily shook her head. "He is helping me leave China because—"

"Your father says that he," Xiong jabbed his finger at me as he had the knife blade only moments ago, "took your mother, too."

"Lily, he's lying." I said. "He wants the reward—or someone's threatened to lock him up for life if he doesn't track you down. You *know* your father wanted you to leave with me."

Lily's eyes shifted between Xiong and me. Was she actually having doubts? With all the stress and fear, was the appearance of her father's trusted bodyguard enough to make her question the decision to leave, our relationship?

"Lily, he's working for them," I said. "They've either bribed or coerced him into turning on your father."

"Them?" she repeated, dropping the rod.

"The Central Government. Your father's enemies. Your father knew when he chose to leave that they'd do everything possible to prevent him from getting away."

She was still glancing at Xiong as if she might trust him more than me. And she'd dropped the metal rod, our only weapon.

"*He's* CIA," Xiong said, pointing at me. "Our enemy."

"You're CIA?" Lily asked me.

"No!" I replied as emphatically as Xiong. "I mean, not really. When we met I was just a teacher."

She stared at me, making no move to come closer, confusion in her eyes.

I offered the only response I could. "I love you, Lily."

Her head moved slowly from Xiong to me. Then she looked past both of us to her mother standing in the cabin doorway.

"Lily, Xiong is lying," Mrs. Jiang said. "Everything your father and I told you was true. China's going in the wrong direction. The best thing we can do is cooperate with the Americans. And you'll be safe from your father's extremist enemies." She stepped up to the injured bodyguard. "You...you have betrayed our family."

He grabbed her by the shoulders and started shaking her. "You know I don't want to hurt you, but you're leaving me no choice. Stop this foolishness. Tell your daughter to behave," he added with a glance at Lily.

As he turned back to Mrs. Jiang, she plunged a knife into his chest, her stern gaze as unforgiving as the blade.

I looked at the floor, where Xiong's knife had fallen near the door, and then at Xiong, where it had now come to rest.

He sank to his knees. Both his eyes were open, the damaged one as red as his shirt. He moaned horribly.

Mrs. Jiang turned and hurriedly locked the cabin door.

Xiong clutched the haft of the blade. For a moment, I thought he'd yank it out and try to stab Lily's mother, but instead he spilled forward onto the floor, driving it farther into his heart.

"Drag him into the bathroom, quick," Mrs. Jiang told me. "Lily, get towels and clean the blood up."

Far from shocked by the violence, Lily's mother had become a field general herself, dispatching her troops decisively.

I quickly wrapped a shirt around my wounded arm, which was crusting over but still seeping blood, then grabbed Xiong's heels and pulled his heavy body into the bathroom. He barely fit. As I reached for his neck to check his pulse, I feared that he'd spring to life. But the only part of him that moved was the stream of blood still seeping from his ghastly wound.

Lily bent over and started to clean up the blood in the cabin. Moments later, she straightened, giving up. There was too much on the floor. Her face was as wet and red as the rags in her hands. Her mother took them from her and threw them into the bathroom.

I looked at the cabin door, worrying who would pound on it next.

CHAPTER 43

The knife in Xiong's chest was our only real weapon.

With a groan that drew a glance from Mrs. Jiang, I headed into the bathroom, closing the door behind me. I was determined to spare Lily and her mother the gruesome scene.

I rolled Xiong over and found that his fall had left only about an inch of the haft protruding from his chest. I figured that would be enough for me to grab. I was wrong. I hadn't anticipated how difficult it would be to dislodge that blade with only my fingertips. Grotesque as it was, I forced my fingers deep into that warm flesh to grab the knife firmly until I could feel the handle in the palm of my hand. I pulled it all the way out, producing a horrible sucking sound and a gush of fresh blood.

My hand and arm appeared to have gone through a meat grinder.

I turned on the faucet and rinsed the knife before washing out the long gash on my forearm. I stepped over Xiong's body and edged out of the bathroom. Lily never looked over, but Mrs. Jiang nodded her approval.

I returned the gesture as I slipped the knife into my jacket pocket, then sat down and took a deep breath.

The ferry crossing was scheduled to take fifteen hours. I was already exhausted, but we couldn't be certain that Xiong had been searching for us on his own. I had to stay alert. I also needed to try to keep my wounded arm functional and not infected. Lily dabbed the long cut with antiseptic hand wipes, then tied a fresh shirt snugly around it.

After a few hours in which every sound made us tense up and exchange nervous glances, we figured the absence of any discernable ship-wide search meant that we *might* be in the clear. But we also had no doubt that the Chinese were employing their increasingly sophisticated technical prowess to analyze every possible point of departure from the country. And we couldn't exclude the possibility that ferry employees—or our fellow travelers, no matter how sleepy-looking— had noticed the arrival of a tall Westerner not long after the boarding of two Chinese women, all of whom matched faces on the news and wanted posters.

Lily curled into a fetal position on a bunk, eyes open, no doubt in shock after witnessing her mother's grisly slaying of a man she'd known and trusted all her life. Mrs. Jiang's shoes lay on the floor beneath her, stained red, one from smashing Xiong's face, the other splattered by my own blood. Mrs. Jiang sat erect on a chair, staring straight ahead at the cabin door, either not noticing her daughter's fraught condition or preparing herself for even worse to come. As for me, I was dazed by all that had happened, but felt no regret—it had been him or us. I just wanted to make it to Incheon, be done with this ordeal, and begin my life with Lily. I kept my attention riveted to the door, determined that no one was going to stop us.

After sailing for another twenty minutes—with Lily still balled up on the bunk, eyes wide, as though she feared the demons of dreams most of all—I sat beside her and took her hand. It felt lifeless. She looked lost.

Someone knocked on the door.

The three of us startled. I squeezed the handle on the knife and extended my right arm—painfully reopening the wounds—to ensure that I could still use it. Then I stepped slowly toward the entry. Bracing myself, I unlatched the door and opened it a crack.

Oh my God! "It's Will," I said to Lily and her mother as I threw open the door. "You're alive!" I ushered him inside. "How—"

He shoved a pistol toward my face. "Against the wall, all of you."

What?

We backed toward the bathroom, hands in the air. Will mule-kicked the cabin door shut—with the leg that had been shot, which made no sense. I must have been staring at it because he read my reaction right away.

"That was chicken blood at the bank, Andrew. Sorry to put you through so much grief, buddy."

Buddy? "What the hell—*who are you?*"

He inhaled so strongly that his nostrils flared, like he was bracing himself for a storm. "China cracked our communications. They caught me and offered a crash course in how joints shouldn't bend and places bamboo shouldn't go. They said I could spend the rest of my days getting tortured, or I could cooperate and help them roll up the CIA's network for trade bait to get the general back—do that, and live happily ever after in Beijing with all my limbs. I chose door number two."

This was *Will?* His anguish and urgency on the sidewalk had been so real. I couldn't believe the depth of his betrayal. "But how?"

"When you used that phone to call Tom, you helped me complete my side of the bargain. He'd been under such deep cover for so long, no one would have known about him otherwise—including me. And then they rounded up Ed and everybody else you led them to on our little trip around China. Tom was smart enough to put a bullet in his own head before they could take him." I might have heard envy in

Will's voice. "But, hey, General Jiang is safe so congratulations—mission accomplished," he added cynically.

"You don't have to do this," I pleaded. "Let's get the fuck out of here. All of us."

He kept his gun leveled at me. "You don't get it, Andrew. I had no choice—and now you don't, either. Once Xiong tracked you down he radioed for help and they sent a warship after this tub. Now I know why he went silent." Will glanced at the blood smears on the floor. "I guess I trained you well, but now you're done. There are a dozen Chinese marines onboard. I did you a huge favor by convincing them to let me bring you all out peacefully. If you want to do this the hard way, Andrew, you'll be the first one to get shot."

Mrs. Jiang was glaring at him. "Don't do this. You can't trust anything the Party leadership says. They'll keep forcing you to do their bidding—then discard you when you're no longer of use. And now you know what they'll do to us." She looked at Lily.

For a moment, I thought he might be listening to her, but I was deluding myself.

"There's no other way!" Will shouted. "You think we're going to fight off those Marines with one gun and a knife? We're going on deck, all of us, and then we're taking a little boat trip. And I swear I'll shoot you if you take one step out of line."

He marched us out of the cabin, where two Chinese marines with bullpup rifles were waiting on either side of the door. Will was right— there was no way we could have made it to Korea.

One of the soldiers mumbled into a radio, then they led us down the corridor in close formation—Lily and Mrs. Jiang side by side, then me right in front of Will, who was so close behind that the muzzle of his pistol kept brushing against my back.

No one said a word as we climbed the stairs to the main deck, where a half dozen more armed Chinese soldiers were ushering passengers down a separate stairway. "That's it, you're doing fine," Will said to us as we moved into the open air. He sounded friendly, a man whose job was almost done. He pointed off the stern. "Now you can see where we're headed." Trailing a mile away on the starboard side was a massive Chinese destroyer, so large it seemed to fill the horizon.

"Just a little farther to that rope ladder." Will prodded me with the pistol.

I was trying to look over the side for the boat that would take us to the warship when we heard the helicopters. All of us turned to the bow as two gray choppers, not more than fifty feet above the water, streaked toward the ferry.

"What the..." Will mumbled as one of the copters climbed and circled the vessel, "Navy" on the tail. A gunner was visible on the open side. The other chopper rose almost directly above us, a large antiship missile mounted underneath pointed directly at the Chinese destroyer.

There was a gunshot, then several more. One of the Chinese marines on the deck was firing at a SEAL scrambling over the starboard gunwale in full combat gear not more than thirty feet from us— before the shooter was cut down in a hail of fire from the circling helicopter. Two other SEALs climbed aboard the port side. The marines started firing at them.

Mrs. Jiang suddenly turned and leapt at Will. "Run!" she yelled at Lily.

As Lily raced toward the SEALs. Mrs. Jiang grabbed his gun. It went off. Will looked startled as she staggered backward and fell, blood darkening a small hole in the front of her coat.

I jumped him from the side, gripping his trigger hand. He got off one wild shot, which grazed the bloody bandage on my wounded arm, before we crashed to the deck behind a lifeboat. Bursts of gunfire came from behind and above us. I heard Lily scream and then glimpsed several more Chinese marines emerging from below deck to fire at the SEALs as I clung with both hands to Will's pistol.

"Let go!" he growled as he punched my head. "I don't *want* to kill you." I was smashing his hand against the deck, trying to break his grip, but might as well have been trying to hold back the tide.

All around us a fierce gunfight raged. I heard glass shattering and bullets pinging off the hull and saw wood chips exploding off the lifeboat.

Will seized my hair and tried to yank my head back. Maybe he didn't want to kill me, but he was doing a fair imitation of trying.

I strained forward and sank my teeth into the base of his thumb so hard I was down to the knuckle bone in an instant, trying like hell to tear his thumb off.

He grabbed at my face with his left hand, though with my jaw grinding down harder he didn't get to my eyes, if that's what he had in mind. But then he bashed his forehead into my temple, stunning me almost senseless and popping the gun from my hand. The weapon slid to a stop several feet away.

Will climbed on top of me, punching the back of my head. When I rolled over to defend myself, he hammered a hard punch that landed right above my eye. I tried to turn away and cover up, but he locked onto my throat. Gasping, I made another futile attempt to throw him off but failed. I was only dimly aware of the gunfire all around as the world began to turn black.

"I'm sorry," he said, easing the pressure slightly on my neck. "I really am. I'm gonna make a run for it. You're one of the good guys. I wanted to be, too."

He looked up at the gunner in the helicopter drawing a bead on him, then launched himself toward the gunwale on the starboard side.

Several bursts from the helicopter overhead chewed up the deck, trailing his sprint until he dove headfirst over the guardrail, a twenty-foot drop to the sea. I saw a splotch of blood on the white paint. He'd been hit, I assumed. How seriously, I didn't know.

I was trying to recover my senses when a final exchange of fire rose from an upper deck and the circling helicopter, which was placing what sounded like individually aimed rounds.

Seconds later, the gunfire ceased and I heard only the *whup-whup-whup* of the helicopters' rotor blades.

"Bridge is secure," one of the SEALs said nearby.

I rose to my feet, searching for Lily. A medic was leaning over her prone body. I raced over to them, hoping the soldiers wouldn't shoot me. Fortunately, they'd been well briefed. Two men rushed to my side.

"Name?" one shouted.

"Andrew Callahan."

They pulled me away from Lily, but not before I saw her open eyes and read her lips. She was saying my name.

"Put these on," one of the SEALs said to me as he pulled harnesses, goggles, and large ear protectors out of his pack. I saw the medic putting the same gear on Lily.

A massive *boom* erupted from the Chinese warship. Puffs of smoke drifted above the main gun battery. *They're ordering us to stop.* The ferry slowed but remained on course.

"Time to go," the SEAL said to me.

Right then, the Navy gunship overhead, still staring down the Chinese destroyer, dropped what appeared to be a heavy rope. I was prepared for them to winch us up one at a time, but as soon as that line came within reach, Lily and her medic, Mrs. Jiang's body, and I were all clipped with carabiners onto it and yanked skyward off the stern, the others dangling above me.

Our helicopter was in the lead, the other following behind. But with that destroyer looming below I felt like we were the world's easiest targets, even after the second chopper deployed an array of flares to try to fool any missiles fired at us.

Both helicopters were racing farther from the destroyer. Clipped to that rope, we trailed behind the first one like the tail of a kite. The medic had his arms wrapped firmly around Lily, her wounded leg bleeding through the bandage. A few feet below them, Mrs. Jiang's lifeless body drooped, her head bobbing in the turbulence. I clutched onto the rope, expecting at any second to be blasted from the sky.

The door gunner in our chopper was aiming through the clouds of smoke at the warship. His weapon was no match for the Chinese armaments. And I feared for those SEALs who had rescued us, the last of whom were now descending into two rigid-hulled inflatable boats that they'd hooked to the sides of the ferry. With the wind whipping me side to side, I tried to watch as they roared away from the stern.

The destroyer was racing after the SEAL boats and the helicopters—all straight toward whatever American carrier or fleet was just over the horizon. There was a long pause as the destroyer's largest cannons rose and aimed right at us. I was looking at that little carabiner, smaller than my hand, the only thing keeping me tethered to the sky, when two unmistakable American F-18s dove from above and screamed alongside the big ship, bow to stern, as if to say "Back off," before again climbing straight up into the clouds.

The destroyer slowed.

I heard no more gunshots as we continued on, still clipped to that rope. Thirty or forty minutes passed in a blur of pounding air currents, open ocean, and palpable relief.

We reached a large flat-topped ship. Swaying about fifty feet above the deck, I felt myself slowly lowered, dizzy as I neared two combat-ready soldiers waiting to grab me. As soon as I touched down, they unclipped me and moved me quickly aside. Mrs. Jiang's body arrived next and was laid onto a gurney and wheeled away. When I looked back, Lily was settling into the arms of two more Marines and supporting herself on one leg.

"Welcome to the USS *Belleau Wood*," said the officer who was unbuckling my harness. "You did some good work out there—everything considered."

Good work? I kept my doubts to myself even as I thanked him. I was grateful to be alive and ran to Lily's side. She'd been shot in the front of her upper leg when she ran toward the SEALs. Possibly friendly fire. She took my hand as her medic shouted to a doctor rushing up, "No arteries, but she's hurting."

The doctor nodded and edged me aside as Lily was loaded onto a second waiting gurney. I watched them race off with her, the air still stirred by the chopper blades.

Before I could follow them, a SEAL took me by the arm and started leading me in a different direction. I didn't know where we were going.

I moved along, thinking about Will. *Why did he turn traitor?* Was it really a case of blown communications, torture, and the threat of spending the rest of his life in a Chinese dungeon?

What would I have done in his shoes? I would have liked to believe I would have adhered to the military code of conduct—continued to resist, given no information, done nothing disloyal—but my brief experience behind bars in Beijing had left me unsure whether I could have been any stronger than Will if it would have meant certain torture and a lifetime of imprisonment.

Then I asked myself just how much of his relationship with me was phony, part of the deal to unravel the CIA's network in exchange for his freedom. But that had to have been very recent—once the general was already out of the country. There was no way the Chinese leadership would have let a senior military officer out of their sight if there was even a whiff of betrayal in the air. So maybe Will's friendship with me was genuine. I wished I didn't care, but I did.

With the SEAL still leading me away from the scene, I was left with one final, all-encompassing question about Will: Did the answers to who he was—and what he did—die with him at sea, or had he been rescued by the Chinese marines?

The *Belleau Wood*'s captain rushed across the deck to the gurney with Mrs. Jiang's body.

"I need to talk to that officer," I said to the SEAL at my side.

He nodded and walked me over to him. "Captain Wilkins, this is Andrew Callahan."

The grey-haired captain looked at me through dark glasses and nodded. "How did she die?"

"She lunged at an American double agent who was trying to turn us over to the Chinese and the guy's gun went off." It felt insane to reduce Will's horrendous betrayal to one sentence, but those were the brutal facts. I asked if General Jiang was safe in the US?

The captain looked around, as if he wanted to assure himself that all the threats had been eliminated. "We have him. He's alive."

"Where is he?"

The captain shook his head. "I can't tell you that."

"Really? I just risked my life for that man and his family, and you can't tell me?"

"I can tell you that you have the enormous gratitude of your country, from the commander in chief on down. And that includes me." He stuck out his hand and I shook it. "You will be briefed, I assure you. This is not the time or the place."

"I'm just glad to hear that the operation was a success."

"At a very high cost." As he looked down at Lily's mother, I realized that only her daughter and I had found a safe harbor so far out at sea. "And, in this business, missions have long tails. I don't think we'll know the full ramifications for years to come."

I followed Captain Wilkins across the deck, then insisted to the SEAL officer still by my side that I wanted to see Lily.

"I'm afraid that's not possible now," he replied.

Captain Wilkins about-faced. "Lieutenant, take him to her."

Moments later, I saw Lily lying on an infirmary bed, IVs already in her arms. I took her hand, squeezing it gently. "How are you?"

Her eyes were wet and I could see that she'd been crying. She shook her head.

"I'm so sorry about your mother."

Lily squeezed her eyes shut. Tears spilled down her cheeks. "We were so close to making it out together." She looked up at me. "She tried to stop Will so that I could get away."

"I know. She never hesitated. I think she's probably been doing that one way or another most of your life."

Lily nodded. I dried her tears with a tissue.

"They want to X-ray my leg," she said. "But they don't think it's bad. It could have been a lot worse. A soldier said you tackled Will."

"Something like that."

"I guess I was wrong about you. You *did* come to China to fight." She smiled as she had months ago, after our night at Solutions. "Maybe you should challenge that big Russian to a rematch."

"I have bigger ambitions now." *Including you.*

"You were amazing. I can't believe what you did."

Of course, I hadn't done it alone. Hardly. But when Lily took my hand and pulled me close, I didn't object. I hoped to have a lifetime with her to set the record straight.

EPILOGUE

Present Day

The Signal notification lights up my screen as my plane touches down at Tokyo's Haneda Airport: "Got time for an old friend, China Hand?"

Only Professor Lin still uses that handle. After seventeen years of marriage, not even Lily knows it—one of the details I spared her after the trauma of the exfiltration and the standoff that followed, with China demanding the return of her father and the US insisting on Ed, the two agents who helped with our passports, and the older woman at the safehouse. Neither side got what they wanted, and to this day the general remains under US protection in a location unknown to anyone but his handlers at the CIA. Will's status has never been determined by US intelligence; in the face of all evidence the Chinese deny that he ever worked for them. Only the Englishman Owen made it out—in the sludgy hold of a cargo ship, an indignity I hear he's been dining out on for years.

"Sure," I text back to Lin.

The old professor and I exchange messages every month or so—generally news about China, updates on his research, or the latest in my life—but I've otherwise moved on, burying what happened all those years ago in the deepest recesses of my memory. My own government threatened me with an espionage conviction if I ever talked. And who knows what China might do? So even as the consequences of our actions continued to reverberate in the US and China, the facts of what we did have remained in the shadows.

It's been five years since I last saw Professor Lin in person. That was by happenstance—*perhaps*—while I was killing time between flights at London's Heathrow Airport. I was at a news kiosk browsing headlines when I heard him say, "If it isn't the old…" and then he looked left and right before whispering far too dramatically to be serious, "…China Hand."

I laughed and so did the normally staid professor, whose black hair had turned nearly white. We had about an hour before our connections. We settled at a bar abuzz over a rugby match on a wall-sized screen. He said he was returning from an "academic conference." I knew better than to ask what he was really up to. We respected each other's secrets.

As much as I liked and admired Professor Lin—the years had done nothing to diminish those feelings—I was glad our communications never veered into the shadowy demimonde that he clearly thrived in. The scar on my arm is a daily reminder of our shared past, but I was grateful to have traded that in for my shared life with Lily and the Seattle-based tech startup where I'd landed after completing my computer science PhD—the mission having blown up any aspirations of working for White & McInerny. Lily had gotten her opportunity to study at Harvard after all and was now an Associate Professor of Political Science. Fortuitously, she received a grant to conduct research at the University of Tokyo right when I was tasked with launching our company's Japan operations. So we were back on the road together again—this time, it seemed, in much less perilous circumstances.

"How about now?" Lin texts back as my Boeing 777 taxis up to the terminal.

"Sure. Just landed. I'll call you after immigration."

"Better face-to-face," he texts. "I'm in Tokyo."

I'm not surprised that he knows precisely where I am. That ability surely comes with his job description.

"American Club?" I suggest. It's just around the corner from where we live. I'd told Lily I'd be home for dinner.

"I was thinking more low-key," he replies. He gives me the name of a small whiskey bar, which is also nearby.

I message Lily that I need to meet someone for a drink. "Won't be long." I save the details for later. Then I add a goofy selfie for her to share with Kai, our son.

When I climb out of the cab at the bar, Lin waves as he walks down the narrow cobblestone street, under cherry blossoms illuminated by the streetlamps. He looks unchanged, despite God knows how many missions. We each take a stool and order a Hakushu 18 from the stocky barman. There are no other customers.

After all these years, I'm emboldened enough to ask Lin if he ever wonders whether the risks he takes are worth it. "How do you keep going? Don't some of the failures leave you depressed?" While getting Lily out was life-changing and wonderful for me personally, it's not easy to see how well my own mission accomplished its other objectives. Even if General Jiang helped expose and deter some of the more extremist elements in China's government—for a time—our two countries seem to be on a collision course now more than ever.

"Of course, it would be easy to get depressed," the unflappable professor says. "Especially these last two decades. But after all the places I've been, I still think America is worth defending. I've seen what *real* totalitarianism looks like. I admit that our fellow citizens seem a little too fragile these days. But *you civilians,*" he pats me gently on the forearm, "don't get to hear about the successes, right?"

If he's trying to pique my curiosity, it's working. "You want to tell me about some of them?" I'm smiling because I know he will remain tight-lipped as always.

He diverts me with an unusually personal query. "You happy?"

This is so unlike Lin that I wonder if he'll follow with a crushing revelation—"I've been diagnosed with leukemia," or something equally dire. I wait for him to say more, but nothing dramatic follows.

"Happy? You bet." I offer a bright demeanor to match those words, though I know at best it's a subtle disguise. I love my life now, but I am conscious of my past, and I never know when it might reach out from the darkness and grab me or—my greatest fear—Lily or Kai. With the regular hacks and leaks of national security secrets, I've long feared it was just a matter of time until I was unmasked, too.

Lin has undoubtedly inferred all that—he's got a spy's sixth sense—and I suspect he also knows another truth: I've become restless, plagued by the "what now?" that can follow accomplishment or the approach of middle age.

"Right," he says, swirling his whiskey before cutting to the chase. "We need your help."

"We?" I know what he means, of course. After we had been airlifted off the ferry and finally back in the States, we were rushed to Langley for a debrief. Professor Lin was there. At the end of the sessions, he fixed me with his steady gaze and said, "Every mission has long tentacles."

I had dreaded—but also, every so often, secretly waited for—this moment. All those old events in China suddenly rush back to me.

Now he leans closer and lowers his voice, much as he did at that kiosk in London. But this time he's deadly serious. "It's time to come in from the cold."

THE END

ACKNOWLEDGMENTS

The idea for *China Hand* evolved from a series of experiences, encounters, events, and speculations with a group of friends in Beijing and Shanghai. For these people who still live or work in China, there is no upside to being associated with an espionage story—even this work of fiction—so I will be discreet. But you know who you are, and I thank you for sharing some interesting times and inspiring this book.

Thank you to the former intelligence officer and Navy SEALs who explained how an actual exfiltration and the seizing of a ship might have gone down in Asia in the late-1990s. While you must also remain nameless, I could not allow your help and professionalism to go unacknowledged.

I also owe a great debt to the guidance and thorough editing of Mark Nykanen, Stephanie Gangi, and Jodie Renner, who helped this novice writer turn a collection of loosely connected stories into its final form. Thank you.

Finally, my deepest appreciation to my wife, son, and daughter for their patience and support while I wrote and tinkered with this manuscript for far too long, and to my parents, brother, and sister who have encouraged and supported my travels and writing over the years.

Any errors are my own.